Illusion

by

Sonia Deane

Dales Large Print Books
Long Preston, North Yorkshire,
BD23 4ND, England.

British Library Cataloguing in Publication Data.

_____

Deane, Sonia
    Illusion.

    A catalogue record of this book is
    available from the British Library

    ISBN   1-84262-133-5 pbk

First published in Great Britain in 1952
by Hutchinson & Co. (Publishers) Ltd.

Cover illustration © Ben Turner by arrangement with
P.W.A. International Ltd.

The moral right of the author has been asserted

Published in Large Print 2002 by arrangement with
Rupert Crew Limited

Dales Large Print is an imprint of Library Magna Books Ltd.

Printed and bound in Great Britain by
T.J. (International) Ltd., Cornwall, PL28 8RW

To
DOROTHY

Looking back over twenty-three years of great friendship, darling, and repeating every word written to you in the dedication of *Secret Interlude*.

S.D.

CHAPTER 1

The auctioneer's hammer came down with a bleak finality and Lot 543, a pair of early Georgian side tables, passed into the keeping of the anonymous highest bidder, thus marking the end of the auction of furniture and of the house itself, Old Meadows, Berkshire home of the Waynes for the past four generations.

Vicki (christened Victoria) who had, such a brief while before, lived there with her parents, stood tensed and disconsolate, watching the scene with resentful, yet mesmerized, gaze. She could not leave, even to spare herself pain. The avariciousness of the people pressing covetously around her, awakened a certain disgust and revulsion; their determination to pay only ten per cent of the value of the goods offered for sale, not only dealt her and her stepmother a financial blow, but evoked within her a certain, cynical disillusionment. This was her first contact with the bargaining public, who appeared to her to have neither conscience nor heart.

The lofty, Georgian drawing-room, with its stately windows, its exquisitely gilt-beaded, tapestried walls, was now crowded with what had become a rabble as the sale ended. Women peered into each other's faces, congratulating themselves on this antique, that carpet or suite, all of which were 'an absolute gift, my dear!' Dealers, pocketing their notebooks, with smirking satisfaction on their plump features, were mentally totting up their future substantial profit and congratulating themselves accordingly.

Vicki gazed about her, stunned by the impact of tragedy. Soon, treasured possessions would leave the sanctuary of those walls and pass into alien hands...

Now, only a few stragglers remained, staring at her and whispering among themselves, while hoping to hear a little more gossip about the family, whose fortunes had crashed with the death of Henry Blake Wayne, Vicki's father, some two months previously.

And then, suddenly, Vicki met the steady gaze of the man who loomed as an arch-enemy; the man who had bought Old Meadows itself and a considerable amount of its furniture. The hostility in her eyes was as clear and distinct as the flash of steel in the sun. She stood there, faintly imperious, contemptuous and aloof, hardly realizing that they were entirely alone in the room. He moved nearer, watching her with interest and she said involuntarily:

'You've been very lucky today.'

He glanced about him appraisingly and she noticed, even as he did so, that his features were well cut, his mouth firm, his voice was low, and held a warmth, even encouragement, in its resonant tones.

'Very lucky,' he agreed. 'It's a lovely old house, isn't it? Or perhaps you haven't been all over it?'

Vicki's smile was ironic.

'Yes, I've been all over it. And agree with you.'

He brightened and then sighed.

'Somehow, I can't help thinking of the family who have had to leave it. Perhaps I'm a romantic, but it is as though their reproachful glances have been haunting me. The price, too, was unexpectedly low... Why do you look at me like that?'

'I was,' she said, not without disdain, 'contemplating the somewhat unusual spectacle of a man almost regretful of having acquired something for nothing. You will recover from the shock.'

He looked at her more closely, aware that she was expensively dressed in a smartly cut, cream linen suit; that her hat was a model, because of its classic simplicity, and that she was beautiful, haughty and, in some inexplicable fashion, oddly pathetic. He realized, too, that there was fire behind the coldness of her eyes.

'No doubt,' he said shortly.

She *had* to ask one question and did so, almost abruptly:

'What are you going to do with the place now that you own it?'

He didn't hesitate.

'Turn it into flats.'

'What!'

'Is that such sacrilege?'

Despite herself, Vicki was shocked; she had appreciated his earlier sentiments, while being too wretched and unhappy to admit it. This vandalism, however, hardly sustained her judgment.

'Yes.' Her eyes flashed him an accusing glance. 'I didn't realize you were a builder,' she added hotly.

At that he laughed.

'I'm not a builder.'

'Speculator, then. I'm not very well acquainted with the specific terms.'

He held her gaze somewhat unnervingly.

'Would it appease your artistic sense if the government had purchased the place to house a few more of its surplus ministers?'

Vicki was angry with herself and she hastened:

'I'm sorry; it is not for me to pass any opinion.' A pause, then: 'Flats! How many?'

'Three.'

'Will you live in one?'

'I hope to do so.' He took a cigarette-case from his breast pocket and, clicking it open, offered her a cigarette, which she declined. 'Do you mind if I do?'

'Not at all.' She returned to the former subject. 'I suppose this place would convert very easily?'

'Very; without, I am assured, in any way spoiling its character.' He made a sweeping gesture. 'I shall leave all this intact – practically the whole of this ground floor.' He paused briefly. 'I've no earthly use for the house as it stands – far too big. And since I have two friends, each of whom would take a flat ... what could be simpler? That way, also, by pooling the expense of the grounds, we shall be able to maintain them. It would be criminal to mar this setting.'

Vicki felt slightly better.

'You evidently haven't a family.'

'Nor a wife,' he finished coolly. A wry smile touched his lips. 'I'm an orphan, too,' he added absurdly.

Vicki didn't laugh; she was moving, slowly towards the door. This conversation served no purpose. At least now she knew the ultimate fate of Old Meadows ... and she most certainly wasn't interested in this man's private life.

'At least I wish you luck with the project here,' she said in clipped, precise tones.

13

'Thank you … do you live in the district?'

'Yes; a mile or so away from here – at Ascot.'

'My name's Evans – Guy Evans. I'm a radiologist – quite harmless – perhaps you'll come and approve the finished building when it is converted.'

She gave him an intent, but not encouraging, look.

'I think not, Dr Evans – I believe all radiologists are doctors – thank you all the same.'

And with that she walked out.

The auctioneer's clerk entered the room as she left it. Guy Evans asked abruptly:

'You don't happen to know who that lady was?'

The clerk answered swiftly:

'Why, yes, sir; that's Miss Wayne.'

'You mean,' Guy gasped, shocked, 'the–'

'Yes, sir; this must have been a sad day for her an' no mistake. Her father dead, the home in which she's lived all her life – sold.'

Guy felt uncomfortable.

The clerk continued:

'Bad job her father dying so suddenly. Death duties and the rest of it, have just about finished them. And the sales here won't exactly keep them in luxury.' He gave a wintry smile. 'Never known worse prices. Queer thing that: things never do seem to fetch anything like their value when they've *got* to be sold and when the owners are relying on every penny of the money. But when it doesn't really matter, one way or the other, to the owners ... things make a packet. Noticed it often. Always people ready to take advantage of—' He stopped realizing that he was hardly being discreet and then adding, as he hastily retrieved a notebook and made towards the door, 'Lovely old place, isn't it, sir? They say that the Waynes have owned it for generations. Ah well, that's life.'

Guy Evans stood there uncertainly. So that was Victoria Wayne! How she must have loathed every word he uttered.

The house had become deathly silent. He gazed through the long windows across smooth lawns to arbours, festooned in profusion with roses – crimson, yellow and pink to break up the blue and gold of the June day. In the far distance, pine woods rose darkly, their more subdued hue providing a sombre tapestry. He stirred restlessly, his footsteps echoing with a certain ghostliness across the shining, parquet floor. The auctioneer's rostrum remained on an improvised dais, its cold, business-like appearance almost an affront. Guy thought swiftly of the people who had once lived and laughed in that very room and Byron's words came swiftly: 'Gone – glimmering through the dream of things that were.'

Now, all was still; death had come, not only to the head of that house, but to a tradition... There would be no more Waynes at Old Meadows. Odd, he reflected, that, as their fortunes had deteriorated, so his own, on the other hand, had vastly improved through the death of his uncle, thus enabling him to achieve many ambitions, without in any way creating within him the urge to retire from his practice as a radiologist – work in which he was deeply interested and extremely successful. He decided, as he made his way slowly to his car, that it was useless worrying himself about the fortunes of a family – whom he did not know – simply on account of the fact that he happened to be in a position to buy the house they wanted to sell!

Vicki, meanwhile, was driving back to the small cottage which she and her step-mother, Nadia, had salvaged from the wreckage. Her thoughts were turbulent, her nerves taut. Old Meadows had gone, leaving an emptiness indescribable... *Flats*, that man Evans had said, she reflected bitterly, hating the very sound of his name. She sobered slightly as she reached White Cottage and braked at its latticed gate. Nadia needed comfort, not rebellion.

A matter of seconds later Vicki faced her stepmother in the small sitting-room, acutely conscious of her pale cheeks and pained, dark eyes; of her exceptional beauty, even for a woman of fifty and, above all, of her quiet dignity and courage as she asked, striving to infuse a note of brightness into her voice:

'Well, darling?'

Vicki didn't prevaricate in the hope of softening the blow.

'The house went for eleven thousand; I doubt if the furniture fetched three.' She added, breathlessly: 'Oh, Nadia, I'm so *sorry*. There'll be hardly anything left when the estate is really settled; certainly not enough to keep Emma on here and–'

Nadia interrupted gently:

'It will work out, Vicki; I have at least my own tiny income and Emma has already made it quite clear that nothing would induce her to leave us – wages or no wages. She's served the Waynes for fifty years and she intends to die serving them – that would seem to be her motto… Do you know who bought the – the house?'

'A man named Evans.'

'What sort of a man?'

'Doctor – radiologist – but he's turning it into three flats.'

'*Flats!*'

'Afraid so, darling.'

Nadia thought sharply and poignantly of Henry Wayne whom she had married when Vicki was barely a year old and whose first wife had died in giving Vicki birth. A disastrous first marriage, that had thrown into sublime relief the happiness of the following twenty-three years during which time Nadia had borne a daughter, Brinda, whose character, ironically enough, was as alien and difficult as Vicki's was affectionate and tractable.

Nadia knew in that moment the oppression of an agonizing loneliness; she reflected suddenly: 'I am alone; without Henry I shall *always* be alone, no matter what my feelings may be towards the children.' Aloud she said:

'It was a very low price. I suppose we ought to have put a reserve on it.'

Vicki said bitterly:

'And then, no doubt, it would not have sold at all – which in a way would have been worse.'

'Of course.' Nadia added: 'Regrets will avail us nothing, darling. And the house without your father–' There was a catch in her voice.

Vicki cried:

'It's like some nightmare. I couldn't believe any of it this afternoon. All those people! I hated them being in our room–' She flung out her hands. 'But that won't help. My next step is to find a job and to persuade some unsuspecting person that I'm capable of doing it.'

Nadia was grateful to change the subject.
'What have you in mind?'

Vicki lit a cigarette.

'I'd like to do something useful, but the first thing that occurs to me as in any way practical is modelling clothes, which I should detest.' She looked earnest. 'Or I could teach riding. I just don't know, Nadia.'

They lapsed into silence. Emma served their tea and they drank it gratefully, aware that every service now performed for their benefit had a special significance. Vicki stared out through what to her seemed minute windows, to a garden equally minute, but at least secluded and shaded with tall beech trees. She knew they were exceedingly lucky to have such a sanctuary and in no way disparaged it. For all that, after the spaciousness of Old Meadows, adjustment was inevitable.

Nadia said abruptly:

'Brinda will not take very kindly to all this; she'd imagined Old Meadows producing something in the nature of legacies for us all.'

Vicki nodded.

'Brinda has never been a very happy person – has she?'

'No.'

'And being widowed after only three years of marriage and at twenty-two.' Vicki spoke

19

reflectively. 'I'm glad she went on that cruise after Daddy died. She would have hated all this – the upheaval – oh, just everything.'

Nadia studied Vicki thoughtfully:

'You've always been very good to Brinda.'

'She's your daughter and Daddy's and, besides, I always hoped that, in the end, she would really think of me as a sister. That word "stepsister" has its sting all too often, even though we did grow up together and I'm only two years her senior.' Vicki paused, then: 'She has always seemed to resent our relationship, Nadia, and to force home the fact that you were not my mother. Heaven knows I could not feel any greater affection for you if you were. Perhaps that is the answer.'

Nadia could not stay the thought that, although Brinda was her own daughter and Vicki a stepchild, the bond that bound her to Vicki seemed the greater; theirs had been a rich and satisfying companionship, entirely lacking in her relationship with Brinda.

Suddenly, sharply, Vicki cried:

'Good heavens, here's that man!'

Nadia started.

'What man?' she cried, astounded by the outburst.

'The man who bought Old Meadows. What on earth can he want?' she added somewhat aggressively.

Nadia could not resist a smile.

'He has, after all, a right to *live*, darling!'

'But not to intrude here,' Vicki insisted. 'I'll—'

Nadia interrupted.

'We owe any caller courtesy, Vicki.' Her voice was gentle.

Vicki subsided.

'You are right, of course.'

Guy Evans was shown into the room some seconds later and Vicki presented him to Nadia.

'This,' he said instantly, 'must seem an unwarranted intrusion. Please forgive me.'

'Not at all,' Nadia assured him politely. 'Do sit down.'

Vicki said pointedly:

'What can we do for you, Dr Evans?'

Guy was aware of the faint hostility of her attitude; aware of the fire and spirit dominating her and liked her the more for that reason.

'My mission is exceedingly delicate,' he began quietly; 'and I would ask, above all, not to be misunderstood.'

Vicki flashed:

'We can hardly give you our assurance on that point without knowing the reason for your visit, can we?'

'Naturally not,' he said briefly. He addressed himself to Nadia. 'The fact is, Mrs Wayne, that I have been offered a profit of three thousand pounds on Old Meadows. I've just come from the agents and, apparently, the man most interested in the purchasing of the property was prevented from attending the sale by some unforeseen circumstances.'

Vicki said swiftly:

'I cannot see how this affects us, Dr Evans.'

Guy selected and rejected phrases, striving to find just the right and most telling to express what was in his mind. Then:

'I would like to suggest that I repudiate my contract and that you, Mrs Wayne, accept this new offer.'

Nadia gasped.

'But if you are anxious to be free of the property, then you have an excellent chance to make three thousand pounds. Why–'

Vicki added breathlessly:

'Yes, why come to us?'

'Because,' he said very deliberately, 'I am not really the type of person who enjoys getting something for nothing.' His gaze met hers and Vicki knew that he was still smarting under her indictment earlier that day. 'And much as I would like Old Meadows I should find little pleasure in it at your expense. Three thousand is a considerable improvement on my offer.' He looked from face to face: 'My ceiling price was twelve-five. I cannot, justifiably, go to fourteen thousand. Otherwise I would.'

'But,' gasped Vicki, 'you already own – at least technically – the property at eleven thousand.'

'While knowing that it could fetch fourteen and that your family has to stand the real loss.'

'You could have walked away with three thousand pounds' profit,' Vicki insisted.

'True, and while that might be termed "good business", it would still leave a nasty taste in my mouth in the circumstances.'

Nadia said weakly:

'You are being most awfully generous, Dr Evans. But, of course, your contract stands.'

Vicki felt a sudden lifting of her heart as she sat there. Since her father's death there had been ample evidence of the greed of human beings; this gesture appeared suddenly to redeem each act of avarice.

'Of course,' she said and her voice held a note of warmth for the first time, 'we could not possibly do as you suggest.'

Nadia asked:

'And this prospective purchaser? What are his intentions concerning the property? Do you happen to know?'

'Yes; he is, quite definitely, a speculator; he wants to convert it into flatlets – probably a dozen.'

Vicki burst forth:

'Then, in any case, we don't want him to

have it and since you have no desire to sell–

'None,' Guy admitted, 'but that still does not affect the moral issue.' He looked at Nadia. 'That concrete offer emphasizes the fact that I have gained very considerably at your expense – not a very comfortable feeling.'

Vicki said apologetically:

'I'm afraid our conversation this afternoon was ill-timed, Dr Evans. I spoke in the heat of the moment. Forgive me.'

Their eyes met and interest quickened.

He persisted:

'That has nothing to do with it.'

Nadia exclaimed with finality:

'We shall not forget your generosity, Dr Evans, and in declining your offer we in no way belittle, or misunderstand, the motive behind it.'

Guy could not rightly have said just why it seemed so imperative that he should not benefit at the expense of the Wayne family. Had he not insisted, earlier that day, that their fortunes were no concern of his?… Yet here he was anxious to ease their burden, even at his own expense. He said with a quiet confidence:

'Very well; I can settle any other details with the agents.'

'There is nothing to settle,' Vicki remarked.

'On that we agree to differ,' he murmured,

inclining his head.

Vicki found herself studying him with a new interest, her former prejudices giving place to approval. Few men would have resisted a profit of three thousand pounds and fewer would have offered to step out of the picture so that the original owners of the property could benefit. It was a quixotic gesture that appealed to her.

Nadia said earnestly:

'I am very glad that, since we had to lose Old Meadows, Dr Evans, you are the one to gain it. I know that in your hands it will not lose its character.'

'Not even when converted as, alas, I must convert it?'

'Not even then,' Nadia said gently.

Guy was conscious of the smallness of the room in which they were sitting; conscious of a tug at his heart as he imagined just what a loss Old Meadows must be to them and how restricted – despite its quaint charm – this cottage would appear, how lacking in convenience.

Vicki hastened:

'I appreciate that, in these days, the larger houses are impossible to run. I suppose, with us, the staff had just seemed to grow there and we were hardly conscious of their being half as old as they were in actual fact.'

Guy said jerkily:

'They will miss you.'

25

'Yes, I think they will. Fortunately, they will be taken care of and are mostly going to retire.' She sighed. 'I've realized what a world apart it all was.'

Guy looked at her reflectively.

'For all that, I hate to see these old homes being relegated to the past. They gave life, colour, dignity, romance; there is nothing to compensate for that loss.'

Vicki smiled.

'For all that,' she admitted honestly, 'we are a dying section of society, Dr Evans, and while perhaps decorative, certainly not useful. I hope I'm broad-minded enough to accept that fact. I've loved my life; I've danced through the years, both here and on the Continent; I've been spoilt shamelessly and revelled in it ... well, that's over.'

'Not for good,' he insisted.

'Definitely for good,' she said firmly. 'I want a job and I want it quickly. That brings me face to face with the realization of my uselessness!' She paused. 'I'm sorry; I'm wasting your time and–'

There was a second of silence which Guy broke by saying:

'What kind of a job had you in mind?'

'Since I am fitted for none, I can hardly afford the luxury of being selective ... why do you ask?'

'I was wondering if I might help.' He added hastily: 'I have a practice in Wimpole Street.

26

My receptionist is leaving shortly to get married. If you cared to try it out under her guidance to begin with–' He broke off. It was impossible to forget that he was talking to Victoria Wayne and offering her a *job!* 'But, of course, you wouldn't be interested.'

Vicki hastened.

'I should – terribly interested. I love dealing with people and have very special ideas of how receptionists should behave! Having been the patient on one or two occasions. And I might well know quite a number of yours!'

'The assets are piling up on your side already,' he said with a laugh. He looked at her with interest. 'Would you consider dining with me tomorrow evening – just to settle the details?' He glanced at Nadia, seeking her approval and finding it in her smile.

Vicki didn't hesitate.

'I'd love to.'

'Then I'll call for you at eight.'

Vicki inclined her head. She was enjoying herself for the first time for many dreary weeks; excitement surged within her. It was like being poised on the brink of adventure.

She walked with him to the front door and so down the narrow, cottage pathway to the grass verge flanking the lane in which his car stood. It was a new Jaguar and she said instantly:

'They're a joy – aren't they?'

'Yes; I waited years for it!'

'And I mine,' she said quietly. 'I hated parting with it. Still, I have an ancient Morris that gets me about, so I mustn't grumble.'

Guy's eyes met hers.

'I'm so terribly sorry about everything.' His sincerity lent eloquence to the conventional remark.

She smiled wistfully. There was an abrupt pause during which time the flame of anticipation flashed between them. A matter of hours before they had not known each other; now they hovered on the brink of friendship.

Guy wanted to make some comment upon the charm of the cottage but could not, honestly, do so, realizing that she would scorn banality. By comparison with Old Meadows it was like a soap box after a golden casket; its clematis-covered walls were conventionally picturesque but no more; it had no special period to give it any claim to distinction and provided, as he well knew, merely a roof – a sanctuary.

Vicki held out her hand.

'Thank you for everything, Dr Evans. You have been most kind. And I was unforgivably hostile this afternoon.'

'You were forgivably human,' he said slowly, holding her gaze. 'When I realized to whom I had been talking I felt that I had been treading on satin while wearing hob-nail boots!'

Vicki laughed. She was aware of his strong, firm grip as his hand held hers for a fraction longer than was strictly necessary; aware, too, of a certain comforting, even reassuring quality in his attitude, as of an ally. She wished suddenly that they might have met in the happier days at Old Meadows when life was gay and carefree and she could have offered him hospitality.

He slid into the driving seat. She remained standing beside the open window.

'Until eight o'clock tomorrow,' he reminded her. A pause. 'And you will be hearing from the agents regarding the house,' he added in more business-like tones.

'That,' she said firmly, 'is settled, Dr Evans.'

'It is not,' he countered, 'if you will pardon the correction. And it is not, also, a fact that the woman always has the last word!' With that, he slid swiftly away.

The following morning at eleven o'clock the estate agent duly phoned and spoke to Nadia. He sounded slightly bewildered. Dr Evans had sent a further deposit for one hundred and fifty pounds, insisting that the purchase price should be twelve thousand five hundred. A most unprecedented

29

occurrence. Of course, the property was worth far more and he still had a bargain ... had a reserve been put upon the sale and so on... Nadia listened and made suitable comments and from those Vicky gauged the trend of the conversation. As Nadia finally put down the receiver Vicki said:

'So that was what Dr Evans meant when he spoke last night of seeing the agent.' She stood immobile, looking out across the small lawn. 'Strange how one finds that rare person who redeems all others.'

'Yes,' said Nadia, deeply moved.

'What are you going to do?'

'Accept it,' said Nadia, thoughtfully, 'because not to do so would be rather like throwing a wonderful gesture in Dr Evans's face. Later on, we must find ways of making it up to him, Vicki.'

Vicki nodded, hearing those words and yet feeling they were coming to her as from a great distance... Guy Evans. ...'we must find ways of making it up to him.' ...Curiously, unbidden and irrelevant, the only thought that came to her, the only reaction, embraced the words of Omar Khayyam:

The Moving Finger writes; and, having writ,
Moves on:

Moves on...

A little shiver passed over her; a shadow touched her heart; a strange, uncanny presentiment. Now it would seem that Fate had smoothed the immediate pathway... But it was as if this calm was merely that before some violent, destructive storm.

Defiance flashed into her eyes.

Why peer into the dark glass of tomorrow or look back to yesterday...

Nor all thy tears wash out a Word of it...

Nadia said gently:

'Vicki! What is it?'

She started.

'Someone walking over my grave...' A light laugh. Then: 'I'm going to run into Ascot. Anything you want?'

Nadia laughed.

'Nothing I can possibly afford.'

Vicki forced a smile.

'Lack of money certainly simplifies life from that angle.' She paused. The day suddenly loomed ahead bleakly. The thought of Guy Evans obtruded again and she cast off the former depression. It would be pleasant to dine with him. She found that she was, after all, looking forward to it.

CHAPTER 2

Guy arrived punctually at White Cottage and Vicki greeted him with genuine friendliness. They set off immediately for a hotel mid-way between Ascot and Windlesham and it was not until they were actually sitting at dinner that Vicki began:

'The agent rang this morning ... my mother asked me to thank you; yet that seems so totally inadequate.'

'Please.' He looked at her with a steady and searching gaze. 'I ask only that you do not resent my buying the place, Miss Wayne. It isn't easy to express what I feel; but I want, above all, to preserve its atmosphere and win your approval for any changes that I must inevitably make. If I could take it over and run it in its present form – I would.' He smiled ruefully. 'But I'm sure you appreciate the impracticability of that from my point of view and in these days. It is true I have inherited a certain amount of money, but I want to use it to widen my horizon and not merely to marry me, as it were, to a house.'

'I do understand,' Vicki said instantly. 'In truth, my father could not afford to run it during the past seven or eight years – if not before then. But to have parted from it and uprooted himself–' Vicki shook her head. 'I realise now how indifferent I was to that phase of things, but it is so terribly difficult when one has been used to things, suddenly to become *aware* of them as luxuries.'

Guy studied her intently; she seemed to be an entirely different personality; her expression more gentle, her eyes friendly, the cynicism gone.

'It is human weakness to take for granted the comforts to which we have been accustomed and to imagine that one's parents' income is as elastic as one's desires. I know.'

Vicki said softly:

'And you are an orphan! I remember that.'

'Yes; I lost my father during the last war and the shock killed my mother. It was better that way. Some people are fitted to face up to life, to meet its blows; my mother was one of the "little Dora's", shall we say. I could not wish her back.' Their glances met. 'Odd how we meet people; how little I dreamed, when I came down to the sale yesterday, that I should be sitting here like this with you of all people.'

'The unexpected is so often more satisfying than that which is planned.'

They dined and moved into the lounge for coffee, sitting in the deep armchairs and talking easily and naturally, without strain and then, encouragingly, Guy said:

'And now, what about helping me out with my work?'

Vicki smiled.

'That's a very generous way of putting it!' She found her gaze persistently drawn to his, noticing every expression and aware that his eyes were disarming, sympathetic, admiring in turn. Useless denying that he was a most attractive and charming man, whose personality was so strong, so forceful that she realized it would be exceedingly difficult to win any battle against him.

'Not at all. An intelligent, inexperienced person can often be more helpful than an inefficient, experienced one. I do not want a receptionist-cum-secretary-cum-nurse,' he added. 'I want someone to receive my patients, set them at their ease and tell them what is required of them. I am confident that you, after a week or so, would be excellent.'

'I should try to be.'

'And what about the routine? The hours,' he said without compromise. 'It would have to be nine-thirty until five-thirty and in any special case, or emergency, longer than that.'

Vicki didn't hesitate.

'I have to earn my living, or at least supplement a minute income in order to live,' she said frankly. 'I ask no quarter.'

34

'I have other assistants, a secretary...'

'Have you a lurking fear that I might not mix?'

He looked at her steadily and unflinchingly.

'You have been accustomed to giving orders all your life, Miss Wayne; the point is, how will you feel about *taking* them?'

She didn't prevaricate.

'Undoubtedly very strange at first; but that is inevitable. But I shall, at least, be fortified by the knowledge of how I expected to be treated *myself* in the past and behave accordingly. I may be quite wrong, but I should say that anyone who has been used to being in command would more readily know what was expected of them when they found themselves in the inferior position! What one's personal reactions might be, do not affect the issue.'

Guy allowed the flicker of a smile to cross his face.

'You have something there.' He looked at her. 'I could not give you any concessions – in that I must be perfectly frank.'

'I appreciate that and I can assure you that when I step over the threshold of your consulting-rooms I shall leave Victoria Wayne outside and become, I hope, an efficient and interested member of your staff – that and no more. Does that sum it up?'

'Neatly.'

'Splendid. I like to know where I stand in all things.'

He arched his eyebrows.

'Practical?'

'In many ways, yes; I hate loose ends, untidy situations. But materially practical–' She smiled. 'Alas, no!'

'That makes two of us,' he said and laughed.

She gave him a tender, appreciative glance.

'You do not have to tell me *that.*'

He looked slightly confused, and swiftly changed the subject.

Vicki said unexpectedly as they left the hotel:

'I wonder if you would gratify a whim of mine?'

'Name it ... but, first, we've not really settled the job. When could you start?'

'Monday? This is Friday–'

'Excellent.' He added swiftly: 'Three-fifty a year?'

'Is that–'

'The precise amount I am in the habit of paying.'

Vicki flushed.

'Oh, I wasn't quibbling *that* way; merely making sure–'

'No favouritism,' he said briefly. 'Very well then. Monday.'

'A month on trial?'

'If you prefer it that way.'

She laughed.

'I'm making it easy for you to get rid of me!'

He looked down at her and some spark ignited between them that made him say hoarsely:

'I shall not seek that concession.' A pause, then: 'And now for the whim?'

'To go over Old Meadows with you. I'd like you to see it through my eyes.' She glanced up at the sky. 'We have another hour yet before sunset ... or have you to get back to town?'

'No; and I can think of nothing I'd like more than to do as you say. You're sure you can bear it?'

'Quite sure. Yesterday it was agony; but now I know you—' she added slowly, 'it is rather like having handed over a favourite pet to a friend.'

'I appreciate that.'

They set off, driving through rhododendron-lined lanes, past deep pine woods and so to Old Meadows which stood secluded from the road and approached by a long drive. In the softer evening light, it loomed in shadow, its bowed windows and impressive colonnades, testimony of a period of grandeur in architectural beauty and dignity.

Guy's pulses quickened at the sight of it;

the pride of ownership stirred within him. It was his first taste of buying property and he was not prepared for the thrill it now provided. Yesterday, curiously enough, had seemed a hateful anti-climax; today, he was at peace with himself and the presence of Victoria Wayne added just the right note calculated to dispel the disharmony of his anxious pity.

'It looks wonderful,' he said, hoarsely. He embraced the grounds in a sweep of his hand. 'That view over the Berkshire Downs; the fringe of beeches shadowing the lawns – and what lawns! And the cedar trees...' He stopped abruptly.

'I had a swing just over there,' Vicki said quietly. 'My hair was in pig-tails, then. And I used to hide from nannie among those rose arbours. I can see myself, too, in my first evening frock on the occasion of the first dance given for me... I was sixteen. And at twenty-one–' A sigh. 'A world of fairy-lights; an enchanted world that I fondly imagined would last for ever.' She looked up at Guy. 'What a pity it is that we never quite realize how happy we are until that happiness has passed... I was so gloriously *young*, so wildly romantic, too. Always poised on the brink of some ecstatic infatuation that died–' She paused and added: 'Yet left no scars, but only an indulgent memory.'

Guy looked down at her, his gaze searching.

'Nothing serious – ever?'

She laughed. There had been a long list of would-be suitors who still pursued her, but in whom she had little interest beyond genuine friendship.

'Nothing from my point of view.' She thrust a hand deeply into the pocket of her loose powder-blue gabardine coat as she added: 'I've a horrid suspicion that if and when love comes to me I shall be intense over it. And that is fatal. One should never give all.'

'A dangerous reservation,' he said softly; 'since only all could ever be enough.'

'All the same,' Vicki said guardedly, 'I've seen the tragedies of these really great loves; the tearing heart-ache of them … love gaily, lightly and be loved just that much more than you have to give in return. There lies happiness.'

'Even so, there must be one who gives all,' he reminded her.

'Then I shall studiously avoid the role,' she insisted.

He shook his head.

'You're not the type to calculate the cost once your heart were involved. I'd stake my life on that.'

'A rash pronouncement after so brief an acquaintance, surely.'

Their eyes met, half startled, inquiring, disturbingly revealing.

'So be it,' he said softly: '"Nor all thy Piety nor Wit Shall lure it back to cancel half a Line."...'

Vicki caught at her breath.

'I thought of the Rubaiyat this morning... It seemed that, somehow, today was fateful. And now you finish the quotation from those immortal words.'

'You will not deny them and you will not deny yourself all the power and the passion that lies, perhaps dormant now, within you,' he said tensely. 'Not for you the half-measures of caution, the fear of being hurt. Your life is cast in a sterner mould and you'll never change it.'

Vicki stared up at him questioningly.

'Is that professional instinct or effective guesswork?'

'Neither.' It was a clipped utterance, almost stern. He held her gaze. 'A challenge, perhaps.'

She said with quiet authority:

'Suppose we go inside... I still have my key.'

The door opened and cold, stale air rushed at them. Already the house had become a shell. Litter remained from the sale; furniture, as yet uncollected, was stacked in readiness for removers. Yet none of this could mar its essential beauty; its

40

spacious rooms, exquisitely carved wood-
work, imposing staircase.

Vicki showed him every corner. This had
been her especial sanctum; this wing, their
nurseries and so on. The light began to fade,
but still their footsteps echoed hollowly, still
their voices could be heard.

'And now,' she said as once more they
returned to the lofty hall, 'your family will
take over ... your children play on those
lawns and run through these old rooms. I
am so grateful, now, that it happened to be
you.'

Guy said comically:

'I hate to disillusion you, but I've every
intention of remaining a bachelor.'

Vicki stared up at him.

'Are you serious?'

'Perfectly. I've managed to keep in that
enviable state for thirty-three years.'

'On the principle that "he travels fastest
who travels alone".'

'Exactly.'

'I rather wondered if you might not have
had marriage in mind when you bought this
house,' she said a trifle subdued.

'No: I have a splendid housekeeper who
will take over here and, with daily help –
once I have this ground floor as my flat –
what could be more ideal?' He smiled at her
indulgently. 'But I'll have to see what my
friends, who are hoping to have the other

two flats, can do about providing the family atmosphere. They are both married.'

Vicki said swiftly:

'What have you against marriage?'

'Nothing – for other people.'

Spirit flashed into her eyes.

'Yet you talked like that about me – my future.'

'Why not?' It was a cool, calm question. 'One can be a romantic at heart without wanting to *marry*.' He added: 'And, if I may say so, a reasonably good judge of other people's emotional make-up.'

'I take it that you are not against *all* emotional ties.'

'I'm not against *anything* that contributes towards human happiness.'

'The enviable state of man,' she said with a trace of bitterness. 'To love without ties–'

'You disapprove?'

'I haven't, honestly, given the subject much thought.' She felt suddenly irritated as though the conversation had lost its harmony.

'The world will be a shock to you,' he said warningly. 'Oh, I'm not suggesting that you have been brought up in a nunnery, or that you are not fully aware of the weaknesses of human beings; but being aware of those weaknesses and being plunged into a world where they are the rule and not the exception – a vastly different matter. Textbook sex and reality are as apart as the poles.'

'I don't doubt that fact.'

'You're angry,' he said quietly.

'Don't be ridiculous!'

'There's ice instead of fire,' he added tensely. 'Believe me, I'm not a Casanova.'

Vicki said shortly:

'You are not answerable to me for your actions even if that were so.' She added: 'It's getting dark; there's no point in our staying any longer.'

They went out into the cool, night air. Above them the sky still quivered in the radiance of the afterglow; below, soft crimson light was diffused upon the grounds around them as though invisible limes were pouring their magic upon every flower, every blade of grass, giving it new life and an unearthly beauty.

Guy said:

'"The setting sun and music at the close."'

'Richard III,' Vicki murmured. 'You're fond of poetry?'

'I like to remember it when words fail me,' he said simply. 'To see beauty through the great minds of the past.'

'But you would fiercely resist any suggestion of sentimentality?'

'Yes.' He shook his head. 'Very definitely.'

'You are an exceedingly complex person.'

'We are all complex and a mass of contraditions,' he insisted.

An intense loneliness stole upon her in that moment. She told herself that it was no more than reaction to her surroundings, but a certain fierce and ungovernable yearning stirred within her as she looked out upon the glory of the scene around her. The suggestion of unity – with which her earlier discussions with Guy Evans had been marked – vanished, leaving a rather desolate isolation. She resisted the idea to no avail and her silence as they returned to the car and drove away prompted his:

'Miss Wayne ... have I annoyed you? Upset you?'

Instantly, she was alert.

'Of course not.'

'Then I ought not to have agreed to take you back to Old Meadows; it has depressed you.'

She cried:

'No, really. One has moods and beauty – a night such as this – does not always inspire happiness.'

'No,' he said hoarsely; 'all too often the indefinable yearning is nearer to pain.'

She glanced at him in surprise.

'You understand that?'

'Why shouldn't I?'

She shook her head, bewildered and confused.

'I thought–'

He interrupted her:

'You thought – jumping to conclusions like all women – that because I said I intended to remain a bachelor that I was either a hardened sinner, or a hardened cynic!'

Vicki's spirits were raised slightly.

'Not that,' she insisted.

Guy went on:

'One of these days I'll tell you my life story,' he said, and there was a note of seriousness underlying the banter.

Vicki said unexpectedly:

'I'd like that.'

'But not in office hours!'

She glanced at him, seeing the clear lines of his profile in the semi-darkness of the car, and finding that her heart was beating slightly faster than its normal rate. It both annoyed and disturbed her to realize that he had the power physically to stir her. Her mood was a treachery of the senses and she recognized the fact. Emotion surged after weeks, even months, of misery and repression. Life burst through the dam of its restraint, demanding to be heard – the life that throbbed within her, eager, youthful, desirous. Her voice shook a little as she repeated:

'"Not in office hours" and I am sure you are a very busy man outside your professional sphere.'

'That fact will not prevent my asking you to dinner. Will you come?'

She smiled in the darkness.

'When you ask me you shall have my answer, Dr Evans.'

They drove back to the cottage.

Vicki said:

'Daddy bought this property to house any retiring staff, later on. We're terribly cramped, but it is a home rent-free and that will make all the difference.' She turned to him. 'Unfortunately a very great deal was owing to the Inland Revenue or we should have benefited greatly by the sale of Old Meadows. As it is–'

'You mean that–'

Vicki shook her head.

'Nadia has a small income and I a smaller one left in trust for me by my grandfather. But the tax on unearned income today... Otherwise, none of the money made yesterday will come to us.'

Guy groaned.

'On the other hand, had the sale realized less, or had you been less generous, we might well have had to sell this little place also. So please understand just how we do appreciate your gesture.'

He turned, his expression solemn as he faced her.

'If ever there is anything I can do – anything, please don't insult me by not regarding me as a friend. I cannot think in terms of time and the fact that we did not know each other yesterday, has nothing to do with what I am trying to say now.' He drew her gaze deeply, masterfully to his: 'Either we go on from here in under-standing, or we become purely two people associated professionally only. And I would much prefer the former. I'm not intruding; you have your solicitors and all the rest of it, but you and your mother are alone–' He stopped. 'You haven't any brothers or sisters, I take it?'

'One sister; she will not be home until August; she's on a cruise at the moment. A widow.'

Guy said swiftly:

'Funny; I can't think of anyone else in the circle.'

Vicki smiled.

'You will have to do so, then.'

'But that is beside the point...' He spoke softly.

'I know it is and I promise that we will not insult you by refusing any help – no matter what its nature – you so generously offer to give.'

'Ah,' he said with satisfaction. 'That's better.'

'Will you come in?'

'No; thank you all the same. I have some plates I want to study tonight and must get

back. I have a flat just off Harley Street –
fortunately. It saves a great deal of effort.'

'Will you keep it on afterwards?'

'Yes; this will be my week-end heaven and
my sanctuary in old age.'

Vickie laughed.

'I'll come to visit you then and, who
knows, follow your example and "travel
alone".'

He shook his head.

'Never; I'll dance at your wedding.'

'Is that a bet?'

'No; I never bet on certainties.'

She began to get out of the car and he
swiftly moved to assist her.

'It's been a most pleasant evening,' she
said sincerely.

'And I'm restored to favour?'

'Have you been out of it?'

'I rather think so – just for a brief while
tonight.' He looked at her intently.

'You are far, far too discerning.'

'All part of my professional training,' he
said blithely. 'Good-night…'

Vicki ventured.

'And on Monday–'

'Yes,' he said briskly; 'at nine-thirty.'

She wondered just what he was doing over
the weekend and almost as though reading
her thoughts he said:

'I'm going up to Stanton this week-end;
but I'll try to set you a good example and be

48

at Wimpole Street early!'

Vicki cried:

'Stanton near Broadway?'

'Yes. Lovely spot...' He opened the gate for her and stood there while she passed through it. 'Good-night,' he said again. 'Let me see you into the cottage; it's getting chilly out here.'

Vicki did as she was told and from the open doorway watched his car glide away, his headlights throwing bright fans of light seemingly for a mile down the lane.

Monday, at nine-thirty... Stanton... Was there someone special whom he visited there? Colour flamed into her cheeks. What was it to do with her and what did she care if he made love to fifty women. He was a free man...

The philosophy, however, did not remove the depression from her heart...

CHAPTER 3

The following two months brought an almost fantastic change in Vicki's life. During that time she took her place as a working girl and, after the first week or so, merged herself completely into the mysterious world behind the doors of Dr Guy

49

Evans's Wimpole Street rooms. She was immediately popular with his patients, anticipating their fears and soothing their jagged nerves. Her smile and air of 'I know just how you feel, but there isn't anything to worry about,' won their gratitude and appreciation. The intricacies of radiotherapy, the complications of the massive X-ray apparatus, the incredible skill and medical knowledge that informed the work of Guy Evans, provided an interest both absorbing and satisfying. Above all, she was accepted by the other members of his staff, enjoying their light-hearted banter, their confidences, to say nothing of their astringent and witty comments about certain patients.

Vicki saw very little of Guy during those months, beyond what was necessary in the course of her duties. He treated her with precisely the same courtesy and consideration shown to the rest of the staff, but there was nothing to indicate a former, or more intimate, acquaintanceship. And no suggestion came from him regarding any outside meeting. Her month on trial passed and her appointment was approved permanently by his saying:

'You've been excellent, Miss Wayne. I hope you feel disposed to remain.'

To which, somewhat abashed, she had replied:

'If you wish.'

He had looked up from an X-ray plate which he was intently studying and, for an instant, their eyes had met.

'Then we can take it as settled... Would you bring me Mrs Watson's file?' And with that he had turned away, her presence apparently forgotten.

Well, Vicki had thought defiantly, he had warned her that it would be a strictly official appointment.

It was Thelma Minton, his secretary, who said to Vicki at the end of that second month:

'He never changes a scrap, that man. Attractive devil; inscrutable, impersonal; yet fair and considerate to work with. I'd all manner of ideas when I came here four years ago. You know: secretary marries boss ... and they say he's bought the most marvellous place down near Ascot ... but, if you ask me, no woman will hook Guy Evans. He loves 'em all a little.'

Vicki liked Thelma; she had a forthright approach to life and was very kind. She had known poverty and hardship and had struggled to reach her present position.

Vicki found herself asking, breathlessly:

'Isn't there anyone special? No woman with whom his name has ever been linked?'

Thelma flashed a smile. She was dazzlingly blonde, impeccably groomed and sophisticated.

'Not at the moment. There was a time, about two years ago, when he went off to Sweden for a holiday; they say he had a pretty hectic affair then and certainly he came back rather nervy and we all went through it – the only time things changed around here. I don't think the lady could have treated him very well – amazing, but there it is. The woman was supposed to be married and very glamorous.' Thelma shrugged her shoulders. 'Whatever he's done since then, he's been mighty discreet about, believe me.' A sigh. 'Absolute crime for an attractive brute like that to be a bachelor.'

Vicki felt suddenly cold; she hated the idea of anything sordid touching this man whom she had come enormously to respect.

'I should think the story about Sweden was most unlikely or exaggerated,' she said with some spirit.

Thelma smiled good-humouredly.

'You carrying the torch too, my dear?'

Vicki looked perplexed.

'I don't follow.'

'Skip it,' said Thelma. She patted Vicki's shoulder. 'You're a sweet kid ... and *that* is dear Lady Frozen Mitt ... don't keep *her* waiting!'

Vicki found herself reflecting upon Thelma's story throughout the rest of the day while at the same time telling herself that it had nothing whatsoever to do with her. In fact, it was becoming increasingly obvious that he had no wish, or intention, of pursuing the friendship of which he had spoken so earnestly on the night of their visit to Old Meadows. Just why, since her coming to Wimpole Street, had he not mentioned anything connected with the house? Why had he behaved as though she were as complete a stranger to him, outside consulting hours, as the other members of the staff? Useless denying that it had caused her unhappiness, but she had argued that he might well consider that to mix business with pleasure would be dangerous and had thought better of his earlier, impulsive gesture. She was now, she knew, an efficient receptionist, learning far more, in actual fact, than her job entailed. From his point of view it was not important who she was, so long as she served him well.

Vicki reviewed those two months dispassionately. She had learned much about life and people in general; realized how sheltered her own existence had been... She had tasted the first discomfort of standing in bus queues; the frantic struggle in the rush hour to catch her train; the gloom and depression of Waterloo between five and six, when its hordes flooded up from escalators and poured into already packed carriages ... the weariness, the apathy and sometimes the gaiety, too. She had ached in every limb at first; her feet swelling, her back apparently breaking. The leisure and luxury of the past loomed like a dream; the present, a nightmare. But, gradually, she rose to meet the changed circumstances and to realize that there was zest and interest in a life no longer filled with amusement and pleasure, but mostly with work. No one at Wimpole Street was aware of her former position; they knew only that she lived with her mother in a cottage at Ascot.

One evening when Vicki had stayed behind a little later than usual and undertaken a few routine jobs in order that Thelma might leave early, Guy, in search of Thelma, strode into the room and, seeing Vicki, stopped abruptly. Swiftly, she explained her presence there.

He said almost curtly:

'I will not have the other members of the staff imposing on you.'

Vicki smiled.

'Quite frankly, I like the work. I want to learn.'

The memory of that night at Old Meadows seemed suddenly to be flashed between them as on some invisible screen.

'I'm glad you're happy here.'

A little of the proud spirit of the past reared its head. She might be employed by this man, but that did not mean utter subservience, or fear of displeasing him. She said deliberately:

'I'm told that the work at Old Meadows is proceeding very well.'

Guy jerked his head up, becoming instantly on the defensive.

'I'm satisfied with it,' he said briefly. 'Would you be good enough to get Dr Orlong on the phone and switch the call through to me?'

'Certainly, Dr Evans,' she said coldly.

A pained bewilderment gripped Vicki as she watched him stride away; she felt faint and sick without knowing quite why. She drew herself up sharply. Was she going to hang on his every word, live only in the hope that he might extend their present, formal relationship? The whip of scorn, self-administered, returned her to near-normality. She got the call and said icily:

'Your call to Dr Orlong.'

Then, swiftly, she tore off her white overall and began to put on her coat and hat. She had reached the door when a voice startled her and she turned to meet Guy's tense, compelling gaze:

'Will you have dinner with me?'

Her expression remained coldly forbidding, although her heart missed a beat.

'I hardly think we have any reason–'

He interrupted her.

'Please. I *must* talk to you.'

She didn't relax as she said:

'Very well.' And her tone made it a concession.

'Do you mind coming over to my flat?'

'Not at all.'

'It would be simpler and I hate talking in a hotel lounge or restaurant.'

She said flippantly:

'You do not need to invite me to dinner in order to dismiss me, you know.'

'And is that the only reason you can think of that would prompt me to invite you to dinner?'

'Shall we say the one that comes most readily to mind?' she answered coolly.

He drew her gaze to his with a masterful penetration.

'Then you have yet to learn how far from the truth your deductions are.'

They walked the short distance to his flat and were admitted by his housekeeper, a motherly looking woman approaching fifty, to whom Guy represented a whole world, since she had begun as his nurse.

'Dinner for two,' he said smilingly.

He led Vicki into his sitting-room; a comfortable, yet artistic room with rich burgundy carpet and deep blue velvet curtains. A man's room, but without the drabness too often associated with the term. The windows were screened with silk net and, despite the heat of the evening, a breeze stirred, giving a suggestion of coolness.

Vicki made no comment, remaining tensed, wary.

'What can I get you?' he asked going to a cocktail cabinet.

'Sherry,' she answered simply, 'please.'

He poured out two, handed her one and then sat down opposite her. And suddenly he sighed.

'At last,' he murmured. 'You are here.'

She stared at him.

'I'm sorry,' she said calmly, fighting to maintain a rigid control, in face of his somewhat unusual attitude. 'I cannot be expected to appreciate the implication of that remark.'

He studied her earnestly.

'No,' he agreed; 'you cannot.' He got up from his chair restlessly and stood looking down at her, one elbow resting on the mantelpiece. 'My attitude during these months must have seemed very odd.'

She did not capitulate.

'You warned me that there would be no favours; I have received the courtesy and consideration given to the rest of your staff. I make no complaint.'

A wry smile touched his lips, which faded into an expression of near regret.

'I, also, said once that either we went on in understanding, or became two people associated professionally.'

Vicki caught at her breath.

'It hasn't been difficult for me to recognize your choice, Dr Evans. I am merely your receptionist and so long as I prove efficient and am satisfied with the position, why concern yourself further?'

He drew her gaze to his.

'And you're serious in this attitude – aren't you?'

'I have no "attitude", I have merely behaved in a manner I considered to be expected of me,' she added a little ironically. Then, because her heart was thudding so fiercely that it seemed liable to choke her, she tried to change the subject. 'This is a very charming room; I love the richness of the colours.'

He might not have heard her as he said hoarsely:

'And you really believe that my behaviour during those past months has meant my indifference to you – as a person?'

She raised her gaze to his:

'Naturally.' She added: 'That is rather an overstatement; after all, there was no reason why either of us should be unduly interested in the other. Our association was of the briefest and concerned only with the sale of Old Meadows.'

'And did you imagine that our second meeting that evening would prove to be our last – at least in that capacity of friendly acquaintances?'

Vicki felt a curious thrill creep over her body; an excitement not to be denied. Colour rose to her cheeks as she answered him, clinging to the last frail thread of her pride.

'I cannot see that the question is in the least important.'

'Then I must have been a far better actor all these weeks than I had dared to hope,' he exclaimed startlingly.

She made a helpless gesture.

'You talk in riddles.'

'Do I? Can't you guess what I'm trying to say?'

Vicki was conscious of a certain shock; of a sudden electrifying of the atmosphere.

'No–' It was a half-inquiring sound.

'Haven't you realized that all these weeks I've been fighting to resist you; doing everything within my power not to acknowledge the fact, even to myself, that I was in love with you?'

Vicki's lips parted.

'In love with me,' she gasped as though the utterance were the most fantastic she had ever heard.

'Yes,' he said slowly and with increasing passion, 'in love with you. At first I ridiculed the idea ... but I've fought a losing battle. I foolishly imagined that by regarding you simply and solely as a part of my staff – and treating you as such – that the emotion

59

would die. Well, it hasn't and I cannot go on any longer; I cannot endure the strain of seeing you all day and every day and loving you, my darling, until I cannot think beyond that love.'

Vicki was trembling; every limb, it seemed, every nerve quivering with the realization of his words. She could not grasp them in a matter of seconds, accept the explanation of his conduct... Was it that she dared not, lest she awaken and find it all an impossible dream? Her voice was unsteady as she whispered:

'I never for one moment *thought*–'

He said almost harshly:

'That was my objective.'

She drew on her courage, her dignity.

'I think I understand. You're the confirmed bachelor and your – your feelings for me cut across every desire, every plan, threatening to wreck all that you had so surely built as foundations for the future...'

'I admit that,' he said tensely.

Her heart felt suddenly leaden within her as she went on:

'And having found my presence a distraction, a menace, shall we say, you now want me to leave in order that you can cut out the sickness that afflicts you – forget me and, in time, go on–'

'Are you mad?' he cried.

'Quite probably,' she replied.

'Oh, my *dear;* don't you see? I can't go on without you... I don't *care* about my plans, about anything in this world except you – *you...* I love you – love you far more deeply than I could ever make you realize with any words. Oh, darling ... marry me; that's what I'm trying to say – to ask – and I'm afraid, terrified, that your answer might be no.'

He remained standing, looking down at her, aware of her hesitation, her bewilderment, as she gasped:

'It doesn't seem real – I–'

'Meaning that you are not in love with me,' he said with a desperate gentleness.

Vicki raised her eyes to his.

'No,' she whispered and her heart beats quickened as she spoke; 'that I *am* in love with you, even though I wouldn't admit it to myself until this minute...' Her expression was suddenly radiant, her eyes starry. 'Oh, Guy,' she finished shakily.

He drew her swiftly to her feet, then passionately found her lips, holding her with a fierceness that met the sudden need within her, awakening every instinct, every desire, as her arms crept up around his neck and she felt the tensing of his body against hers, the desperate longing.

He lifted his mouth from her warm, soft lips and, for a second, looked down into her misted eyes:

'I adore you, Vicki, adore you.'

'And I you.'

'No reservations?'

'None.' She moved, craving his kiss that almost suffocated with its intensity, leaving her breathless, exhausted and ecstatic. A thrill shot through her body at his touch, seeming to bring her to throbbing life; to light some invisible lamp within her heart; so that she was transformed by a radiance beautifying and all sufficing... She was loved ... and she loved – completely, and with that intensity that was a part of her volatile, passionate nature.

She felt his lips upon her eyes, her throat and clung to him in frenzied need. Then, abruptly, he released her, so that she swayed even as she stood there and then sank down in her chair, her cheeks flaming, her mouth bruised and burning.

'And you,' she said unevenly, 'are the cold, phlegmatic man about whom I've been imagining so much!'

'And you the enchantress whom I sought to resist and look at me now!' He laughed softly and lit his cigarette. 'Even my hands are shaking like mad!'

Vicki said with earnestness:

'I couldn't bear regret, Guy; regrets because of your lost freedom. Before I promise to marry you–'

He started.

'You've already promised!'

'Not in so many words.'

He held her gaze.

'Don't actions count?' He added softly: 'There are no regrets and there never will be any. It is easy to talk of being a bachelor and of avoiding marriage when one has never really been sufficiently fond of anyone to want to give up one's freedom.'

Vicki thought of Thelma's words and said hastily:

'And hasn't there been anyone like that – ever?'

He stood before her and unflinchingly met her gaze.

'No, my darling; never anything even approaching this. Oh,' he paused for a second, 'I am not going to deceive you into believing that there have never been any women in my life, but if I say that in my opinion the past is dead – for both of us – from this moment, is that enough?'

'Quite enough ... and I hope I understand life sufficiently to know that you are far too attractive never to have had any love affairs, Guy–'

'You're very sweet, my darling.'

'That I just *haven't* any past–' she shrugged her shoulders, 'is of no consequence; my life was so gloriously simple and restricted in one sense that any lovers – as *such* – definitely, no!'

'I don't deserve you,' he said gravely.

'That is for me to say.'

He bent and kissed the top of her head.

'I suppose I must gladly concede you that,' he said gaily. Then: 'Vicki … do you realize something?'

'What?'

'That you will go back to Old Meadows and that, after all, there will be—'

'Children playing on the lawns,' she said softly, almost with reverence.

'*Darling.* Strange how loving you has made all those things important; as though, before, only half of life was visible to me and now, suddenly, it has become a full circle – complete. Never until this moment have I blessed the fact of my uncle's legacy; now I do … I want to give you so much.'

She smiled up at him.

'And just when I was learning to do so well on so *little*.'

'You've been magnificent,' he said softly.

'And you were quite the most frigid—'

'I know! Don't say it!' He laughed.

'I think I'm glad,' she said unexpectedly. 'You've had time, at least, in which to study me and argue with yourself about me.'

He picked up her hand and held it against his cheek.

'I could have asked you to marry me that night in the car, my dearest, had it been merely the desire to do so. Then, I distrusted my emotions and afterwards struggled to preserve what I foolishly imagined to be freedom.' He said swiftly: 'Darling, not a long engagement – please.'

She looked innocent.

'How long?'

'A week?' He was laughing.

'Three months,' she said.

'Are you serious?'

'Shamelessly so. I want to be with you ... watch our home grow...'

'And you'd be content to begin with me here, if Old Meadows is not ready?'

'*Content!*' A sigh. 'You've starved me of your company for so long. Oh, darling, I'm so *happy!* Do you think that such happiness can possibly last? Or is it–'

'It is our heritage, my darling, so long as we make it so. We are its custodians and it rests with us.' His voice was low and earnest. 'We should hate failure, Vicki.'

She shivered; a little cold wind of apprehension blew across her heart.

'Yes,' she whispered.

He said anxiously:

'What is it?'

She threw off the unexplicable mood of depression.

'Stupid fear. I suppose, just lately, so much has been new and strange to me that I almost distrust this – this bliss.'

He sat down on the arm of her chair.

'Don't,' he whispered, 'distrust anything,

Vicki. It attracts misery. And what have we to fear?'

'Nothing,' she admitted and relaxed with a little sigh of content. Then, looking up at him, she said: 'Do you realize how little we've actually been together during these months; how little we know about each other?'

'What one knows about another person is not governed by time,' he said thoughtfully and with conviction. 'Affinity is there, or not, from the instant two people meet and, mostly, they are aware of that fact.'

Vicki laughed softly.

'When we first met I most certainly did not welcome you as *that!*'

'Didn't you?' His voice was low. 'Be honest: suppose that night at Old Meadows I had made love to you, would you have repulsed me? Can you deny that, as we sat in the car together during those last moments, that there was something intense, even passionate, that could so easily have brought us precisely to where we are now?'

Vicki didn't resist the suggestion because she knew it to be so near the truth.

'I could not deny, or wish to deny, that, darling,' she said with a fervour that stirred him anew so that he leaned down and kissed her, with a lingering tenderness.

'I wanted desperately to do just that,' he said as he drew away from her. 'But I felt quite certain that you would hate any clumsy, precipitate action.'

'You certainly haven't taken any risks in that direction since,' she said with a little laugh that echoed gaily through the silence.

'Such commendable restraint on my part,' he teased.

'Such fierce self-preservation,' she corrected. 'To resist me at all costs! And I did nothing, you must admit, to encourage you, or make my presence felt in any way.'

'You were capably frigid – the Victoria Wayne of the sale day,' he agreed. 'But I still adored you! The more distant you became the worse I felt. And the inflection of your voice tonight when you put that Orlong call through ... was more than I could stand.'

'*You* could stand ... oh, Guy!' She sighed ecstatically.

'And you are serious about our being married in three months?'

'Yes, but–'

'But, what?'

She looked entrancingly confused.

'If you feel as I about it.'

'My darling, there is nothing so eager or so rabid as a convert, and I, being a convert to the idea of marriage – well, I want desperately to begin living in that world which I have so studiously avoided.'

She looked up at him and smiled.

'You will be a great surprise to everyone –

particularly my sister who should be home next week – just in time for a little informal engagement party.'

'I hope she and all your friends will approve of me,' he said and there was content and gaiety between them.

'And your friends – me.'

He looked down at her eager, radiant face, aware anew of her charm and gentle beauty that lent such vivid contrast to the more passionate depths of her character.

'That is a foregone conclusion. I wish so much that my parents could have been alive to know you, Vicki.' He picked up her hands as he spoke and held them caressingly. Then: 'What will Mrs Wayne think?'

'Nadia? All the right things, provided I am happy. She will be amazed, of course!'

'And are there any special friends – particularly the males?'

Vicki said honestly:

'Quite a few; chief among them Digby Graves.'

'The persistent type – eh?'

'Yes; but not the placid.'

'Too bad; the placid are so much simpler.'

'Digby is a very wealthy young man,' she said. 'Too wealthy for his own good. His father built up a vast engineering firm in the north; Digby inherited the results of his labours.'

'And he wants to marry you?'

Vicki laughed.

'He proposes to me with regularity and I decline him. His argument is that "water dropping on a stone—"' She shook her head. 'I've always felt that there was something unsteady about Digby ... you know how you get the idea that the lives of some people are doomed to end in tragedy?'

'Yes. All the same I'm sorry for Digby.'

Vicki said, not ungenerously:

'So am I, but up to a point; he finds all women irresistible and there are so many to console him!'

'Cynic!'

'Never; I hope merely a good judge of character.' She raised her eyes to his. 'And that conviction has never more forcibly been brought home to me than at this moment, as I look at you, darling.'

His lips on hers gave silent answer.

They dined and afterwards Guy said:

'I'm going to run you home, my dearest.'

She sighed.

'That will be heaven.'

'And explain to your mother that I am very, very much in love with you,' he added lightly, yet with that underlying note of passion that sent a thrill through her body.

'No one in the world will better understand all we feel than Nadia,' she said gently. 'She and my father remained lovers to the end. It was a perfect relationship.'

'I hope,' Guy said thoughtfully, 'that we shall not hurt her the more because of our happiness and because it follows so closely upon her sadness ... are we being selfish in–'

'Wishing to marry so soon?' Vicki swiftly gauged his thoughts. 'No, darling. And Daddy would have loathed any conventional mourning; he had very strong views on the subject and' – she looked at Guy appealingly – 'we don't want any formal wedding, or any fuss – do we?'

He smiled indulgently.

'I thought all women wanted both!'

'Then I am the exception,' she admitted. 'I always feel that the greater the fuss the less the sincerity. I couldn't bear the emotional strain of the "big" wedding, anyway.'

'Nor I.' He breathed deeply. 'You are quite unique, my dearest.'

Vicki smiled knowingly:

'Just so long as you keep believing that.'

'Just so long as you make it possible for me to do so!'

They looked at each other and laughed. Life seemed, just then, so simple, so ecstatic as to be almost unbelievable.

Guy stooped and pressed his mouth against her parted lips. For a second his kiss was fiercely passionate. Then, abruptly, he drew back:

'Come along, my sweet; this is where I take you home,' he said hoarsely.

CHAPTER 4

Nadia welcomed them, somewhat surprised to see Guy Evans standing there beside Vicki. Tactfully, she had refrained from mentioning him, keeping her romantic hopes to herself and feeling that Vicki's silence regarding her relationship with him should be accepted without questioning.

'Dr Evans,' she said smilingly. 'How nice to see you again.'

Guy replied swiftly:

'I hope you will still feel that when you hear the news that Vicki has consented to be my wife.' His intonation removed any formality, or coldness, from the phrasing.

Nadia gasped; she was completely surprised.

'But–' She made a helpless gesture, then: 'Oh, bless you both. I'm so *happy* for you.' She peered into Vicki's face.

Vicki hastened:

'Nadia, I didn't have any opportunity, whatsoever, of confiding in you before... I'm marrying the confirmed bachelor who, apparently, held out against me with sadistic cruelty.'

They laughed together: three people

instantly in harmony. Guy relaxed and felt completely at home. The early wedding was discussed and the possibility of a small engagement party in a fortnight's time.

Nadia said gently:

'And so you will go back to Old Meadows, Vicki.'

Vicki said in a hushed voice:

'Does that hurt? I mean—'

'Darling – no! It makes me very content. Your father would have been so happy. At least the tradition will go on and even in these days when tradition counts for so little, it still holds a very precious graciousness which lends colour to life.'

A sudden sadness crept upon Vicki as she sat there, a shadow thrown, as it were, by the reflection of her own almost suffocating happiness. It hurt her that Nadia was now so reduced in circumstances while she, Vicki, was about to marry a comparatively wealthy man. That aspect of Guy had never before registered in her mind; never for an instant had she considered either his financial, or his social, position; now both were, inevitably, thrown into relief. To deny the unutterable joy of a return to Old Meadows – even to a flat, as it would be, there – would have been hypocritical; yet she knew, full well, that no matter what Guy's material assets might have been, or how meagre, nothing would have prevented her decision to marry him.

Her ardour, her devotion, her admiration, was infinitely greater because of her up-bringing; she had not been long enough in the modern, materialistic world, for her ideals to be submerged, her views tainted with either cynicism or sophistication. She had matured in a certain idealism that intensified her conception of love, marriage and all human relationships. It struck her, however, that, as Guy's wife – how madly her heart raced at the thought – she could do much for Nadia – surreptitiously – and was comforted by the belief.

'I think,' said Guy suddenly, 'that now I'm to become a married man, it might be a good idea to have only two flats instead of three.'

Vicki gasped:

'But hasn't the work progressed–'

'Not that far,' he assured her. 'And I've been sorely tempted to keep the major portion and have a maisonette, as it were, for myself. I couldn't part from that staircase! Or some of those lovely, upstairs rooms!' He looked adoringly at Vicki. 'You must come over it tomorrow and give the final instructions.'

Vicki said severely:

'And I must not be carried away by my own enthusiasm; we want a home large enough, but above all, small enough com-fortably to run.' A laugh. 'I don't want to ruin you before we begin!'

Guy chuckled.

'The Inland Revenue takes care of that!'

He left an hour later. Vicki saw him into his car and lingered as though loath to part. It was then moonlight – a night of stars and painted shadows upon a silvered country-side – and a soft, warm breeze touched their faces seeming to hold the shiver of ecstasy in its breath.

'Till tomorrow… I shall tell the staff,' Guy said joyously.

Vicki thought of Thelma. She would find it almost impossible to believe!

'And I'd like to stay on for at least another month,' Vicki said. 'May I?'

'Just to keep an eye on me?' He held her gaze deeply.

'Is that necessary?' She caught at her breath.

He shook his head.

'No, my darling,' he said gravely. There was something intense about him as he spoke which, afterwards, she remembered with a certain anguish. 'Do you believe me?'

'Yes,' she whispered. 'With all my heart.'

He smiled, a radiant, contented smile.

'My heart feels far too small to hold all the emotions surging into it,' he said with a little smile. 'And to think I might have missed all this had it not been for you, darling.'

'Might there not have been someone else?'

She spoke quietly.

He shook his head.

'No; because obviously Fate intended it to be – you–'

'And that we should meet,' she suggested.

He gave a little laugh.

'Do you want to argue it out?'

'No.' She sighed. 'I only want to keep you here a few moments longer.' She stood back. 'But you must go, you've a terribly full day tomorrow and need *some* sleep!'

He kissed her hand, put the car into gear and moved away. She watched him as she had done on that previous occasion. How little she had dreamed, then, that next time he visited White Cottage they would be engaged.

Nadia smiled as she re-entered the sitting-room.

'This is perfect for you, Vicki. I'm so *glad*. Guy is everything any woman could wish for in a man and it may be silly of me, but I am so thankful he can give you the things to which you've always been accustomed – even though I know that, should it have been otherwise, it would not have made the slightest difference to your wanting to marry him.'

'No,' said Vicki, 'not the slightest difference … but to know that Old Meadows is still a part of us… Oh, Nadia, I think I'm afraid. I've realized during these months how very remote I've been from life; there was never any need for me to think about it beyond its normal evolution. Daddy's leaving us was my first sorrow, my first breath almost of *reality*... I cannot explain–'

'You don't have to. But Guy, like your father, will preserve that happiness.'

'And if he did not; or I failed him? I couldn't pretend or be flippant about it. I know myself; I'd die inside – whichever way it was. I'm too intense, Nadia; it's a fault that I must curb. I come up against it every day of my life.'

Nadia understood. She knew Vicki's limitations, not of character, but of experience and she knew that where, for instance, Brinda would toss an issue aside, Vicki would torture herself until she had satisfied herself that it was rightly settled. She had been a solemn, idealistic child; sensitive to a degree, but without any parading of the fact – even as today. Vicki's hurts turned inward to bruise and sear; she could not bewail them and so destroy them. In marriage it would be the same. She would adore Guy and be far too inclined to set him on a pedestal, idealizing his virtues and glossing over his failings. She would, Nadia knew, be faithful, passionate and devoted, but never, in any circumstances, be satisfied with less than complete success. Or less than her own measure of love. She would never understand vengefulness, vindictiveness, only a deep and terrible agony of the soul. Nadia pulled herself up sharply. Why dwell upon such things? With Guy her happiness would be safe and she would be the most alluring, attractive wife. It might be, Nadia thought painfully, her own love story all over again. Nevertheless, Nadia knew just what hell, what anguish she, herself, would have been capable of suffering had she ever known cause for disillusionment. And the courage to meet it; the courage apparently to dismiss it, in no way, she knew, lessened its wound or the depth of its scars. She said:

'Neither you nor Guy will fail... Take this happiness with both hands; don't lose one precious moment of it, Vicki; don't think beyond it, preserve it with your love, your passionate eagerness, and you will find that the years will pass like days that are always as wonderful, as new, as these first, rapturous moments. I've proved it so.'

Vicki smiled ecstatically.

'You're such a comfort, darling; I don't know what I'd have done without you.' She stopped. 'I wonder what Brinda will say.'

Nadia said instantly:

'Not that it really matters, but she will be pleased. Brinda will always roam and look in on us occasionally ... it is better so. And since she was left comfortably provided for, she would be foolish to settle down yet awhile.'

'She will probably marry again,' Vicki said ruminatively. 'And my marriage may draw us closer, Nadia.' The wish was father to the thought. 'I can quite see that there is a great gap between single and married women – even when those women are sisters. Rather like looking at each other across an island of experience that cannot be bridged except by that same experience.' She added: 'And, of course, she may come back here and stay with you.'

Nadia made no comment. Her love for Brinda in no way prevented her facing the inexorable fact that she was incompatible and a disruptive influence and her moods, often lovable and charming, nevertheless could plunge the household into gloom and ill-temper.

Vicki did not notice the silence that fell; she was far too busy with her own thoughts; experiencing that surge of emotion that flooded her heart as she dwelt upon Guy and their love for each other; aware of that sudden, sharp and sweet sense of belonging, as though miraculously, in the space of hours, she had become a woman where before she had been merely an immature and ineffectual girl. Guy's fiancée ... and in three months, his wife. She realized then, that they hadn't told Nadia how soon was their intention to marry. Hesitantly, she exclaimed:

'Nadia ... would you think it very selfish if we were to marry in three months' time?'

'Darling, you know me better than that. Why wait? Why waste the days. Had you said you were going to marry next week I should have rejoiced for you.'

'And you?'

'I shall be perfectly all right here with Emma. I can manage very well.'

'You would say that.'

'It is true, darling.'

'Financially–'

'That extra fifteen hundred that Guy so generously gave for the house has meant so much more proportionately – given that little margin, Vicki, and we–'

'Everything,' said Vicki almost sternly, 'is yours, Nadia, from now on. That must be so.'

Nadia smiled.

'We will not argue about that,' she said with an indulgent smile. 'Now, to bed with you or you'll never get to Wimpole Street in the morning.' She added swiftly: 'I shall give a very modest engagement party for you, darling. Next week some time–'

'That would be perfect. And I suppose it is useless waiting for Brinda and now that she is on that cruise we can't even contact her–'

'You'll probably be married before she returns to England, darling. She will understand.'

79

Vicki nodded and went to bed, there to lie awake dreaming, planning and re-living the ecstatic moments spent in Guy's arms. Impossible wholly to grasp the fact of her own happiness; to realize that the pattern of her future had that day been traced and seemingly in a thread of pure gold. Strange that she had from the beginning been made aware of an inexorable destiny linking her with Guy; that even through the months of his apparent indifference the subconscious belief had lingered.

The week that followed was a whirl of rapturous delight. The staff at Wimpole Street could not have been kinder, or more generous in their good wishes and Vicki was touched by their sincerity, realizing that she would never forget their gay comradeship and oblivious of the fact that her unaffected simplicity, allied to a certain indefinable graciousness, had inspired such emotions within them.

The *last* patient had a tremendous significance as each day ended. Then Vicki could go into Guy's room, meet his gaze and move swiftly into his arms. The house would be still; they would be alone and no patients would be sitting in the waiting-room...

They went down to Old Meadows at the first opportunity, arriving there just before seven, when the August sun seemed to have borrowed the deeper hue of autumn and poured upon it a molten gold that made each window glitter like a gigantic coin, throwing into shadow the cream-painted walls and stately pillars. The grounds, still perfectly kept, stretched cool and green into the distance; the blue-capped hills a frieze beyond them, majestic against the evening sky. Vicki caught at her breath. This had been her heritage and it would be that of her children, after all. Her children and Guy's... Her heart lifted and seemed to throb with the intensity of her happiness. She looked up at Guy, moved by a curious reverence.

'Oh darling,' she whispered, 'to be here with you like *this;* to come home, as it were, and have your love. I ask myself if anyone can deserve all that.'

He took her hand and led her into the still, empty hall. His eyes answered her, the pressure of his fingers more expressive than a multitude of words. Then he said humbly:

'I think, now, that I, too, know fear ... of losing you; losing you when I know that you are my life and that everything that has ever been written about love isn't enough to express all that I feel for you, my dearest. There's so much ahead. So much to achieve and not merely to *buy*, Vicki.'

'I know; I love you to love your work; the fact that you haven't given it up; your attitude towards it all and – oh, Guy, I'm a little dazed by my own joy, my own love for you. Now I know why all lovers think their particular love is "different". I do, too, because I refuse to believe that any woman has ever loved any man just as I do you.' She added gently: 'And if that is what they term all the wrong technique, I don't mind; it is true and I see no reason to hide that truth.'

He drew her into his arms.

'You cannot quite realize how unspoiled you are, Vicki, my dear darling; how untouched by so many things from which this background here, the life you led in this house, have guarded you. There's no guile—'

She looked crestfallen.

'No,' he insisted, 'you can be haughty, aloof, hostile and enchantingly adoring, but never could you pose or pretend, because it was either expected of you, or you imagine it to be the thing to do.' He looked thoughtful. 'Yours has been an upbringing that allowed of naturalness. Thank heaven for it.' He kissed her half-parted lips and held her close for a second, then: 'And this way we shall never settle the house question!'

She looked instantly serious.

'I think we should still make it into three flats; but take the west wing, which has a single suite, and add it to our rooms down here. That would give us the staircase and we could shut off everything to the east of that staircase. That way we should have our own rooms upstairs – bedroom, dressing-room, bathroom and a second bedroom, and downstairs the four reception rooms one of which we could turn into a bedroom. Then we could modernize the servants' quarters to provide, say, two residents with accommodation and leave two other bedrooms for nurseries,' she said honestly. 'The butler's pantry would make a lovely room for children!'

'Still in a hurry I see,' he said comically.

She said sagely:

'It is no use parting with the wrong portion of the house and then wanting it again. I know this house; we had four indoor servants when Daddy died and had cut down then. We want something far, far simpler, Guy. The upkeep and responsibility, today, is out of the question.' She added: 'And I should hate to see you forced to continue in practice long after you otherwise would, because this establishment was too great a financial drain.' She paused, finishing firmly: 'I'd specially like to keep the little west wing suite for ourselves, shut off all the rest and convert it. That would leave us our precious staircase and all this down here. *Quite* enough and to spare.'

'Practical young woman!'

'Concerned for you. It has done me a lot of good to plan a budget on seven pounds a week, including lunches and train fares,' she said. 'At first, I hadn't a penny by Tuesday … now, sometimes, I've a penny *left* on Saturday! And then I tell myself that many people have to run a home on less.'

Guy stared at her. It was she who had lived in this spacious house, waited on at every turn; she who had her car in the garage, her horse in the stable; she who had hunted and indulged her every whim … and here she was budgeting without complaint and instead of persuading him to plunge her back into the old life, was endeavouring to spare him expense in every way.

'You're wonderful,' he said. 'And I've said that before!'

'It always sounds like the first time,' she said softly. 'Guy, I want to be in charge here; to plan your meals, keep my fingers on the pulse of things … no I'm not going to be dishonest enough to say that I want to pose over the sink … but if it were necessary for me to do so, I'd join the millions of other women who are doing just that because they happen to love some man very much.'

Guy put his arm round her shoulders and pressed her face against his shoulder, kissing the top of her head as he did so.

'If I could adore you more – I would,' he said tensely.

She stirred and raised her mouth, inviting his kiss, feeling the pressure of his lips, the fierceness of a mounting passion sweeping them to a wild surrender; an intoxication of the senses that negatived time and place and left them shaken, trembling as he abruptly moved away from her and said hoarsely:

'Let's go, beloved, and I must try to resist you – impossible a task though it is. Now, about this suite upstairs.'

Their eyes met, the emotion of a few seconds before lingered between them like the echo of a haunting melody they could not escape. There was something almost desperate and intense about those moments as of two people on the brink of an agonizing parting. And a certain mute inquiry crept into Vicki's eyes as she whispered:

'It is as if I must hold these seconds... I don't know what it is, Guy... I only know that I love you until it seems to hurt.'

'Darling.' It was a rough sound. Then: 'I know; as though some vital force were demanding from us something which is greater than our strength to give.' He looked down into her eyes. 'I want you so terribly, my dearest.' An almost savage note crept into his voice. 'And that is just why I am going to put the distance of this hall between us and politely, or unpolitely, make my way up these stairs,' he said in an attempt to bring them back to normality.

She joined him on the landing and they

explored the suite, with its lofty, sunlit bedroom, one wall of which was devoted to floor-to-ceiling windows that gave a view over the entire acreage.

'I was born in this room,' Vicki said quietly. She looked at him. 'That seems suddenly to have a very great significance, darling, since I was, twenty-four years later, to come back to it – with you.' She avoided labouring the sentiment and moved swiftly into an adjoining dressing-room and bath-room, exquisitely done in shell pink marble. Nadia's and her father's rooms...

Guy said suddenly:

'Are you sure about this – about coming back here? I mean I can sell and–'

She shook her head.

'I *was* thinking of Nadia, then.'

'I knew you were.'

'And she wants us to be here; it will preserve for her my father's memory; be a – a kind of altar to him always. I can't explain ... but this old house has been loved by so many members of our family for so long, that to desert it would be unthinkable. Fate was very kind when it sent you along.'

'May those words never be less true than you believe them to be at this moment, my dearest.'

'And,' she said again changing the subject and walking on to the wide landing; 'you see what I mean. A door could be put in shutting off completely the east wing–' She indicated a long corridor from which many rooms radiated. 'And there is already another staircase – as you know.'

'It would,' admitted Guy, 'be very simple. And shall be done!' Then as he saw her shiver. 'It is getting late and darkish. Away you come.'

'How long do you think it is likely to take?' she asked suddenly.

'I can't really say in the light of this change of structural plans, darling. But we'll be in for Christmas, I should think. Once our portion is finished we are completely shut away, after all. And we shall have the flat in town if the hammering gets too much!'

'Shall we hear it,' she murmured blissfully.

He drew her gaze to his with a masterful directness.

'We shall be deaf, dumb and blind to all but each other!' He stopped abruptly. Then: 'Good heavens, am I talking like that? You've demoralized me, my sweet! Here I am at your mercy, longing to get married and impatient of the delay even for three months. Before, I'd have scorned the very idea of marriage at any price!'

'Which is just as it should be,' she said complacently. 'And there *is* one thing: you have been surrounded by some exceedingly pretty girls among your staff – do you always pick the pretty ones?'

'Always.' He grinned at her.

'And your patients, too, are often most attractive.'

'And often the reverse,' he countered.

'True.' She paused. 'It must be terrible to be jealous and untrusting.'

'Or to have cause for both.'

Vicki's eyes widened.

'I could not live without trust,' she said gravely. 'It would degrade me. To be jealous without cause is surely an unforgivable vice; to be jealous *with* cause must, equally, be a living hell.' She looked intensely serious. 'I hate sordid emotions that bring out the very worst in people.'

Guy studied her with great tenderness. She was so completely untouched by life in all its ugly phases and her response to love, to happiness, was accordingly spontaneous and uninhibited. To him, after his more brutal contacts with the grim realities of life, she had all the beauty and stimulating force of trapped sunlight; of clean, downland winds sweeping across the countryside, revitalizing and apart... Her appeal, for that reason, was different from that of any other woman he had ever met, or was, he told himself, likely to meet; it was as if, beyond his love for her, she exercised some strange power that held him enthralled and admiring, as each day he found some new facet of her character more lovable than the rest. Yet for all her elusive beauty, her idealism, she was, contradictorily, able to concentrate on practical issues and, above all, even at this stage, to study him to the exclusion of all else.

'Then we must,' he said quietly, 'make quite sure that you escape all of them!'

She made a little face.

'I do not want to escape from life, Guy; it isn't that; merely that I hope that, no matter what my fate, how great the misery I might be called upon to endure, I should at least meet it with dignity and courage and not sink – oh, I cannot quite explain. I couldn't condemn, or criticize, anyone for anything and to be hard or unsympathetic – no! But any wailing in the market place as it were–' She laughed.

'The sordidness of reading your husband's letters or spying on him!'

'Exactly! *That* kind of thing!'

'I'm going to be terribly fortunate, aren't I?'

She met his gaze fearlessly:

'I couldn't stand a relationship that relied on anger and quarrelling to awaken passion,' she said deliberately. 'This business of people whipping themselves into a frenzy of rage and then saying that the making up is worth while.' She stood poised, tensed. 'Emotion should not need such pathetic stimulation; its own motive power should be strong enough to swirl people to the heights!'

He said hoarsely:

'You're all fire, Vicki, even as I said – remember?'

'"Not for me half-measures or caution",' she quoted easily.

'When you insisted,' he reminded her, 'that the best way was to love lightly and be loved just that much more than you had to give in return!'

'One breath of experience,' she agreed, 'and where are one's passionate philosophies! All pre-conceived notions are no more than the elementary text book of our lives! And how far from that is life itself!'

Guy nodded. To explore the depths of her fertile, receptive mind, to watch its development, as the pattern of her life changed yet again, would, he knew, be a source of unending delight.

They talked fitfully for a second or two and then Vicki said:

'I can't quite realize that we shall have some of the old furniture here, too. You must admit that it is a somewhat original situation!'

'And the more intriguing on that account,' he suggested. 'I hated to see that rare and exquisite stuff torn from its rightful place. I think I must have had some instinct about it all, as I watched you standing so aggressively at the other end of the room and noticing, also, that you did not bid for anything!'

'I hated you,' she said firmly.

'Splendid! That, at least, was an emotion.'

Their eyes met and she said softly:

'I didn't dream that loving, that being in love, could mean this ecstasy, this glorious sensation as of *belonging* in the world and of having found the most perfect form of self-expression... Oh, Guy, my dear, thank you for making it all possible, for bringing me really to *life*. Nothing can ever take the memory of these moments away.'

'We will,' he said softly, 'immortalize them.'

She slipped her arm through his and pressed her cheek against his arm as they walked out into the twilight. Then, looking up at the façade of Old Meadows, she said:

'I can think only of Keats's words as I stand here with you, my darling:

"If I am destined to be happy with you here – how short is the longest life. I wish to believe in immortality – I wish to live with you – forever".'

Guy said:

'Comment would mar the perfection of those sentiments written to Fanny Brawne. Would that I might have written them to you!'

They lapsed into gentle silence. The cool night breeze stole refreshingly upon them; the canopy of the sky was shot with the roseate tints of the afterglow; it was a vast world encrusted with stars that glittered as diamonds. The moon had not yet reached supremacy and it hung like a golden circle, cut out of sapphire.

Vicki breathed deeply the air laden with the perfume of many flowers and aware of that first tang of autumn, sharpening the atmosphere and misting distant fields as though faint blue smoke had drifted across them.

'It will be November,' she said suddenly, 'when we are married, Guy.'

'Not the ideal month.' He stopped. 'Although—'

'There will still be russets and golds and twitch fires and lamp-light,' she said softly, lovingly, 'in that room we shall have made our room. And logs roaring up the wide chimney... May or June, November or January ... what place has time when every moment is happiness?'

'Darling heart...' And even as he spoke, he took her in his arms.

CHAPTER 5

Nadia arranged a cocktail party with which to celebrate the engagement. Only very old and intimate friends were invited and the number limited to a modest twelve because White Cottage, firstly, would not hold any more and, secondly, the expense of additional numbers was beyond Nadia's means.

Digby Graves arrived early as Vicki and Nadia had guessed he would.

'I just wanted to have a word with you,' he explained to Vicki, 'before the crowd came.'

Nadia smiled and left them alone.

Digby was an attractive type, irresponsible but in no way vicious. His love for Vicki was the most stable emotion of his life and had he been born with less of this world's goods, he might have achieved a great deal more. He was always going to find *something* to do, but never found it. His hair was mid-brown and waved back from a broad forehead; his features were good, his complexion fresh and even boyish. At twenty eight he looked no more than twenty-five.

'It's nice to see you,' Vicki said tritely. 'And thank you for your letter.'

He gazed at her somewhat stormily:

'You know I wish you all the happiness, Vicki. You deserve the best. I envy this chap like hell and make no secret of the fact. But I don't doubt for a moment that the better man has won.'

Vicki was touched. She genuinely liked Digby and there were times, in adolescence, when they had indulged in mild flirtatious periods and then lapsed into self-conscious intensity. But, for the past two years she had been consistent and adamant in her refusal to marry him, knowing that the spark was not there and that to become his wife would be merely a compromise with every hope and ideal she possessed.

'You would be sporting enough to say that,' she said warmly.

'Just my good manners,' he said with a disarming grin. 'But don't forget, Vicki, that if you should ever need me I'll still be there.'

Vicki started.

'That sounds almost prophetic.'

'I didn't mean it ... but, you know what life is ... can't be too certain of anything and while I am not possessed of any virtues, I do claim to be the persistent kind. Oh, you're out of reach now, my sweet, and I honour the fact...'

Vicki said breathlessly:

'Mine isn't going to be one of those marriages with one eye on the divorce court, Digby.'

Digby's smile was rueful.

'Do any marriages begin that way?' he asked with an impressive calm.

Vicki laughed.

'You couldn't depress me if you tried!'

'I'm aware of that. You're really happy – aren't you?' He studied her thoughtfully. 'And deeply in love.'

Faint colour stole into her cheeks.

'Yes,' she whispered tensely.

'It's in your eyes, my dear; you've always been a very lovely person, but never quite so lovely as you are now.' He appraised her as she stood there in an exquisitely modelled powder blue cocktail dress, upon which was a single diamond clip providing the only ornament.

Vicki did not speak, but her gaze as it rested in his was tender and affectionate. It wasn't a question of Digby being dismissed but, rather, of her wishing to preserve his friendship, which she valued. In no way did she regard him as the stodgy, faithful lover, undemanding and content to remain a watch-dog.

'I should,' he went on easily, 'have been along before; but I've had to get used to the idea that I can no longer propose to you, or even delude myself that in the end you will change your mind.'

95

Vicki said earnestly.

'What are you going to do with your life, Digby?'

He sighed.

'I haven't, honestly, the faintest idea. I know I'm a disappointment to my father and that I ought to be taking my place in the works ... but I shudder at the thought of industry. And I know the answer to that one: my present income is derived from its fruits. Fair enough, I admit it. The tragedy of financial independence is that it breeds an idleness which becomes delightful. My time is always full – doing nothing! Now,' he added almost gruffly, 'I'm getting bored with the whole set-up. Incentive,' he said sharply, 'is everything.' He added stormily: 'And don't suggest that some charming girl will come along and take your place. No one will do that – ever.'

Vicki insisted:

'You cannot say that; we none of us know tomorrow.'

'If you were to lose Guy would you think along the same lines? Ah! You see? Oh, I may marry eventually in sheer desperation but–' He shook his head. 'And I hear your guests arriving!'

It was a gay and informal party with everyone intimately friendly with everyone else. Greta Norton, Vicki's old school friend, and her husband, James Norton, were both genuinely thrilled with the news of the engagement and Greta said softly:

'Your Guy Evans is a most charming man, darling. I don't wonder you fell in love with him. I'm so *glad,* Vicki, and that you will live at Old Meadows – well, that is quite perfect... Nadia's wonderful, isn't she? That quiet courage and a curious feeling that, to her, your father is still beside her.'

'She truly believes that he is,' Vicki said. 'I'm quite sure she would never have borne all this without that faith.'

Greta nodded and glanced to where Guy and James were already talking like old friends. James Norton was a barrister for whom a great future was predicted.

'I knew,' she said, 'the moment I spoke to Guy that he and Jimmy would get on ... you know that we've really bought Grey Friars at Bracknell? Of course; I phoned you. My memory is appalling! Ah, Nadia ... and what do you think of this sudden tempest that has swept your daughter into near-matrimony?'

Nadia said unhesitatingly:

'I think it is the happiest thing in the world and I'm delighted. Digby, your glass is empty...'

Digby chuckled.

'A most unusual occurrence,' he said banteringly. 'By the way, what news of Brinda?'

Nadia said:

'She's on a cruise with her Danish friends; we did wire her when she reached Madeira, but have not heard. But then, that's Brinda. I expect she is writing.'

Guy rejoined the little group in that second, his gaze leaping to Vicki as though he would draw her to him and defy anyone to separate them even for an instant. Both found it a form of exquisite torture to have to concentrate upon others instead of being alone together, although Vicki felt that the surging, bursting happiness of looking across the crowded room – as she had previously done – and seeing him standing there talking to others, while yet so specially *hers,* was a wonder to which she would never quite accustom herself.

Guy was, she knew, accepted by everyone as an exceedingly attractive, charming person of whom they wholeheartedly approved. And, in turn, he whispered to her how very much he liked the friends gathered there, and James in particular. Vicki could picture another scene, not too far distant, when she and Guy would give their first party at Old Meadows and her heart seemed to stop beating for a second in order to grasp its own wild happiness.

It was just when conversation was mellowing, when Guy had entrenched himself and felt that he had become a part of all that was going on around him – instead of the

newly introduced fiancé of Victoria Wayne –
that a hush fell upon the gathering and
Brinda walked dramatically into the room,
having counselled Emma's silence, and
crept stealthily upon them as a result. She
stood on the threshold instantly becoming
centre-stage; aware that, though it might be
Vicki's party, she would now steal the
thunder. Then:

'Hallo, Mummie, and everyone!' She
moved forward and pressed her cheeks
against Nadia's; then turning to Vicki and
kissing her, said: 'I had your wire about the
engagement and just couldn't resist coming
home. I flew. Apparently just in time for the
celebrations.' She was smiling in all direc-
tions as she spoke and sufficiently familiar
with all the guests not to greet them in turn.
'And now for my future brother-in-law.' Her
gaze wandered and suddenly she gasped:
'Guy!'

For a second there was a dramatic silence
to which Brinda was oblivious and she
moved swiftly forward and said again:

'Guy! Of all people. To meet you here!'

Guy was aware that all eyes were turned in
his direction and he maintained a rigid
control as he said:

'How are you, Brinda. I happen to *be* your
future brother-in-law.'

Brinda held his gaze in faint mockery.

'Really!' It was a quiet, challenging sound.

Well, well!' She turned to Vicki. 'You didn't mention the *name* of the man to whom you were engaged, darling, and so unexpectedly, too. I hope you'll be very happy.' She glanced again at Guy. 'Congratulations,' she said smoothly.

To Vicki it was as though the sun had suddenly disappeared behind dark, ominous cloud. Brinda brought with her an element of unrest and disunity and never had that seemed more true than on this occasion. She hurried over the fact of her knowing Guy as being no more than normal coincidence happening every day in life; but she knew that, deep in her heart, she would have preferred her to remain out of the country until after the marriage. She looked at her as she stood there; a difficult character to describe since she could be the most delightful and charming person in the world and, equally, the most difficult, even foul. Her moods were ever changing and she would, for no apparent reason, become sullen and uncommunicative, and then confiding and voluble. The strain of her presence was such that nerves became taut, tempers frayed. Vicki, in her present state of happiness could not calmly contemplate the disruption of her home-life with Nadia during these few months ahead and had consoled herself that Brinda was *happy* to be away. And Brinda's being happy meant that everyone else shared that commendable state. Vicki had always found it extremely difficult to gauge Brinda's emotional reactions to her marriage or to her subsequent widowhood which had, to Vicki, seemed darkest tragedy. Brinda had married before she was eighteen – a captain in the Navy, then stationed in Malta. There had been the big, fashionable wedding in London; the reception at Claridges which, now Vicki realized, must have cost her father money he could ill afford. With Brinda poised, confident, glorying in the pageant, knowing herself to be the cynosure of all eyes. Impossible really to know what she had *thought* or *felt* about Raymond Wells; impossible to decide whether the uniform and all that went with it, had not been the main attraction but, now in love herself, Vicki knew, full well, that Brinda had not at any time cared deeply for Raymond. His death – sudden and tragic in an air crash while flying home on leave from Spain to England – only a year before had appeared to do no more than make Brinda a pathetic *widow;* the object of sympathy who, in soft, misty black, looked agonizingly young for such dire suffering. Financially she was well provided for. Raymond had a private income which reverted to Brinda and, after six months, she left England for a tour of the Continent, actually finding widowhood oppressive and determined to escape from its restrictions. Thus had it been immediately following the death of her father... An excuse and she had escaped...

Vicki accepted the truth that Brinda had always faintly resented her and, in a bad mood, never ceased to remind her that she was Nadia's *step*child and her *step*sister. Nevertheless, Vicki had been genuinely attached to her and had overlooked many unforgivable insults of which neither Nadia nor Henry Wayne were aware.

Brinda was striking to look at, having an almost Nordic fairness of hair and skin and deep, china-blue eyes, that could be hard, cold and merciless. Her figure, like Vicki's, was extremely slender, but shapely, and she wore her clothes with the elegance of one accustomed to the best models from the best houses.

To Guy her presence came as a great shock from which he did his best to recover. That she, of all people – Brinda Wells – should be Vicki's half-sister. Only then did it occur to him that very little had been said about her and that he had not been sufficiently interested to ask any specific questions: she was abroad and would be home shortly ... that had more than sufficed. And now... He looked at her and remembered ... and a shiver passed over him.

The atmosphere changed; glances inter-cepted glances; an awareness of some indefinable undercurrent destroyed the former ease and gaiety. Nadia strove valiantly to keep the party spirit alive, to talk generalities and, for a reason she could not quite have explained even to herself, keep Brinda away from Guy and Vicki. James also made a valiant contribution while Digby cried:

'And how long are you going to be home this time, Brinda?'

Brinda stood, glass in hand, and slipped an arm through Nadia's.

'For as long as Mummie can put up with me. I'm tired of roaming. It isn't much fun on one's own,' she added deliberately.

Digby chuckled.

'You could soon alter that, my dear!'

'True,' she retorted with self-confidence, 'but I'm one of those selective people, alas!' She turned to Vicki. 'And where are you and Guy going to live once you are married?' she asked deliberately.

Vicki explained the facts.

Brinda paled.

'Old Meadows!' It was an outraged sound.

Nadia hastily interposed.

'I'm so thankful the house isn't lost to us, Brinda.'

Brinda sipped her cocktail.

'They are not *married* yet, Mummie...

103

Guy, how's the radiology going? I seem to remember that you were just starting a practice in Wimpole Street when we last saw each other.'

Guy's voice was steady:

'I have little to grumble about.'

'And have changed your views somewhat – about marriage?' she added deliberately.

'The privilege of each one of us,' he said, maintaining a deceptive calm. 'The confirmed bachelor has become the convert.' He looked at Vicki adoringly. 'Yes, darling?'

Vicki told herself that this bleak desolation that lay upon her like a pall was sheer imagination and she said laughingly:

'Just you try escaping!'

Brinda gave a cynical little laugh.

'Digby, are you going to wait for the divorce?' she spoke gaily and flippantly.

Nadia frowned.

Digby said sharply.

'No; for the golden wedding. I've an idea that Guy and Vicki are the kind of people who will – if they live – celebrate that.'

There was a cheerful little chorus of approval. Brinda drew in her claws.

'I'm sure that my stepsister,' she said pleasantly, 'would never undertake anything unless she intended it to be a great success. Marriage included.' She sighed. 'I must say that you look very well, Vicki.' Her gaze flicked to Guy. 'Just what the doctor ordered! Is that what you have proved to be, Guy?'

Vicki could not escape from the weight of depression induced by every word Brinda uttered. She felt like a child whose party had been spoiled by some alien influence ... this was to have been her evening and Guy's... But from the moment Brinda had stepped over the threshold, the spontaneous happiness had vanished and in its place had come strain and awkwardness. Where had Brinda and Guy met and why hadn't either of them enlarged on the meeting? Wasn't that, in itself, a trifle odd? Usually, in such circumstances, the two people concerned automatically discussed their former acquaintanceship. And there had been an expression in Brinda's eyes – predatory, intimate and even possessive, as she had looked at him. Vicki mentally cried out against such thoughts and fiercely resisted them. Then, aware that all eyes were upon her, she said gaily:

'He has very definitely. Whether or not, as his receptionist, I can twist the same compliment remains to be seen!'

Greta put in:

'I should love to see you in that neat, white uniform, looking crisply efficient.'

James laughed.

'Do you hold the hand of the patients? In which case I must come along! Guy's a damned lucky fellow – that's all I say … and now we must be going, Nadia, my dear.' He turned to embrace Nadia as he spoke, feeling for her a wealth of tenderness, genuine and deep. He had been devoted to Henry and had spent endless happy days, in the past, at Old Meadows which Nadia had always seemed to grace, rather than merely to live in.

'Good-bye, James dear,' Nadia said softly. 'And thank you for all your help just recently. You and Greta have been a tower of strength.'

Greta said:

'When you get this other daughter off your hands, darling, you are coming to stay with us for a real holiday and no arguments.'

'I should love it,' said Nadia feeling that some automatic gramophone record was speaking for her and that she was, in truth, completely cut off from the scene around her. Poignantly she was conscious of the fact that, in a brief while, these friends would return with their husbands to their own homes … there to relax and to talk as only those two people – a man and a woman in love – can talk, in freedom, understanding and sympathy, leaving no lonely places of the heart or soul, but only the rich ful-filment of comradeship. She was thankful, in that second, that no one would ever guess quite the depths of her own loneliness, or the barren waste of her life without Henry. She detested self-pity or sympathy-seeking.

The house emptied; cars drove away and a luxurious silence fell as Nadia, Vicki, Brinda and Guy sat down and relaxed. At least that was the picture Vicki willed herself to see: four people gloriously content after a successful party ... the man she adored at her side ... happiness wrapping her around with all the warmth of sunlight.

Brinda looked from face to face:

'A homely little scene.'

Vicki fought to accept that as sincere.

'I can hardly believe you are back,' she said eagerly. 'Tell us about the trip. Where did you go?'

'The cruise was a frightful bore and we left the ship and cut our losses at Madeira. After that we toured Europe and' – she paused imperceptibly – 'ending up by staying the last week in Stockholm.'

Vicki felt the burning knife of memory stabbing at her brain as she recalled Thelma Minton's words regarding Guy's trip to Sweden... And the next second despised herself with unutterable loathing.

She said swiftly, almost nervously:

'I think Stockholm one of the most beautiful places. In fact I love Scandinavia altogether. I'll never forget our holiday in Norway, Sweden and Denmark or the sheer delight of meeting their friendly, homely people... Guy, we must make the trip again, sometime.'

Brinda put in softly:

'Guy, I think you will find, has a very soft spot for Sweden – eh, Guy?' She laughed. 'He was very gay when we met there ... was it three years ago?'

Guy felt that his collar was slowly strangling him. But he replied as calmly as possible:

'I think it must be; I'm not very good at remembering time.'

Brinda smiled seductively.

'I hope you are not quite so indifferent towards – people.'

'That,' said Guy, 'rather depends upon the people.'

'The world,' said Brinda tritely, 'is a very small place and one is forever meeting friends from the past and in the most unexpected fashion. I cannot quite believe that *you* are the man whom Vicki is going to marry.'

Vicki said, feeling a certain irritation rising within her:

'I really cannot see, because you happen to have met Guy before, in your many and varied travels, that there is anything really astounding about it. You admit yourself that people are always running into each other in–' she stopped.

Brinda jumped in.

'What are you trying to prove, darling?' A light laugh.

Vicki went cold; a shudder passed over her. Brinda seemed to have become some arch enemy intent upon destroying her.

Guy got to his feet. All he knew was that he must get away and, later, after thrashing the problem out, place all the facts before Vicki.

'I must be getting back, darling,' he said to Vicki, his gaze intense and adoring. 'I've got to go over that Robins's case pretty thoroughly and promised to let them have the results of the plates in the morning. I don't want to prolong their suspense.' He glanced at Brinda and then at Nadia: 'And I'm sure you must have a lot to talk about among yourselves.'

Vicki hastened:

'Nothing to which you may not be party: you're already one of the family.'

Brinda crossed a slender leg.

'I endorse that.'

Vicki saw Guy to his car. She stood uncertainly beside him as if expecting a confidence that didn't materialize and then rebuking herself for imagining it to be necessary. Why should his previous meeting with Brinda have any significance? Just because Thelma had told her that wild story… Her gaze searched his face and the words came involuntarily:

'What a strange coincidence that you should know Brinda... Did you meet her husband?'

'Once,' Guy said. Then, abruptly: 'We must have dinner quietly together tomorrow night, my darling – to make up for these hours tonight. I think I was damned jealous of that fellow Digby!'

Vicki purred.

'I love you so *much*, Guy.' She spoke with a sudden intensity.

Guy, his thoughts in chaos, the realization of the problem that lay inescapably ahead torturing him, did no more than raise her hand to his lips and say hoarsely:

'Bless you, my sweet.'

She asked, and the sickness returned:

'Is there anything wrong, Guy?'

Instantly, he was alert.

'Good heavens, no!' Why should there be?'

'I don't know.'

'Woman's famous intuition?' He forced a smile.

'If you like.'

He pressed the starter button and put the car into gear.

'Until tomorrow, darling.'

Vicki stood, like a statue, as she watched him drive away. It was, she argued, an ordinary enough procedure which never varied on his visits to White Cottage and yet, on this occasion, it appeared to be fraught with drama, almost as though it were something she might well be doing for the last time. A cry escaped her lips. She was behaving in the most ridiculous fashion, she argued furiously. If this was evidence of her intensity then she had better curb it, in case every woman who had met Guy previously, produced the same devastating effect as Brinda. But the bleak little wind of a desolate fear touched her heart and the sun faded from her world. Misgiving, sharp and insistent, pursued her while her thoughts swung like a pendulum between that fear and sudden, illogical reassurance. *Brinda!* What did anything matter except the fact that Guy and she were in love and going to be married? She *was* behaving like some gauche adolescent. And thus comforted, she returned to the sitting-room of the cottage in gay spirits.

Brinda smiled.

'Seen your adored one off?'

'Yes.'

'He's attractive – isn't he?' Brinda reached for a cigarette which she lit from a previous one.

Vicki bristled at the possessive implication.

'As attractive to me as I am sure Raymond was to you,' she said and then felt mean since Raymond was ... dead.

Brinda didn't withdraw from what she

knew to be a silent battle.

'I don't think that Raymond was ever as attractive as Guy – quite frankly,' she said startlingly: 'And just in case either you or Mummie may be jumping to the wrong conclusions about my attitude since Raymond's death ... well, it wasn't a very successful marriage and my grief was tempered by the fact. So now that I've come home, don't impose any restrictions on your conversation fearing that I may be hurt. He was not the man with whom I was really in love,' she added significantly.

Vicki looked at Brinda in startled dismay. Nadia said:

'I'm sorry, Brinda; I didn't guess.'

'I didn't intend you should,' said Brinda. Life at Old Meadows was so shut away from all the realities that I knew it would distress Daddy.' She went on pointedly: 'Daddy's own disastrous first marriage was brought so conveniently to an end by your mother's death, Vicki, that it left no scars. Fate is not always so kind.' She looked jealously from Vicki's face to Nadia's. 'Thank heaven, *my* mother atoned to him for everything. Oh, Mummie, it's good to be *home.*' She glanced around. 'Even if "home" has become this tiny cubby hole.' Then: 'Tell me about Old Meadows.'

Nadia explained the facts, finishing with:
'Guy was most generous–'

112

Brinda cut in:

'That was, of course, just like him ... ah, well, don't worry, darling; there will be a great many changes, believe me. It so happens that I've been very fortunate on the Stock Exchange recently and now have all that I am ever likely to need – and well invested – even if I didn't marry again.'

Vicki said:

'But you will marry again?'

'That,' Brinda replied lightly, 'would be giving away secrets.' She looked at Nadia. 'We can get rid of this cottage, darling, and buy something more comfortable.'

Nadia's voice was low and a little shaken:

'It's generous of you to think of it, Brinda, but I can manage perfectly well here and I've grown to like it; Henry bought this little place after all and I can maintain it on my modest income. Emma and I have come to a satisfactory arrangement, so that I have no staff worries. If and when you marry again – and with Vicki soon married – what do I need a larger establishment for? Quite apart from the fact that I should hate not to be really independent!'

Nadia knew that, should the choice be given her, she would accept help from Vicki, knowing that never would she be reminded of the gesture; whereas, with Brinda ... in a bad mood it would be the first thing that would be, as it were, thrown in her face.

113

Whether or not it would be meant was another matter, but that in no way altered the fact of the hurt.

Brinda cried:

'But that's absurd, Mummie! After all, this place–'

'Has become "home",' Nadia said quietly.

Brinda looked at Vicki.

'You agree with me, don't you?' she demanded.

Vicki said:

'I think that Nadia's point of view is the only one that is really important. I know how she feels ... there is much of the past enshrined here and–'

Brinda said hotly:

'Of course, you two were always siding with each other.'

Nadia felt the old pang, the sudden awareness of peace shattered the moment Brinda reappeared.

'It isn't that, Brinda dear; but shall I say that Vicki and I have lived here during these past months, even dug ourselves some roots. We haven't any illusions about the place but, from my point of view, better to live in a cottage I can afford, than in a larger house which I cannot.'

Brinda said shortly:

'I have already told you I have more than enough money to buy something different.'

'Then you spend it, darling, on having a

good time.'

Brinda was irritated; she liked her own way and the old jealousy of her mother's and Vicki's devotion reared its head like some monster.

'Is that intended to suggest I am selfish and do nothing but have a good time?' she demanded.

Nadia said patiently:

'Darling, don't be foolish; such a thought never entered my head and how you should arrive at such a conclusion in view of my remark—'

'I don't doubt but that you both criticized me for leaving England so soon after Daddy's death.'

Vicki put in hotly:

'That was the very last thing on our minds.'

Brinda snapped:

'Allow me to know a *little* of what my *own* mother thinks.'

Nadia got to her feet.

'Let's not begin an argument just now, darling.'

'*Argument*,' Brinda cried. 'When I was trying to *help!*'

Nadia had reached the door.

'I appreciate your concern for me,' she said with a patient gentleness.

'But you refuse to do as I suggest.' It was an aggressive challenge.

'I'm just happier here,' Nadia said firmly. Then: 'I think I'll have a little rest before having anything to eat,' she added. There was something frail about her as she stood there, her cheeks pale, her eyes darkly troubled as she realized the difficulties attendant upon Brinda's return.

Instantly, Vicki said:

'Can I get you anything?'

'Nothing.' A smile. 'You two have a nice chat together.' She added: 'It's lovely to see you, Brinda, and such a surprise.'

Brinda's mood changed.

'It's lovely to be here. *Home!* Perhaps you're right about this cottage; it is cosy, I suppose.'

Nadia smiled, much relieved. There might well be harmony for the rest of the evening! It struck her, then, that Brinda's luggage had not arrived with her and she mentioned the fact.

'It's coming up from the station a little later; I have all I need with me for tonight, at least,' Brinda explained. She laughed. 'I remembered that there was an attic for trunks, thank heavens! I've literally dozens!'

Left alone, Brinda said:

'And you've a job with Guy. How amusing.'

'I've enjoyed it,' Vicki said, eager and willing to maintain a friendly atmosphere. 'Learned quite a bit, too! I can develop X-ray plates and am getting quite an expert in the dark room! It's fun, Brinda – working, you know.'

Brinda reached for yet another cigarette.

'Of course it is, my dear girl, when you happen to be in love with the man for whom you work! I'd settle for that reward!'

Vicki laughed.

'No, seriously, apart from that. Even after we're married I shall want to be doing something; not just wandering aimlessly from one party to another.'

'The crusading type,' Brinda said. 'Well, I adore being lazy. I hate lifting a finger, or a cup. The old tradition suits me perfectly.'

Vicki didn't intend to argue. Brinda was perfectly entitled to her point of view.

'I'm so glad that you're financially secure,' she said generously. 'I knew, of course, that Raymond had left you provided for but–'

'Unless I'd taken a chance and gambled a bit, the income would have been worth very little and, of course, the major portion of it is trust money as you know. I've dabbled with the odds and ends, as it were. I think I must be lucky,' she said her cold blue eyes flashing.

'I hope,' said Vicki softly, 'that you are also going to be very happy from now on. You look marvellous; that faint tan suits you and makes your eyes seem even bluer!' Affection welled within Vicki as she spoke; above all, she wanted Brinda's friendship and the fears and forebodings of an earlier hour were dispelled in a wave of impulsive expansiveness.

Brinda studied Vicki, unable to rid herself of a sense of irritation. She had no doubts, but that Vicki had always been both generous and affectionate towards her and that she had, in all fairness, no possible complaint to make; nevertheless, being Brinda, that very fact alone constituted a grievance since she loved nothing better than creating a disturbance, or smashing a peaceful mood and then, contrite and genuinely ashamed, being profuse in her apologies. She said abruptly:

'You haven't changed.'

Vicki laughed.

'Should I have done?'

'I mean in your attitude; you were always attractive,' she added coolly.

Vicki sighed.

'One cannot change one's spots, I suppose.'

'I should never have taken kindly to living here, working for my living.' Brinda grinned. 'You *would* have gone through it!'

Vicki laughed.

'It's good to have you back,' she said with a sudden rush of tenderness. 'We must have fun together, Brinda, and once Guy and I are married and settled, well, you know you can come to us whenever you like. And if you marry again!' She paused. 'It would be wonderful if we both had children growing up together.'

Brinda gave a mocking laugh.

'Always the romantic, painting pretty pictures! I can't stand children and thank heaven I wasn't left with any. Even with nannies they are messy creatures and a dreadful drain financially.'

Vicki didn't argue that point, but said lightly:

'Very well! Perhaps you won't mind being godmother to one of mine!'

'So! There's to be a family!'

'Quite definitely.'

'As I remember Guy, he couldn't stand children ... but no doubt he would hate to damp your enthusiasm.'

Vicki struggled to infuse a note of lightness into her voice:

'Just where did you meet Guy?'

For a second Brinda hesitated, then:

'Stockholm ... your ring is very magnificent. I assume Guy has come into money since last I saw him.'

'Yes; his uncle died.'

'Of course... I remember his being ill. And he's bought Old Meadows.' A cynical smile touched her lips. 'Fact is indeed stranger than fiction.'

Again the fleeting shadow of uneasiness

fell across Vicki's heart and again she dispelled it, saying:

'We never know just what the impact of life will be.'

'Indeed – no! And just when we delude ourselves that everything is going quite perfectly...' She stopped and studied Vicki very deliberately. 'Was it your intention to marry quickly?'

Vicki's brows puckered into an inquiring and fearful expression.

'It *is* our intention to marry quickly. How strangely you speak, Brinda.'

'Do I?' Brinda stubbed out a half-smoked cigarette. 'Forgive me.' Instantly she became aloof and unapproachable. 'I must go and do something to my face, have a wash, too. I suppose,' she added, 'we shall be having *something* to eat tonight?'

'Of course; we made it late because one never knows when that last guest will depart.'

'I'm hungry,' Brinda said; 'I lunched on the train and you know how appalling that can be. Is my room ready for me?' She spoke after the matter of one who would like nothing better than for it not to be ready, so that she might have a martyred grouse.

'Always ready,' said Vicki quietly.

Brinda reached the door and stood dramatically posed against it: a striking figure in her black skirt and white jacket.

'By the way, Vicki, it's rather important that I talk to you before we go to bed tonight. Without danger of interruption. Shall I come to your room, or you to mine?' She hastened: 'After Mummie is settled.'

Vicki's heart seemed to become suspended on a very slender thread.

'You sound very mysterious.'

'Do I? Sorry, my dear.'

Vicki cried:

'But what *is* it? I mean—'

'I cannot begin to discuss the matter now,' Brinda insisted. 'I'll pop in to see you before you settle down tonight. I have to remember that, as a working girl, you'll be away from the house before I'm awake in the morning.'

Vicki shivered.

'Yes,' she murmured. 'I most certainly shall.'

Brinda moved out and was lost in the shadows of the hall. Vicki remained standing, one hand pressed against her heart which was throbbing as if from a sudden wound.

Brinda's words echoed sinisterly through the silence:

'It is rather important that I talk to you before we go to bed tonight...'

Vicki pulled herself together. Brinda dramatized everything. Probably some simple problem concerning this prospective husband of hers. It was high time Brinda's moods ceased to have such devastating effect.

Thus comforted she went into the kitchen to give Emma a hand with the meal.

CHAPTER 6

White Cottage settled down for the night, the mysterious quiet, as all activity ceased, merging into complete silence. Doors had been locked; Emma had gone to her room, watchful that everything in her domain was in perfect order. Only Vicki's light continued to burn as though, suddenly, it had become a focal point.

She herself, bathed and in bed, sat propped against the pillows, awaiting Brinda's appearance and what was, she argued, merely to be a confidence between sisters, seemed suddenly fraught with drama. She found that she was trembling and apprehensive and that when, finally, Brinda entered, she jumped as if startled by a pistol shot.

Brinda said:

'Your nerves, darling!' She moved to the dressing-table and looked at herself in the mirror, aware that she was glamorous and that her tiered chiffon *négligé* was as

122

beautiful and alluring as any Vicki was likely to see. Even Vicki's admiration pleased her and she thrived on it.

Vicki exclaimed:

'That *négligé* is beautiful – a most heavenly blue, too.'

Brinda smiled and turned, sitting down gracefully in an armchair beside the bed.

'It has,' she said deliberately, 'known some romantic moments.'

Vicki relaxed slightly. Of course Brinda was in the throes of some new love and wanted to discuss it. She said with interest:

'Tell me about yourself, Brinda; the things that have been happening that *mattered*. We've talked so little during these past few years.'

Brinda put a white hand into a lacy pocket and drew forth a small jewelled cigarette case. Deliberately she took from it a cigarette, lit it and blew a tiny cloud of smoke into the air. It seemed that she was building up the suspense as she said, finally:

'That is just the trouble now, Vicki.'

Vicki started.

'But – why *trouble?*'

'Because you are entirely ignorant of my life, or of the people in it.' Brinda's eyes met hers very deliberately. 'I should have confided in you more, perhaps, only I was by no means certain you would understand.'

Vicki said gently:

'That's not quite fair. No one can be accused of not understanding when denied the privilege of confidence.'

'True,' Brinda admitted. 'Unfortunately, now it will require a very great deal of understanding on your part.'

Vicki, warm-hearted, impulsive, generous, cried instantly:

'There isn't anything you could tell me, or ask of me that—'

'Don't,' interrupted Brinda sharply, 'be rash, my dear. You haven't yet heard what I have to say.'

There was a second of tense silence. Vicki said quietly:

'I'm listening, Brinda.'

Brinda took a deep breath, her eyes flashed, her lips parted a second before any words fell from them, then:

'Has Guy ever told you anything about his past?' she asked with studied calm.

Instantly, Vicki became alert; her heart thudding.

'All that I want to know,' she replied with a certain precision. 'I do not, for one moment, imagine that he has not loved other women, or lived after the fashion of most men, before he met me. We are both agreed that the past is dead.' She caught at her breath. 'I really *don't* see that such matters, in any case, can be any concern of

124

yours.' She added hastily: 'Not that I mind your questions.'

'My questions are not asked idly, I assure you.'

Vicki gasped:

'Why then?'

Brinda glanced down at the cigarette held between her fingers and then back at Vicki's pale face.

'Because it so happened that Guy and I were lovers, my dear. Is that reason enough?'

Vicki was grateful for the pillows supporting her as a hateful faintness stole sickeningly over her; her heart seemed to stop beating and her lungs bereft of air. She tried to speak, but her lips felt stiff; only the anguish settling upon her like a suffocating weight had any reality.

'Well,' snapped Brinda. 'Do you disbelieve me?'

Vicki making a gigantic effort, said huskily:

'No.' And again, with more power: 'No; I felt there was *something* ... but this–' Her voice trailed away to a whisper.

Brinda sighed.

'We first met in Stockholm, while Raymond was on some scheme or other and obviously away. It was just "one of those things" from the start. We stayed together, lived together,' she added more explicitly, seeing Vicki wince and finding a sadistic pleasure in the torture she was inflicting. 'At the end of the time I went back to what might be termed "duty".' Her voice grew cynical. 'We agreed not to communicate but, never for a moment, did we believe it was the end for us.'

'I see.' Vicki could find no words to convey her feelings and, in fact, beyond the tearing pain she was experiencing, she could not have explained, in any measure, the true nature of those feelings. All she knew was that she had passed from radiance to darkness and that she seemed to lie there quivering in the shadows of a wrecked happiness.

'I came home,' Brinda said, 'intending to go to Guy, to pick up the threads again and, of course, marry him. I've waited this conventional year after Raymond's death out of respect for his family and ours... And I wanted to make quite sure of my own feelings for Guy before taking any precipitate step.'

Vicki said suddenly:

'And didn't it occur to you that *he* might have changed?'

Brinda said calmly:

'It was a possibility, but not a probability. I knew he was not, at heart, the marrying kind.' She gauged Vicki's emotional reaction pretty correctly as she added casually: 'Of course I'd no illusions about his fidelity; and was quite prepared for there to have been, shall we say, "interludes". It is always fatal to expect too much of any man.' She paused. 'I shock you?'

Vicki flushed.

'I am not a child, Brinda.'

'But you are very unworldly.' Brinda spoke with some authority. 'Quite frankly, had Guy not wanted to marry even now it would not have worried me unduly. I've seen enough of marriage not to have much respect for it. But that is beside the point. Don't look so pained, Vicki.'

Vicki could not marshal her thoughts sufficiently to express herself with any degree of adequacy.

'It isn't that,' she murmured. 'I just can't grasp it all. I thought–'

Brinda got to her feet.

'You thought you knew me ... when you don't even begin to understand. You don't understand life in the least; you are as unrealistic as the heroine of a romantic novel.' She snapped her fingers. 'Well, I'm different; I don't care for the veneer of marriage and I'm sufficiently independent financially to please myself, because I do not have to be kept. I'm not, either, the sentimental, affectionate kind and I should loathe any sonnet sung or read aloud to me! My emotions are far more primitive.'

Vicki stared at her aghast, aware of a certain quality within her from which she instinctively recoiled. She said, stunned and shaken:

'This isn't a very pleasant situation, is it?'

'That,' said Brinda coolly, 'rather depends on how you look at it. I am home for good, my dear, and, that being so, I rather think you will agree that I have prior claim to Guy's affections, even his loyalty.'

Vicki felt the knife of jealousy cut into her heart. Guy and Brinda... Guy and Brinda... How easy to dismiss some nameless, nebulous woman; how impossible to do so in such circumstances as these. And Guy had known her to be married... Was he that type – promiscuous, caring as little for the man he dishonoured, as for his own sense of the fitness of things? Was this 'the past' which he dismissed so lightly as being 'dead'?

'Could there be any loyalty in the kind of deception you both practised?' Vicki said slowly.

Brinda gave a ridiculing laugh.

'You are such an idealist, my child. What has loyalty to do with emotion, with passion? You just don't know what you're talking about and as for ever understanding a man like *Guy* – never in a hundred years!'

Vicki said sharply:

'That remains to be seen.'

Brinda's eyes narrowed; her body tensed,

her attitude changed swiftly.

'Suppose we come to the point,' she said and her voice was harsh in its resoluteness. 'I intend to fight you every inch of the way for Guy. All's fair in love and war and nothing can alter–'

Vicki heard her words from a great distance, as the ghostly echo of the words that had haunted her from the beginning came again mockingly. 'The Moving Finger writes… Nor all thy Piety nor Wit shall lure it back to cancel half a Line.'

Brinda cried sharply:

'What is it – what are you staring at?'

Vicki blinked and sighed. Brinda went on sharply:

'Nothing can alter the fact that Guy and I have been lovers – nothing. That alone gives me prior claim. Even were you to go ahead now and marry him, it would not make the slightest difference to my intentions. I just want to make all this quite clear, Vicki.'

Vicki gasped:

'But you couldn't–'

Brinda's eyes gleamed maliciously.

'I'm not a particularly pleasant person when I don't get my own way, my dear – you should know that by now. But I'll not play the hypocrite or pretend. Marry Guy and I'll haunt you both, I'll wear down his defences – if he has any – until you'll be glad to let him go. The only thing I will not do is scheme or plot behind your back, or be driven to lies. I've declared war and you know the terms. Fair enough. This doesn't alter what regard I have for you and if you're wise–' She paused and then thundered. 'Why don't you say something? Lying there like some alabaster statue–'

'I'm not so good at speeches as you, Brinda; go on, I'm listening.'

Brinda tossed her head defiantly; her eyes were flashing and greedy.

'Whatever Guy may feel for you, there is still the memory of me, don't forget, and at any time I like I can fan the flame of that memory and reawaken the passion we once knew. 'She added brutally: 'And don't overlook the fact that had Guy known I was free, it is very doubtful if he would ever have asked you to marry him.' Her insolent gaze rested upon Vicki's deathly white face. 'You and I may bear no resemblance physically to each other, but it might well be that, without knowing it, he was drawn to you because of that *something* which reminded him of me.'

Vicki's hands were clenched; with every scrap of her strength she struggled to maintain the semblance of calm; to avoid the degradation of a violent argument. Yet Brinda's words seared her, stripping from her that veil of beauty, of faith and illusion to which she had clung so tenaciously. She said, her voice shaken:

'You are, in fact, suggesting that I break my engagement so that you can marry Guy.'

Brinda smiled confidently.

'My dear innocent, I'm not "suggesting" anything; I'm merely making my own intentions perfectly plain.' She studied Vicki with a cool insolence: 'You're not the type to stand up to this kind of thing; your life has been fantastically sheltered and while it isn't a question of your being narrow in your criticism of other people, you just don't begin to appreciate what life is.'

'That,' burst forth Vicki, 'is absurd. I know–'

'By theory and not experience, my child. A vastly different thing.'

Faint colour stole into Vicki's cheeks; her body seemed on fire as she maintained:

'I have imagination, emotions–'

'True; but you'd shrivel and die in any sordid situation – or what you deemed to be sordid. Marry Guy – he'll probably tell you about me. And then what? I shall be around. Oh, not blatantly: I know Guy too well for that, but just sufficiently to be a reminder … and men are awful fools where women are concerned, my dear – even the best of 'em. I've told you that I mean to seduce him from you – should that require any effort and *that* remains to be seen.' She smiled slowly and hatefully. 'And you couldn't confide in Guy about it all, or it would make it an issue and suggest that you didn't trust him and were jealous. I defy any two people to live in harmony with the past on their doorstep, my dear – least of all one of your temperament.'

Vicki put her hands up to her face as if to shut out the hideous picture. And Brinda went on:

'Every time he made love to you, you'd remember me and wonder if I might be in his thoughts also. You'd torture yourself every moment that he and I were together and you'd end up by being insanely jealous, no matter how hard you tried not to be.'

Vicki burst forth desperately:

'But you're not in love with Guy.'

Brinda said sharply.

'I'm sufficiently in love with him to want him back. Had I not been married we should never have parted, anyway. But we were both wary of the divorce court. Ours was one of those perfect interludes, my child. And, believe me, Guy is not the kind of lover one easily forgets.' She sighed. 'Don't look so pained.'

Vicki said with spirit:

'How do you expect me to look?'

Brinda showed a row of even teeth.

'You have a point there, certainly. I'd hate to be in your shoes, I must admit. You'll never be able to say, though, that I didn't warn you; or that I schemed behind your back.'

Vicki said in a strangled voice:

'I almost wish you had chosen that way.'

'Couldn't be bothered, darling. Intrigue has never appealed to me.'

'And yet–' Vicki's voice shook with indignation.

'Oh, deceiving Raymond! That didn't count. I doubt very much that he was faithful to me, either.'

Vicki said amazed:

'But, Brinda, you can't really think like that about life and marriage?'

'Can't I? This eternal fidelity rot; this moonshine and roses and poetic nonsense! I told you before my emotions are far more primitive.'

'Then why,' Vicki demanded firmly, 'won't any other man do just as well?'

There was a second of dramatic silence. Then Brinda replied, her voice low and throbbing:

'Because, my dear, Guy is rather different and, oh freely I admit it, has become ten times more desirable now that he is engaged to you. I want to recapture the delights and enchantment we knew before... I might even be prepared to settle down and marry him and become a dear little faithful wife.' She added with telling emphasis: 'Although you are well aware how dead against being married Guy was.' She smiled. 'I can understand your attraction for him: the new experience, dewy-eyed innocence and all that. But, one breath of challenge from a more experienced woman, and where would you be?'

'Seeing that Guy is in love with me—'

Brinda laughed outright.

'And how far does that take you? How long will that last?'

'It lasted a lifetime between Daddy and Nadia.'

Brinda made an impatient sound.

'In their world – yes. And Guy is not Daddy! Oh, be your age, Vicki. Your idea of love is the kind you read about in novels; you see your life with Guy through a series of pretty pictures... You and Guy at Old Meadows, bringing up the family... Ah, I'm so *right*, aren't I? And just what power do you imagine all that would have against my onslaught ... the senses are so much more insistent than the soul, my sweet.'

Vicki stared at her.

'You're so different... I can't believe all this, Brinda.'

'Then you'll have to,' came the sharp retort. 'And this is getting us nowhere. You can, of course, go ahead and marry Guy assuring him that his affair with me will be forgotten, wiped out between you. I shall make no move to thwart you.' She sighed.

'But, as the rather lonely little widow I shall plead for a flat at Old Meadows and since you can hardly broadcast the fact of our previous relationship in order to cut me out of your circle, equally you could hardly deny me that sanctuary! And living, as it were, *with* you ... what could be simpler? Think well, my child. I hold all the aces, really. And I should never be foolish enough to allow Guy to suspect for a moment that I had any ulterior motive and ... could *you* tell him that I had?'

Vicki's stricken face, the deathly hush that fell upon the room, touched faintly a chord of sympathy within Brinda's heart. She said in a somewhat rough and brisk tone:

'I'm sorry about this, Vicki; but I shall break you in the end if you try to thwart me.'

Vicki heard those words and, knowing Brinda, in no way dismissed them lightly. Brinda was the type to stop at nothing to gain her own ends, even if ultimately she was the loser.

Vicki spoke in a bewildered, incredulous tone:

'I can't quite grasp the fact that anyone – least of all a relation – could behave as you are doing. Had our position been reversed–'

'I know,' Brinda cut in, 'you would have retired gracefully. Only you wouldn't have been in my position – ever. You would never have allowed Guy to become your lover in the first place, or connived with him to deceive your husband–'

Vicki felt the sting of those words as they affected Guy. It seemed impossible that he could ever have entered into a liaison of that description. The mere fact of his having been Brinda's lover was, she appreciated, without particular moral significance, because he had not posed to her as an inexperienced celibate. But that, behind Raymond Wells's back, he had lived with Brinda during those weeks and then, doubtless, behaved to Raymond as the trusted friend ... that seared her.

'I think,' she said with sudden spirit, 'that we have said all there is to say, Brinda.'

Brinda shrugged her shoulders.

'Very well... Oh, I know I'm a nasty piece of work, my dear. I wasn't blessed with your disposition or character, but at this moment I'm glad of that fact. I'm not vulnerable like you; I haven't your pride or, for that matter, your moral courage. So much more comfortable without. I'm sorry for you.' She eyed Vicki with speculation: 'If you go through with this marriage you will live in the shadow of fear and jealousy and never really know if Guy is unfaithful to you with me ... and if you break with him, all your moonlight and roses will vanish. Ah, well ... that's life. Good night, darling. Sleep well.

I've no doubt that Guy will tell you all about me tomorrow. And I shall play whatever role the results demand and be most sympathetic.'

With that she swirled from the room; then, putting her head round the door, said lightly:

'By the way, this *négligé* is a relic of those perfect weeks in Stockholm. You *see* … you'd never stand up to it, Vicki. It's too close, my dear.'

Vicki said in a last, desperate throw:

'But can't you see that Guy no longer wants you? What can you hope for even if I dropped out of the picture tomorrow?'

Brinda's teeth flashed in a half smile.

'My dear innocent, Guy will want me… I've been out of reach for quite a while and, although I say it, my technique is rather good.'

Vicki heard the door shut and Brinda's footsteps falling softly along the landing … the echo of them was like a death knell.

She lay throughout the night wrestling with the situation. Her heart throbbed in what seemed to have become a vacuum; there was a sickness at the pit of her stomach that made her cold and shivering. Hope died in those hours. She knew Brinda; she could see the subtle implication behind her every word. She had delivered her ultimatum and would not modify it no matter what the circumstances. She would create an atmosphere of mistrust, whip jealousy to a fierce crescendo; begin for Vicki a slow death. Vicki struggled to be realistic. And she knew her own limitations; she could not fight in an atmosphere of sordid intrigue; she could not live at Old Meadows with Brinda, predatory and enchanting, sharing that same roof and she had no illusions that such an impasse could be avoided. Brinda would see to that in her cunning fashion even to the point – should Guy resist the idea of her as a tenant – of challenging him and suggesting that he was afraid of the propinquity. Could she, Vicki, exist in that world of sordid uncertainty even were Brinda but a few miles away? Was it possible to wipe out the past in such circumstances and build securely for the future?... Imagination could be a deadly companion... Guy and Brinda... The flame being fanned by her desire. How diabolically clever her conception of it all; her plan for victory. She stood squarely in the sunlight, throwing all else in shadow, like some avenging monster.

She had prior claim... Knives stabbed at Vicki's brain. Suppose Brinda should have reappeared before Guy had met her, Vicki. What then? How impossible to guarantee that he was now utterly indifferent to all that had happened in the past. Simple to describe that same past as 'dead' when its influences were no longer active. But what now, with Brinda always there – glamorous, desirable, experienced; Brinda, the relative claiming naturally certain rights. She groaned aloud and buried her face in the pillow, exhausted, ill with the conflict. It could, she argued, never be other than an exceedingly delicate situation; but with Brinda and her brutal resolves, it was a sordid and impossible one. It wasn't a situation where she, Vicki, could fight defiantly ... there was no visible enemy to fight. And if Guy had been capable of deceiving Brinda's husband ... why should he have any compunction about betraying his own wife?

Harsh, tearing sobs rose to choke her and she beat them back frantically. This was not her conception of love, of marriage; marriage lying within the shadow of a past that could never be dead... She had not the flippant casualness to ignore Brinda's threats, but the fertile imagination to envisage the wreckage and ruin which the carrying out of those threats would bring. And to live every second of her life at Brinda's mercy ... to be reminded almost hourly of her relationship with Guy...

Vicki closed her eyes. She knew, then, precisely the decision she must make...

There was only one detail which Brinda had deliberately withheld that night: the fact that she had represented herself as a single woman during the weeks of her association with Guy and that Guy's discovery of her deception had resulted in bitter recrimination. Nothing daunted, at this stage, Brinda argued that this fact might well not come to light and, thus, Vicki's opinion of Guy would be lowered accordingly. Should it, however, be a matter of discussion, it still in no way altered her intentions as Vicki knew them.

CHAPTER 7

Vicki was thankful that she always left White Cottage before Nadia was awake. She had no illusions about her appearance on this particular morning; her eyes seemed to have receded far into her head; her features were pinched so that her face appeared to be a fraction of its normal size. Hers was the temperament to fight overwhelming odds, but not physically to escape the results of the struggle. Emma said, mouth agape:

'Miss Vicki ... what's the matter? You'll never be going to work today – looking like that. I mean,' she corrected herself, confused and anxious, 'you're not well. I–'

Vicki forced a smile.

'Nothing more than a late night, Emma. My sister and I talked into the small hours and I'm so *tired*.'

Emma gave her another look, and arrested by an expression in her eyes, tactfully said no more than:

'Ah, well then ... and I suppose that means very little breakfast.'

'Just coffee,' Vicki said and smiled again, feeling that food would choke her.

A moment or two later she went out into the freshness of the August morning and her heart seemed to stop beating as she gazed at the magnificent tapestry of the countryside she knew and loved so well, realizing, with a poignant sense of tragedy, that its beauty hurt... Yesterday, she had been a part of its glory; it had reflected the magic of her love for Guy and breathed of a future happiness... She bit fiercely on her lower lip and ran for the bus which took her to Ascot station. The familiar road, with its fringe of silver birches and towering, stately firs, seemed to have lost all reality as she gazed upon it aware of the deep golden shadows, herald of autumn, that touched the scene, as with soft limelight. The bus went on, down Coronation Road, through South Ascot and so to the station. Fellow travellers nodded to her as she stepped on to the platform, but she saw them through a haze, praying that she might not meet any particular friend and thankful when, finally, after a journey of which she was not conscious, she reached Waterloo.

Thelma Minton looked up from her desk a little later, when Vicki walked in. Then:

'Vicki! What on earth's the matter?'

Vicki, desperately anxious to avoid discussion or sympathy, said:

'Nothing except a night of talking instead of sleep! Dr Evans in yet?'

'Yes.'

'Of course; I remember he had an early patient.'

'He looks grim,' said Thelma and her eyes were watchful. 'Or perhaps upset would be a better word.'

Vicki laughed; the sound hollow and lifeless.

'We all have our moods.'

Thelma shot her a swift glance.

'I've never known you to indulge them – thank heaven.'

With supreme self-restraint, Vicki managed to continue her job throughout the day, avoiding any possible contact with Guy alone, until, at last, there came that inevitable silence as both patients and staff had gone and she, as had been her custom went into his room. She noticed that he was pale; his expression tense as he said:

'Thank heaven, this day is over, Vicki.'

She was shaking so violently that she

prayed her lips might utter the words that were tumbling through her brain: words she had rehearsed mechanically during the long, interminable hours. Then, as though drawing on some obscure power, calling upon every scrap of courage and dignity, she said slowly, striving to keep her voice as steady as possible:

'Suppose we do not prolong its discomfort, Guy.' She nerved herself to meet his gaze. 'I know the truth about you and Brinda – she told me last night.'

Guy lowered his eyes and then raised them, meeting hers very steadily as he said hoarsely:

'I'm sorry *she* told you... I'd hoped to spare you a little–' He broke off. 'Oh, my dearest, what can I *say?*'

Vicki felt that she was slowly dying as she stood there, watching him, seeing him for the first time as Brinda's lover – the man who, knowing her to be married, had carried on a despicable intrigue behind her husband's back. She felt suddenly spoiled, degraded and yet, in her love for him, compassionate.

'Let's,' she said thickly, 'say as little as possible – shall we? By a strange twist of fate the past is not – dead.'

He started.

'What do you mean?'

'What I say ... had it been any other

woman but Brinda...'

Guy was shocked into a fierce outburst.

'Are you suggesting that because of this you and I–'

She cut in, hardly daring to allow him to utter those dreaded words:

'The situation would be quite impossible. I'm sure you must realize that. Even if you have no wish to – to marry Brinda now that she is free.' She spoke with great deliberation, watching every shade of emotion that crossed his face.

Instantly he said:

'There can be no question of marriage between Brinda and me. Ours was not a serious–' He broke off awkwardly: 'These things are not pleasant, Vicki; but I didn't pretend to you about the past.'

'No,' she said dully; 'but perhaps it might be a little easier to respect you if now you did not dismiss Brinda quite so lightly.'

He flung up his head.

'You just don't understand these things, Vicki.'

'Perhaps not,' she admitted her lips feeling stiff and cold. 'All I know is that I cannot live within the shadow of yesterday. Brinda is home for good. Do you seriously think I could forget, escape from the sordid implication of it all or,' she added in a breath, 'quite convince myself that your attraction for each other was – dead.'

144

Even as she spoke she recoiled, hearing the echo of Brinda's mocking voice: *'Every time he made love to you, you'd remember me and wonder if I might be in his thoughts and you'd end up by being insanely jealous, no matter how hard you tried not to be. I defy any two people to live in harmony with the past on their doorstep – least of all one of your temperament.'* Hadn't the poison of those words already begun to work.

Guy felt that his heart was becoming too heavy for his body; a desperate awareness of his own powerlessness to convince her, brought a frustration that was agony. He cried:

'Brinda means nothing to me – whatever you may think about the rights or wrongs of that fact. You must see reason, Vicki and not build up the situation out of all proportion.'

She shook her head and sat down heavily as though all strength had drained from her. He drew her gaze to his and a sudden violent, tearing jealousy gripped her as she pictured Brinda in his arms... Emotion, fierce and destructive, swirled and eddied, stabbing at her heart.

'It's no use, Guy,' she said, her voice rising. 'This isn't one of those things that responds to reason, or argument; it goes so much deeper. A dead past – yes. But never this.'

'And our love for each other?' he asked tensely.

Brinda's ultimatum, the whole of their fateful conversation, was echoing through Vicki's brain as she sat there and it was as if, suddenly, the shock, the agony of suffering, brought a deadness of spirit, even of emotion. The scene was no longer real. She murmured:

'Love must have a background of faith, of trust. Perhaps I'm too inexperienced, too idealistic; but I don't want a marriage shadowed eternally by the ghost of my stepsister. Her presence could never fail to have significance – never. You once told me I was the type never to be content with half-measures and *I* know that I'm too intense ... but I cannot alter, Guy, and to drag our love down to some degradation– No!' It was a fierce cry. 'Anything but that.'

He looked at her and a great gentleness crept into his gaze.

'Then you have never loved me, my darling,' he said solemnly. 'For love will endure anything rather than the possibility of parting.'

At that Vicki weakened; her lower lip quivered, sobs rose in her throat, but she beat them back, aware that if she yielded but a fraction, she would be lost; that her only hope was to cling frantically to the decision she had made. There could be no retreating; any truce, and Brinda would be ready to strike in her own damnable way and, in the end, she, Vicki, would suffer beyond even those limits now reached. She said, with a supreme effort:

'Perhaps we know a different kind of love, you and I.' In that second, looking at him, he seemed curiously remote ... she had credited him with high ideals, integrity; his association with Brinda upheld neither and the fierce hurt of disillusionment overwhelmed her.

He held her gaze masterfully:

'To you, love is all poetry and romance, Vicki. I think perhaps that you have been desperately in love with love and named it ... Guy. Now, your ideals seemingly smashed, your illusions destroyed, you long to run away lest further ugliness await you in the future. Let's face it, my darling. You are too sweet, too generous to come here today in anger or bitterness – and how gladly would I have borne both because they are momentary. But I know, even as I look into your eyes, that I am defeated.'

A terrible silence fell. Vicki wanted to rush to his arms, to pour out the truth, but the ghost of Brinda barred her way. Something had gone from her; some magic spark that had been all fire and ecstasy. She said tremulously:

'It isn't a question of being defeated.'

'I think it is,' he insisted gravely. 'One day you will see all this in its true perspective,

Vicki; one day when love tears aside the veil of illusion and leaves you helpless, and at its mercy. Then and only then, will you come to know life as it is and not as you would like it to be.'

She could not, dared not argue; she was almost at breaking point as she whispered:

'This has nothing to do with the depth of my love for you, Guy; you must *see*–'

He said almost harshly:

'I see that if your love for me had been like mine for you then not all the Brindas on earth could have separated us.'

Vicki, desperate, beyond coherent thought, got to her feet.

'It will not help to decry that love, Guy.' She slipped the engagement ring off her finger and handed it to him.

'Just like that,' he said cynically.

Their eyes met, his passionate, challenging, hers afraid, wounded.

'I did not will it thus,' she murmured.

He caught her roughly by the shoulders.

'Do you seriously think this is the end – that we can part like this, wiping out all that has been–'

Like the lash of a whip came her words almost before she realized their utterance:

'Are you quite sure that those words are not a repetition from the past?'

She saw him flinch as from a physical blow, his hands dropped from her shoulders, his face paled. Then, drawing himself up and moving away from her, he said with a quiet, impressive dignity:

'Now I realize that it would be quite impossible for us to go on. Without your faith, marriage, in these circumstances, would be utter hell.' He paused imperceptibly, then: 'One day, my dear, you will look back on all this and realize how *little* you really cared for me at this minute.'

Vicki tried to speak, but the muscles of her throat seemed to contract; a numb misery lay upon her like an illness. She knew only a longing to escape as the fear of breaking down haunted her. When she spoke it was in a whisper.

'You don't understand.'

His gaze was anguished yet tender:

'I understand only too well, Vicki,' he said remorsefully. A great sigh broke from him, his endurance almost at an end. He knew that, at this stage, pleading was useless and that to seek to influence her through the power of sheer emotion, of an appeal to the senses, would avail them nothing. He added, deliberately seeking to end the torment. 'I don't think there is anything more to say.'

'No.' It was no more than a catch at her breath. She moved to the door, shaking, her legs seeming incapable of supporting her. Then, almost absurdly as she afterwards realized, she whispered: 'I'm sorry about letting you down here … I mean–'

'We shall manage,' he said almost stiffly.

She glanced up at him and now, he was stern, aloof. Her resolution faltered…

He opened the door for her and in silence they walked down the long, familiar corridor. Now, in the evening gloom, it seemed peopled with the ghosts of their former selves; they who had been lovers – Guy and Vicki – here, so many kisses had been stolen, so many words whispered. Their laughter re-echoed, in Vicki's imagination, through the now deep and unfriendly stillness. And she had become an automaton, incapable of action, or of speech. A merciful unreality gripped her almost as though she were standing back and watching herself in some fantastic play.

The door clicked open, Guy held it; for an instant his gaze met hers, remorsefully, sorrowfully.

'Good-bye, Vicki,' he said hoarsely.

For a second, her defences were down as the aching, agonizing longing for his arms weakened her. Then, like mud rising from the bottom of a clear pool, the thought of Brinda obtruded to stab and threaten.

Without more than an inarticulate murmur she ran down the steps. And so down the street, blindly and struggling only to fight back the tears.

Was it possible that the end had been written ... that a few words and a relationship, so sweet, so intimate, could be destroyed. Twenty-four hours ago the stars had quivered at her feet ... now there was only a dark abyss from which it seemed she could never escape.

Guy returned to his room. A sense of inevitability lay upon him like a pall. To try to see ahead, to formulate some plan of campaign, was impossible at that stage. And suddenly the door bell rang, setting his nerves on edge while yet making his heart leap with the force of a new hope. She had come back; of course she had come back. He found himself running down the corridor and flinging the door open without thought of propriety, the smile already on his lips, the light of adoration in his eyes, then:

'Brinda!' It was a lifeless sound, as hope died.

Brinda stared at him.

'I'm sorry to be such a disappointment, my dear ... may I come in?'

He said swiftly:

'I was just leaving.'

'Then,' she said coolly, 'perhaps we might have a meal together. Or isn't that convenient?'

'Quite convenient but,' he added deliberately, 'is it necessary?'

She flashed him a provocative smile.

'There surely is no law against it.'

'True.' It struck him that he might enlist her aid with Vicki and then despised himself because, he told himself, fiercely, obviously Vicki's regard for him was but a fraction of his for her. 'I have a few papers to collect.'

'I'll wait,' she said patiently.

They left Wimpole Street some minutes later and drove to the Ritz. It was not, however, until their meal was ordered and the first course served, that Guy said abruptly and disapprovingly:

'Why did you tell Vicki?'

Brinda met his gaze very steadily. She was, she knew, looking her best in a shade of blue that emphasized the glowing tan of her skin, at the same time deepening the colour of her eyes.

'Wouldn't *you* have done so,' she replied calmly.

'Yes.' It was a rather curt sound. 'But that would have been vastly different.'

She looked impressively thoughtful.

'That's where you are wrong, Guy. And, anyway, Vicki already had her suspicions. Women are curiously intuitive in these matters.'

Guy sighed.

'I suppose,' he admitted gloomily, 'it does not make very much difference.' He studied Brinda intently.

Brinda said softly:

'I'm sorry about all this. If Vicki were more experienced... I did my best, Guy.' She was thinking ahead as she spoke, calculating the effect of her every word. 'Strange that, of all people, it should be – you!'

'That is the irony of fate,' he retorted.

She preserved a calm at great expense to herself, anxious to know all that had passed between him and Vicki, yet sufficiently wise to realize that questioning would only antagonize him.

'Vicki has high ideals; she is an incurable romantic and a very lovely person,' she said deliberately; her smile flashing and challenging was designed to attract him. 'I fall far, far beneath her, but of course in circumstances such as these, *I'd* defy the past to take you from me.' Her voice was low, husky. She added regretfully: 'It wouldn't have worked, my dear. You are a man of the world; Vicki has been sheltered, reared, as it were, in a hot-house. She is not the type to be at the mercy of her emotions... Intense, yes; but disciplined.'

'A great virtue,' he said gently. 'And the man of the world always, in the end, seeks the freshness of someone untouched and unspoiled.'

Brinda flashed him a smile.

'A reformed character – eh?'

'One can weary of the flesh-pots, Brinda.'

'True.' A subtle pause. 'I'm glad you're not as angry with me tonight as you were the last time we were together. Then—' She laughed softly: 'Oh, I'm not going to bore you with reminiscences, but I had deceived you about being Raymond's wife and you'd every justification for your fury... It may sound dreadful, but I never *felt* his wife; nothing between us had the faintest reality. His death, no doubt, spared us the divorce court.'

'A succession of interludes,' Guy said somewhat cynically.

'No.' She spoke tentatively. 'A few minor flirtations.'

'And now what?' He studied her with some interest, having no illusions regarding her character, but wholly deceived by her ultimate aims. To him, Brinda was of a world of women to whom a lover was as essential as breathing; women, not of deep emotion, but strong sex instinct and love of conquest.

'I haven't any plans,' she said, adding deceptively: 'Of course, had Vicki not taken this as I presume she has, I should have gone off abroad again and left you in peace.'

Guy asked earnestly:

'Did you tell her that?'

'Naturally. I did my best to make her see reason; to make her understand that you could have been my lover and then almost forgotten my existence – after the fashion of men! All she could see was what, to her, represented sordidness and, in all fairness to her, the fact that I, unfortunately, happened to be the woman emphasized that.'

Guy nodded dejectedly.

Brinda primed her guns further.

'You cannot fight against that wall of convention,' she went on quietly. Then: 'You may hate me for what I am going to say, Guy, but Vicki was not in love with you, the *person,* but her ideal of you and of love, itself.'

Guy said solemnly:

'There is no more bitter thing than to hear the truth and recognize it as such, Brinda.'

Brinda oozed satisfaction. It was simpler than she had even hoped.

'I wish I could say something helpful, Guy.'

He studied her intently.

'Why did you come to see me?'

She read, correctly, a faint suspicion in his voice.

'Firstly, because I wanted you to know how I felt about all this; secondly, to make my peace with you. I've never ceased to regret the fact that I deceived you about Raymond.' Her gaze held his: 'But being unashamedly primitive and feeling as I did about you, I knew that once you realized I was married–' She sighed and shrugged her shoulders. 'And how right I was proved to be on that point.' She finished hastily, mortifyingly aware that he showed not the slightest interest in past history: 'I hope I'm forgiven.'

Guy looked at her.

'The issue has no point; suppose we forget it.'

It didn't occur to him even to ask himself if she had the power again to stir him – so dead was all emotion towards her. She had become merely a woman whose part in his life had wrecked his every dream and hope. Resentment, anger towards her would, he realized, have been ridiculous and unjust, since she was no more responsible for the *débâcle* than he, but he had no desire for her company and no desire to associate himself with her in any way whatsoever in the future.

Brinda concealed her frustration, conscious that his power over her, far from diminishing through absence, had vastly increased. She saw him then as the man she wanted and was determined to have; the man, what was more, she wanted to marry. In the space of seconds, she saw herself back at Old Meadows ... with her income and his combined, there would be no need to turn it into flats. Mrs Guy Evans... He stirred her as no man had ever done; and as far as she was capable of loving anyone she knew that

she loved him. A faint depression stole upon
her and then dissipated. After all, she had
not made such poor headway in twenty-four
hours... Obviously, Vicki's engagement was
now broken ... the first and most vital
stumbling block removed. The rest would
require tact, charm and infinite patience, as
well as great subtlety. Guy was not the type
of man impulsively to be swayed by
momentary passion and he was, she realized
– not without bitterness and chagrin –
deeply in love with Vicki.

'By all means ... and don't be too
despondent about all this. If Vicki really
loves you she will soon find life intolerable
without you and her ideals come hurtling
down and if she doesn't love you ...
marriage on those terms can be pretty
bleak, Guy.'

He nodded. Everything she said registered
and then slipped from his mind; he was
incapable of concentrating except upon
Vicki and the anguish that assailed him;
anguish, new and the more terrible on that
account. This was not a love to be dismissed
or argued out of existence; it was a love cut
deep into his heart, ever to remain there. He
tortured himself with the fear that he had
not made sufficient effort to keep her; or
had not said the right things and then
scorned himself for what seemed a pitiable
weakness. She would not have had him

cringing or crawling before her in ignominy. Anger stirred; that his association with Brinda for whom he felt absolutely *nothing* should be responsible for all this seemed insane and fantastic. And he thought, bitterly, of how life was always wrecked on the little rocks, never the big ones and that human relationships would stand tempest and fire, but never the pin-pricks of Fate.

This wasn't the kind of reunion Brinda had envisaged, however, and while she dragged out the evening as long as possible, Guy was as remote and aloof at the end of it as at the beginning, completely distracted to the point finally, of silence. She made a last effort:

'I'm glad you have Old Meadows at any rate, Guy.' She hung on his answer.

He started and awoke from his reverie.

'I shall probably sell it,' he said sharply.

Brinda's gaze was meltingly tender.

'Don't do anything hastily, Guy. I know how you feel but emotion is a bad guide by which to steer in these cases.'

'Perhaps you're right.'

She thrust home a telling barb.

'There is *one* thing, if ever you did want to sell, I'm perfectly certain that Digby Graves would buy it from you.'

Instantly, he jerked his head up.

'Why Graves?'

She laughed softly.

158

'Rivalry and all that.'

'He didn't want it before when it was on the market,' Guy said flatly.

'He didn't know, then, that you were going to buy it and become engaged to Vicki ... but now that you are no longer engaged to her–' She caught at her breath. 'Am I right in assuming that?'

'Naturally.' His expression became grim. 'I see ... perhaps you are right.' His depression increased; in the conflict and chaos he had forgotten Digby Graves who suddenly loomed as a hateful and formidable rival. Then: 'I'll go through with the original plans,' he said fiercely.

Brinda dared to say:

'Would you consider me as a possible tenant for one of the flats?'

Guy said instantly:

'Suppose we get the place converted first. I do not want to seem ungracious, but I never believe in allowing yesterday to intrude into tomorrow.'

She caught at her breath, smarting under what she knew was a gentle rebuff.

'And, in any case,' she said airily, 'I may well be in Timbuctoo by then.'

'Exactly.' He was impatient to get away and chided himself for the folly of clinging to the hope that Brinda might be able to help him. 'Shall we go?'

'Of course; if you wish.' She paused

effectively: 'And Guy ... don't despair.'

He said briefly.

'I have no intention whatsoever of accepting the situation as it is now, if that is what you mean. On the other hand, I know that, at this stage, there is little I can do about it and that argument is useless.'

'We are a stubborn family,' she admitted. 'But Vicki is up against something she cannot understand; something so far removed from her own life that–' She paused. 'So you intend to fight?'

'Very definitely.'

She started.

'That hardly seemed to be your attitude when we came out tonight.'

'One can never gauge precisely one's reactions until one has had time to stand back from the problem, without the deceptiveness of emotion, anger, frustration.'

Brinda managed to conceal her annoyance and to look duly sympathetic.

'How true that is; we never *do* say the right thing at the right time – only think of vital truths left unsaid, afterwards.' She held his gaze. 'I think it is well that we, at least, understand each other.'

He resisted any suggestion that their lives were interlinked.

'That is not important or necessary, Brinda.'

She said in a breath:

160

'You are not exactly gallant, Guy.'

'I have no wish to be,' he retorted. 'The past–'

'You still hold against me,' she said painfully, 'don't you?'

He looked at her with a frank and steady gaze.

'It is no longer of the least significance, Brinda. But you know that I cannot be expected to have any illusions about you.'

She flashed at him.

'Isn't that rather smug?'

'You know also,' he said sternly, 'that I was not talking of your morals, but your attitude towards life in general.'

'All right, Guy,' she said quietly. 'But surely we can be friends enough to–'

He looked at her with a brutal honesty.

'My dear, I doubt very much if you could ever be merely the *friend* of any man–'

'Guy!' She rather liked what she conceived to be a compliment. A shrug of the shoulders. 'Very well, have it your own way.' She got to her feet as she spoke, realizing that his patience was wearing a little thin and that she had made no progress whatsoever.

A little later, having driven her to the garage in which her car was parked and having handed her into the driving seat, he said with an air of finality:

'Good-bye, Brinda.'

'Good-bye, Guy,' she said coolly. And

added as she moved slowly away: 'There may come a time when I can redeem your poor opinion of my character.'

CHAPTER 8

Vicki reached home in a state of near collapse, while striving desperately to convey the fact that she was perfectly well. The realization that she must tell Nadia of her broken engagement was a torment because she knew that Nadia would suffer with her and that, worst of all, she, Vicki, could not give any reason for the parting.

The thought of Guy was an agony; the uncertainty that possessed her an anguish of mind and soul. Had he been right in his judgment of her? And yet ... he didn't understand... He didn't know the depths to which Brinda would sink... 'One day, my dear, you will look back on all this and realize how little you really cared for me at this minute.' Her heart turned over sickeningly. Was that true? Yet how could she measure this love she had felt for him? A love that now seemed to lie in the mists of doubt and despair. She had no precedent by which to judge; the whole situation was beyond her ... it revealed, at once, her strength and her weakness... How could she go on in the face of Brinda's threats knowing – she hated the truth of the fact – that her own faith might well be destroyed by jealousy and fear... No; she had no alternative. Better to end the association now than remain to watch it disintegrate into a sordid battle between herself and Brinda. And could she doubt but that was what it would ultimately be? Brinda's threats were neither idle nor dramatic; they were calm and reasoned. Already the thought of Brinda's relationship with Guy had begun to assume gigantic proportions. Before, she had dismissed the women who might have been in Guy's life with hardly a thought; now, even at that moment, she could picture the whole scene and derive no comfort from the fact that the ending of the affair was from choice instead of necessity. They had not wanted to risk any divorce, Brinda had said, and the circumstances would seem to lend support to the statement. Was it lack of courage, of love, of faith on her part that made her recoil from a future lived in Brinda's shadow? Would another woman, more experienced than she, ignore the past, defy the present, and fight for the future? On, on, revolved her thoughts, stabbing, mocking and swirling finally to a bitter, sickening jealousy. Did she want to marry a man who had intrigued and cheapened the very name of love? A man who, after all, had not desired marriage. Colour burned her cheeks. Had Guy's capitulation, so far as she was concerned, been a genuine desire for marriage as such, or because he knew that it was the only relationship she would consider...

Nadia, looking up from her book as Vicki entered the sitting-room, caught at her breath, saying:

'Darling! How tired you look.' Her gaze was tender and full of solicitude. A smile. 'I heard you and Brinda talking into the small hours and knew you'd be worn out today.'

Vicki's mouth felt dry; her stomach hollow; she had not eaten all day and felt that she never wanted to do so again.

'Must be getting old,' she said lightly. 'Can't stand late nights...' Then, abruptly: 'Where's Brinda?'

Nadia gave an indulgent smile.

'She went up to London after tea. Terribly restless, Vicki. I wondered if she might have called for you and run you back.'

'No,' said Vicki dully; 'she didn't call.' But her thoughts were racing: had Brinda gone to see Guy?

Nadia concealed her anxiety, aware that there was something wrong; that Vicki's usually fearless, honest gaze, avoided hers until, at last, she looked down at her ringless engagement finger and Vicki intercepted that gaze.

The silence was electric; it seemed to encompass them and defy all sound. Then, almost stridently, Vicki said:

'No, I haven't lost the ring, Nadia. Guy and I have broken our engagement.'

The words, even as she uttered them, seemed ridiculous and she appreciated that the shock of them would deal Nadia a crushing blow.

'Oh *darling*.' Nadia's voice was low and gentle, yet horrified.

Vicki bit on her lip; her hands were clenched.

'Do you mind just not saying anything,' she asked desperately. 'I couldn't stand up to sympathy, Nadia.'

Nadia's thoughts went to Brinda and then turned back to chide her for imagining that, in so short a time, Brinda could possibly be in any way responsible. She whispered:

'I know, darling.'

Vicki rushed on desperately.

'I'm not being secretive, or deliberately keeping you in the dark, Nadia – please believe that; if there was anyone in the world whom I could tell it would be you ... but this is just one of those things between Guy–' her voice broke, 'and myself.' A catch at her breath. 'Don't think the wrong thing because I cannot confide in you as I have always done.'

165

'Vicki, of course not. I don't need to *say* anything; you know what is in my heart.' She felt that a knife was turning in her breast as she spoke; that this scene was being played in her imagination. Guy and Vicki – not to be married ... and when it had seemed that they had touched the very stars in their happiness.

Vicki said huskily:

'Bless you. There'll be talk, Nadia... I hate the idea of your being–'

'Don't be silly, darling ... *talk!* What does that matter! It will not be the first engagement to be broken.' She studied Vicki's tense, pale face. There was something in her eyes that precluded any possibility of hope and forbade the utterance of any banality which might suggest that things would work out, or any other well-meaning platitude or cliché.

'No,' said Vicki. 'I wonder why, in this life, one just never imagines these things happening to oneself... Nadia, would you say my ideas of life are lacking in understanding? That I'm too much of an idealist?'

Nadia looked thoughtful.

'That isn't easy to answer; the very nature of your environment and upbringing have created the sensitivity that is *you;* you cannot change all that. On the other hand, experience, great suffering, mellows ... oh, you could never be hard or unforgiving, I

166

don't mean that.' She hastened: 'But, for instance, Brinda would skim over life, take what she wanted from it, and not necessarily *see* the stars, or feel any need of reaching up, spiritually, towards them. Life takes on a different tinge, a different form, to each one of us ... and our capacity for feeling deeply is the barometer of our actions. You cannot generalize; you may know that a certain person would act entirely differently from you in a given situation, but that does not make you right and him or her wrong.' She paused. 'I'm making a speech,' she said trying to lift the weight of the depression that lay upon them as a pall.

Vicki cried:

'I don't seem to know what I *do* feel any more. My mind is so torn and twisted that nothing emerges clearly. One minute I think I'm wrong; the next, right... Oh, Nadia ... if only it were yesterday,' she said with a pathetic childishness that made Nadia's heart turn over.

'I know, my dear; in any great emotional strain there is always that element; perhaps it is that we actually feel so *much* as to reach a point of satiation. Like looking forward to a thing and being in an agony of suspense and excitement and then, suddenly, on the actual day, just not feeling anything at all.'

Vicki nodded.

'How well I know that,' she whispered.

167

'Will Brinda be back for dinner?'

'I doubt it; she said something about dining with a friend.'

Instantly, Vicki said:

'A man?'

Nadia, quietly discerning where Brinda was concerned and tactfully blind, observed:

'I rather imagine so. I cannot quite see Brinda driving up to London just to have dinner with a woman.'

Vicki's eyes had a sudden, hunted look.

'No,' she said. Then, almost sharply: 'I wish I were like Brinda; she knows life and how to handle it; she's lived in the real world and not just in a beautifully pleasant world of illusion. I'm out of my depth the moment the tide becomes treacherous, Nadia.'

Nadia said softly:

'We learn more from what we feel, darling, than from any other experience that life has to give.'

'How little you loved me...'

Suppose she were to defy Brinda ... to rush to Guy now, at that very moment... Her heart leapt and then became lead in her body... Suppose she did that and found him with ... Brinda.

'The tragedy is perhaps that we learn too late,' Vicki said sharply. 'I don't know... I'd thought of life, seen it in clear sunlight – with the shadows those that could be understood, like death – not the subtle, vicious problems, sordid, cheap–' She caught at her breath. 'It isn't narrowness, Nadia; I wouldn't criticize anyone because their ideals were not mine ... but–'

'That doesn't mean that you could survive in their world,' Nadia said gravely.

'I could defy convention, conceive of almost any situation if I knew it necessary to preserve love ... but I couldn't drag that love into the shadows of suspicion and mistrust knowing that, in the end, its beauty would vanish and hatred, perhaps, take its place.' She found herself adding involuntarily: 'Is it that I care too much or – too little, Nadia?'

Nadia didn't make an instant reply; she knew that whatever had happened had shaken Vicki to the very depths, shown her a new world and destroyed much of the old. She said slowly:

'Only time can give you your answer.'

Vicki caught at her breath.

'So you *see* my point?'

'Yes.' Nadia was trying to build up a possible case while, at the same time, fighting to resist the strange suspicion that was taking shape in her mind.

Vicki, despite herself, was goaded to ask:

'And the past ... how important do you think it is?'

Nadia said instantly:

'Oh not the slightest importance – just so

169

long as it *is* past.'

'Ah.' Vicki leaned back and closed her eyes. Why torment herself, criticize herself? Wouldn't any one in her position know beyond all doubting that she could not go on with a marriage already undermined by the avenging presence of Brinda, of whom she could not fail to be jealous and mistrustful, since she was aware in advance of her plan of campaign?

Nadia wrestled with ghostly possibilities. Had Brinda, knowing Guy before, betrayed some unworthy phase of his past? It was feasible and she was not consoled by any belief that Brinda was the type to spare Vicki hurt or maintain any discreet silence. That Brinda, herself, was involved did not enter Nadia's calculations. No one had cause to suspect Brinda's moral character; her life, on the surface, had been normal and marred only by the tragic loss of her husband. If Nadia was a trifle amazed at the calm and philosophical manner in which Brinda had accepted Raymond's death, she attributed it to the fact that Brinda was, by nature, a cold, unloving person. No one would matter to Brinda more than, or half as much as, Brinda herself. She said softly:

'If I were you, darling, I'd go to bed. I know you won't want a meal and the rest would be soothing.'

Vicki relaxed slightly.

170

'Nothing could be more soothing, or helpful, than talking to you, Nadia ... but I'll do as you say, for all that. I am tired.' She said abruptly: 'I'll have to find a new job, of course. I thought I'd go to see Dr Adamson in the morning. He might either need someone or know of someone who does. And I want to avoid the journeys if I can – and the expense of them.'

Nadia said encouragingly:

'Peter Adamson is extending his practice and has just taken a new partner ... he's a dear, too; and a friend. You'd be happy with him.'

Vicki forced a wintry smile. It seemed to her that she would never know happiness again.

She bathed and slipped into bed; her limbs leaden and aching; her heart suspended on a breaking thread. Nadia appeared with a glass of brandy and milk.

'Drinking does not require the effort that eating demands, darling, and this will at least prevent your sinking through that bed. Be a dear and take every drop of it.'

Vicki promised.

'You're so wonderful to me,' she said. 'Oh, Nadia, and I wanted to do so much for *you*.'

Nadia smiled a little wistfully.

'When you are happy again, you will have given me everything that can be given me, darling.'

She left quietly, a sweet, serene figure who, nevertheless, Vicki knew to be sharing her own tumult.

It was just before ten that the purring sound of Brinda's new car came to Vicki's sensitive ears; a sound for which she had listened, tensed and fearful.

Brinda came into the cottage, kissed Nadia and said casually:

'Vicki not back yet?'

Nadia replied, endeavouring as she spoke to take the measure of Brinda's mood and realizing that it was on the borderline of truculence.

'Yes; but she went to bed early.'

Brinda arched her brows.

'Not well?' A smile. 'I must look in on her.'

Nadia hated the idea of questioning Brinda behind Vicki's back; of trying to probe more deeply into a problem that while concerning her, was not strictly her business.

'You've had dinner?'

'Yes, Mummie; at the Ritz, as a matter of fact.' She sat down and idly lit a cigarette, having thrown her light coat aside. 'I've been taking stock as I drove back tonight.'

Nadia asked:

'Stock of what, darling?'

'My life; my plans for the future.' It was said coolly and confidently.

'It isn't always possible to make plans,' Nadia suggested. 'We never know tomorrow.'

172

Brinda's teeth flashed in the subdued light.

'I always know mine, Mummie ... oh, of course, events happen that one does not foresee; but the thing is to know what one wants and ... get it. At the moment, I want a comfortable furnished house within reasonable distance of you.'

Nadia started.

'So you were serious when you spoke of coming home.'

'Never more so.' Brinda held Nadia's gaze. 'On the other hand, Mummie, my living here at home with you, taking up the threads again as the daughter of the house, as it were. No, it wouldn't work. I haven't Vicki's temperament, nor good temper. In the end, fond though you are of me, I'd make you unhappy.' She added frankly: 'Also, I should be forced, more or less to live a family life instead of an individualistic one. Can you understand?'

'Perfectly.' Nadia hated the fact that she felt a certain relief at the decision. 'When a woman has once had a home of her own she does not take kindly to living in someone else's – not even that of a parent. In fact, least of all, in that of a parent.'

'You're a darling; you always see the other person's point of view... I thought if I could find something with about an acre of ground and have a resident and daily to look

173

after me; or, should the place require it, a man and his wife...' She glanced around her. 'Are you sure about staying on here, Mummie?'

'Perfectly sure, Brinda.'

'I'd–'

'I know you'd do anything for me, darling, but I can manage quite well – honestly. When you get settled I can come to stay with you sometimes for a week-end!'

Brinda smiled approvingly.

'I know all the people around here and it will be rather fun renewing old acquaintances.'

Nadia didn't quite know why she said a trifle breathlessly:

'These plans are very sudden – aren't they? I mean you have always insisted that you would never again *live* in England.'

Brinda's smile was enigmatical.

'The privilege of a woman to change her mind. I hope you're pleased.'

'Of course, and so thankful that you can, financially, do as you desire.'

Brinda lit a cigarette.

'I could not bear being without money,' she said emphatically. 'I'm not self-sacrificing or adaptable as you are. And not to be able to have all the clothes I want–' A sigh. 'Not for little Brinda!'

Nadia said tolerantly:

'You do not do justice to yourself, darling.'

174

'Thus speaks fond mother defending her young.'

As she sat there, Brinda deplored the loss of Old Meadows, reflecting upon that same loss with resentment rather than regret. Her affection for the house had centred around its size and importance. She had never loved it as Nadia and Vicki had done – as a home breathing happiness and love – but had regarded it as a means of acquiring power and domination over those less fortunate. In that second she resolved – a resolve that had gained strength upon reflection – that, one day, she would return to it – as Guy's wife. She had already seen to it that Vicki should never be mistress there and inspired Guy with the desire to keep it... Her eyes gleamed with the fire of ambition and determination. Guy's indifference had further inflamed her emotions but she regarded that indifference as purely a temporary reaction due to the upheaval of the break from Vicki. And it struck her forcibly as she drove home that, without a house of her own and complete freedom of action within it, she could hardly entice him back into her life since, quite definitely, she could not expect Nadia to welcome him to White Cottage.

She got up from her chair.

'I'll look in on Vicki.'

Nadia assumed that Vicki would prefer to

impart the news of her broken engagement. And even as the thought pierced her brain anew, the utter absurdity of it overwhelmed her ... only last evening a cocktail party had been given to celebrate that engagement. She said lightly:

'Amazing that you should have met Guy.'

Brinda shrugged her shoulders.

'Not really; Raymond and I were always bumping into people in odd places. If you ask me, life *is* coincidence. You travel ten thousand miles in order to meet someone who lived in the place where you were born and, if there is anyone whom you do not particularly *want* to see ... he or she turns up with monotonous regularity.'

'Did you know him well?'

Brinda wondered just how much Nadia knew because Vicki had told her, or just how much she knew because she had *guessed*. She respected Nadia's intuition and powers of deduction.

'Just how well,' she answered evasively, 'do we any of us know the other person, Mummie?...' A faint yawn. 'This place makes me sleepy ... 'night, darling. I go straight to my bed when I've had a word with Vicki.'

Nadia hastened:

'If she should be asleep, don't waken her.'

'I won't.' Brinda smirked to herself. Vicki wouldn't *be* asleep!

CHAPTER 9

Brinda went quietly into Vicki's bedroom which was illuminated by a single shaded lamp; a lamp which threw into relief the deathly pallor of Vicki's cheeks and the dark, haunting sadness of her eyes.

'Am I disturbing you?' Brinda, up to a point victorious, felt suddenly expansive. Vicki was no longer the enemy, although she bore her a definite grudge on account of Guy's regard for her.

'No.' Vicki could not accurately have defined her feelings towards Brinda in that moment. In her confusion, her conflict, she found it impossible wholly to decide just how far her threats had been responsible for the present tragedy, or to what degree her own jealousy and mistrust had contributed. A combination of the two had been entirely beyond her power to combat: that she knew to be true. She wished that some violent reaction might set in, but instead only a great weariness assailed her. And suddenly that wish was gratified as Brinda said smugly:

'I had dinner with Guy tonight.'

Vicki's heart seemed to leap a few inches

in her breast and then, misplaced, to thud maddeningly; her body felt suddenly on fire, every nerve tingling as a fierce, ungovernable jealousy leapt to life on the heels of which came a sickening contempt. It had not taken Guy very long, after all, to seek solace with Brinda.

'Really.' It was a clipped, sharp sound. 'I hope you enjoyed it.'

'Thoroughly. I stepped into the breach, my child, when Guy was feeling out of temper with you and life in general. I soothed his ragged nerves, shall we say?' A pause, then: 'I'm glad you took heed of my warning, Vicki; you just wouldn't have stood an earthly against me and it would all have been most awkward–' She shrugged her shoulders – a habit conveying the impression that so far as *she* was concerned there was nothing further to say.

'He told you, of course that I–'

'Naturally.' Brinda sat down and rested her head against the back of the chair. 'He agreed with me that you are far too inexperienced to cope with a situation of this kind, although I insisted that you were a far, far better person than I.' A little laugh. 'Funny how even while knowing the worst about a woman a man clings to her.' She leaned forward. 'Don't take this too seriously, Vicki. I know I've been brutal in my frankness–'

'I prefer at least that to deceit.' Vicki felt that her voice didn't quite belong to her.

'We discussed Old Meadows,' Brinda went on with calm self-assurance.

Vicki held her breath. Guy would sell it; he must sell it now that–

Brinda read those transparent thoughts and exclaimed:

'He's not going to sell it… I'm glad about that. We must keep it in the family, after all.'

Vicki stared at her.

'I never thought there could be anyone like you,' she said in a horrified little gasp. 'Anyone so calculating, so *hard.*'

Brinda laughed softly.

'There are two kinds of people in this world, my dear innocent: the ones who get and the ones who give. I belong to the former. Had I been as soft, as tender-hearted as you, I should have withdrawn gracefully from this scene, as I told you before, and given you and Guy a chance to be happy together. But I happen to want Guy; I came home because of him and having been with him tonight, amid the soft lights and romantic atmosphere, I want him even more. It's very simple. You could have fought me for him… Ah, you shrink from the very idea. That is where I score. I have no such squeamishness. Yours, on the other hand, has served me well.'

Vicki said heavily:

'It's so – cheap; so degrading.'

'Possibly; but I'll take that *and* Guy; you can have your dignity and rarified atmosphere – without him. Simple. I don't believe in kid gloves – you do.' She injected a note of truth to give weight to her remarks: 'Of course, just now Guy is smarting under your dismissal; it will take him a little while to write you off his telephone list, naturally. He was very fond of you and I was absolutely right: the attraction of the hardened sinner for the young, dewy-eyed innocent.'

Colour flamed into Vicki's cheeks.

'Please–'

'But, my dear, Guy and I don't have to mince words; it would be rather absurd, wouldn't it? What more natural than that he should confide in me. A past revived brings instant intimacy of thought and conversation. Quite thrilling, in fact. And don't imagine that Guy has any illusions about me, or that I seek to foster any. He and I are cast in the same mould.'

Vicki felt the tearing anguish of defeat and despair. She did not doubt that Brinda had dined with Guy and the very fact of her doing so proved that Guy's interest was by no means dead. Could he, otherwise, on this night of all night's have taken her out... A fierce flame of anger began to burn within her; anger that deadened a little of the pain,

180

so that she clung to it desperately.

'I'm beginning,' she said sharply, 'to agree with you.'

'I'm glad of *that*,' came the swift retort. 'Guy would never have kept on your level and you would never have come down to his, my dear child. Guy was intrigued, fascinated by your quaint charm; he was in love with the idea of a relationship all frills and rosebuds! But how you would have palled when his more violent emotions came to life. All right, don't look so pained, my child. But, with you, one *has* to use a hammer to break through the purity of that virginal mind!' It was said cynically.

Vicki turned her head away. Then:

'I don't think we have anything more to say,' she whispered tensely.

Brinda ignored that.

'What about Nadia? She knows about the engagement being broken? Only she didn't mention it to me just now.'

'She would assume that I should prefer to tell you myself.'

Brinda didn't want Nadia to suspect the truth and said carefully:

'She asked me how well I knew Guy, by the way.' A challenging look. 'You haven't been telling her anything about me.'

Vicki's gaze was steady and unnerving.

'No; I haven't been telling her anything; you have no need to fear that I shall shed my kid gloves; your secret is safe with me.'

Brinda looked flushed and angry. The thrust went home.

'Damned smug – aren't you?' she retorted.

'I'm very tired,' Vicki said firmly.

Brinda wasn't wholly satisfied.

'I don't want any family rumpus, you know. If you cannot realize that Nadia would be made desperately unhappy if we were openly to quarrel–'

Vicki met those hard blue eyes and said sharply:

'You've had your victory, Brinda, and now you want the battlefield smoothed and serene. Having got your way you are prepared, as of old, to be magnanimous. No, I will not quarrel with you, but I should be without spirit, or character, if I could fawn. I despise you; not because Guy was – was what he was to you, but for the tissue of lies that must have been your life with Raymond. And as for all that has happened since yesterday ... the unpleasant taste of it will never leave me. We don't speak the same language and we never shall. Suppose we leave it at that.' She caught at her breath: 'Yesterday, you accused me of being an idealist ... well, you've successfully cured me of that folly. And now, would you mind leaving me?'

Brinda hesitated, then flinging Vicki a cynical glance, went from the room.

Only one fact burned in Vicki's mind as she lay awake throughout most of the night ... that Guy had dined with Brinda. That fact seemed an indictment against which nothing could be argued in mitigation. Whatever the circumstances, he *could* have made an excuse; that he had refrained from doing so, betrayed the fact that Brinda definitely had not ceased to interest him, proving also that their separation had not been estrangement. Nevertheless why believe Brinda? Yet had not her brutal frankness regarding her intention lent added weight to her words? Vicki's mind went back over all the weeks. Hadn't Guy been drawn to her because of her lack of sophistication; because, to him, she was 'different'? *'But how you would have palled.'* Bitter, searing statement, resting it seemed in the shadow of truth.

She cried out against the torment, craving the oblivion of sleep and finding only the horror of wakefulness and of a room peopled with the ghost of a burning imagination. How simple, were Brinda out of the picture... But she was there and Vicki knew, beyond all doubting, that she would continue to be, until she had achieved her objective. Old Meadows with Brinda as its mistress...

She turned her face into the pillow and allowed the choking sobs to burst through the fierce dam of her restraint.

Downstairs, Brinda lifted the receiver of the telephone and gave Digby Graves's number. Then, softly, insinuatingly, said:

'Digby... Brinda. I thought it might interest you to have an item of news that hasn't yet gone to press... Vicki's engagement's gone phut. Fooling you! Why should I? My dear man, your guess is as good as mine. But now's your chance. And keep this under your hat. Don't mention it. 'Night.'

A smile hovered about her lips. She must take no chances since Guy had every intention of continuing the fight. Unless, she thought cynically, Digby were a blithering idiot, he would catch Vicki on the rebound and thus defeat Guy before the battle had even begun.

CHAPTER 10

Digby arrived at White Cottage soon after eleven o'clock the following morning and seeing Vicki, convincingly gasped:

'What, playing truant! Or is it—'

Vicki said swiftly, anxious to impart the news before Brinda appeared:

'It so happens that I'm looking for another job, Digby, and that my engagement was broken yesterday,' she added sharply.

Digby was not unmindful of the dark shadows under her eyes, of the listless air that appeared to add to her frailty. He said, seeming duly shocked and surprised:

'My dear, for your sake I'm terribly sorry... I'd be a hypocrite to commit myself beyond that measure of sympathy.'

Vicki studied him. His loyalty and devotion were balm to her wounded pride and she resolved, even as she met his steady, solicitous gaze, that no matter what the effort cost her, no one must be allowed to suspect how she felt; there must be no 'pathetic figure' angle, even if she drew upon flippancy and cynicism for support. The idea of wearing her heart on her sleeve appalled her and the possibility of sympathy was a horror from which she shrank, knowing how well it might defeat her courage and strength of purpose. She said:

'Just one of those things, Digby. Perhaps I've been living in a glass-slipper world too long. Amazing how one's life can change in the space of a day or two.'

He was not deceived; here was hurt, stark and devastating. He asked himself: Was Brinda mixed up in this, and then ridiculed the supposition. Why should she be; merely that her return and this development were coincidental.

'Perhaps that reflection brings a certain

185

comfort,' he said gently. 'The pendulum can swing both ways, after all – and just as swiftly... What are your plans for today?'

'Job hunting,' she said practically.

'Oh, Vicki,' he said painfully.

She laughed. Then:

'You're a dear, Digby.'

'Have dinner with me tonight,' he said. 'We could drive down to Chiddingfold to The Crown, if you liked. I warn you that I'm not going to give you any respite from my company. And you know the saying: that the best antidote for one man – is another.'

Vicki's laugh was high-pitched.

'I don't doubt but that it is true.'

He arched his brows.

'Don't learn too swiftly.'

She flashed him a deceptive smile.

'I'm the quaint type – eh? Unsophisticated and all the rest of it; out of touch with reality.'

He looked at her very levelly.

'Don't mock yourself, either.'

Faint colour stole into her cheeks.

'I haven't said anything in reply to your dinner invitation – suppose we come back to it?'

'By all means.'

'Gratefully, I accept; it will be good to get away for an hour or two. And I love Chiddingfold.'

'Then I'll collect you about six.'

Brinda walked slowly into the room at that moment.

'Good morning, Digby.' A pause. 'An early caller.'

There was something about her that aroused his distrust, her smooth slinkiness appearing to him feline.

'Actually,' he said, to account for the call, 'I wanted to know if you would all join me at The Majestic Hotel on the thirtieth. There's a charity affair on and I've been roped in. Red Cross. Worthy and all that. My guests,' he added lightly. 'You cannot refuse.'

Brinda looked at Vicki.

'Why should we wish to, eh, Vicki?'

Digby said deliberately:

'I have a special friend of mine I want you all to meet. So unless you have in mind a particular escort, Brinda, may I arrange it?'

Brinda flashed Vicki a meaning look.

'By all means. I am not without an escort but, just at the moment, I'll be very discreet!' There was something in her voice that made Vicki writhe. 'Incidentally, I'm going house hunting this morning. You don't happen to know of anyone who wants to let their house furnished to a most responsible tenant – do you?'

Digby asked breathlessly:

'So you're settling among us.'

'Very definitely. I suppose I was homesick. I always find myself longing to be back near Old Meadows,' she said deliberately.

Digby exclaimed, aware of the sudden, rather tense silence:

'I do know of one house – near Swinley Golf Course. But they want a let of a year. Twelve guineas a week. They have it in mind to leave their resident maid and I believe there's a daily, also. Attractive place; about an acre. Why not go in and see the agents – they're at Sunningdale?'

'I will… I take it the owners are going abroad?'

'Yes, Singapore; he's an army man.'

Brinda smiled.

'I always get what I want,' she said confidently. 'And without effort, too.' Her teeth flashed, her eyes were bright and to Digby, greedy. She looked at Vicki. 'Of course you didn't know that I'd decided to take a house in the district, did you? Nadia understands perfectly. After a home of one's own one just cannot become "the daughter living with mother" again. And there isn't room for all of us here, anyway.'

Vicki didn't speak; she could not express any pleasure or enthusiasm even for Digby's benefit. To her the very idea of Brinda's proximity horrified her. And she knew, even as she stood there, that she would have to make an effort to get away. Brinda was as salt rubbed incessantly into the wound and with the possibility of any developments between her and Guy, the whole situation was unthinkable.

Digby said awkwardly:

'It seems a good idea to find some place of your own.'

'The year is rather a snag,' Brinda reflected. 'But, I don't doubt that I could make some arrangements later on.'

Digby flashed at her.

'I'm sure you could.'

'I don't,' she said coolly, 'quite see myself living alone – indefinitely.' A little laugh. 'But that's another story.'

She went out. Vicki remained standing, her limbs shaking, the sensation of sickness stealing upon her induced by an emotion that was horrifically new to her – the emotion of contempt and dislike. It stole upon her like an illness, making Brinda's very presence loathsome.

Digby said abruptly:

'She's very attractive, isn't she?' He added: 'And very hard. I cannot imagine gentleness, softness or even compassion ever touching her.'

Vicki said, unable to keep a faint touch of bitterness from her voice:

'Surely men are not concerned beyond that physical attractiveness.'

Digby stared at her.

'That sounds foreign to you, Vicki. And

you are wrong, anyway.'

She gave him a smile of warm approval.

'I think you must be different from most other men.' Vicki was not quite sure what she was trying to prove; she merely found an outlet in a cynicism which, until then, had not touched her life.

'Would that the mere fact of your thinking so might change your "no" to "yes", Vicki.' He hurried on: 'And now having made quite sure of your company tonight and at the Ball on the thirtieth, I will leave you in peace… Give my love to Nadia.'

'She's out shopping,' Vicki explained.

'She wouldn't, I feel, want to come along on the thirtieth,' he said gently.

'No.' Vicki shook her head. 'Without Daddy she is far happier at home – at least for the present.' She looked at him intently. 'Thank you for your understanding over all this, Digby.'

He said slowly:

'I'm ready to listen to anything you may want to tell me, my sweet, and perfectly prepared to avoid any questions you would prefer me not to ask.' He smiled. 'Quite a speech.'

'And very worthy of you.' It was as though, in building up Digby's virtues, she was pouring balm on the wounds of her disillusionment, clinging frantically to the ghost of a former faith, a former belief in the essential beauty of life as evinced through the sterling character of those people for whom she had deep regard.

They walked slowly, side by side, from the cottage to the pathways that led to the grass verge of the quiet lane.

'Good-bye, Digby,' she said softly.

'Good-bye, my dear.' He gave her a steady scrutiny. 'I'm going to mouth a maxim of Rochefoucauld to the effect that we are never as unhappy as we think we are.'

Vicki's pale face and dark eyes held a sudden poignant wistfulness. Then:

'Rochefoucauld is someone for whom I rather imagine that, in future, I am going to have an increasing respect,' she said forcing a note of lightness.

Digby flashed her a doubting glance.

'The leopard never changes his spots.'

'But the leopardess might!'

'Least of all the leopardess,' he insisted.

'We shall see.' She lowered her gaze.

Digby glanced around him, almost as if for inspiration, aware that Vicki's mood was courageous and exceedingly dangerous.

'I shall have to keep a vigilant eye upon you,' he murmured impressively as he got into his car.

Brinda sauntered up, having dressed in readiness to go out.

'By the way, you didn't tell me the name of the agents in Sunningdale.'

Digby did so. And with a nod at Vicki drove off.

Brinda said with enthusiasm:

'Now he is just the type of man for you, my dear.'

Vicki bristled; her nerves taut at the very sound of Brinda's voice.

'Suppose you allow me to choose my own husband,' she said sharply.

Brinda smirked.

'But that is the one thing I cannot *possibly* allow you to do, darling. Too bad; but there it is... Care to come with me to see over this house?'

'No,' said Vicki emphatically.

'Very touchy this morning; it won't get you anywhere, you know... Most convenient if this place is any good; after all, Old Meadows looks out over Swinley golf course... I must be near Guy, whatever happens.'

Vicki had turned on her heel and gone swiftly back into the cottage.

Brinda went to the estate agents, got an order to view and drove to Swinley View which proved to be an ideal house, with every convenience, artistically furnished and set in an acre of secluded garden, well stocked with fruit trees of every description and aflame with rhododendrons. Without hesitation she took it, gave names for references and purred inwardly. But, then, of course, she always had her way.

She lunched at the Berystede and then wrote a brief note to Guy which read:

Guy, my dear–
There's a charity ball down here on the thirtieth. Majestic. Vicki is going. You might think it worth your while to be there. Soft lights and sweet music and all that. Tickets practically sold out, hence this ample notice.

Yours,
BRINDA

She smiled as she sealed it. With Vicki in her present mood anything might happen in three weeks and if Guy did attend the ball she, Brinda, would be there to hold a watching brief. And so would Digby. A malevolent gleam came into her eyes. There was one thing: even if she failed to win Guy back, Vicki should never have him. She hated Vicki. Why try to deny it? She always had; if she could hear of her death, she thought violently, she would be thankful. But even *her* luck wouldn't stretch that far. She sat back in the comfortable armchair in the lounge and sipped her coffee and liqueur. Once she was settled at Swinley View life would be simple and she would be able to entice Guy back into her world. Her inordinate vanity would not admit of failure… She'd been mad to think, but a few moments before, that there was even a possibility of it. Patience; unfortunately it was not one of her virtues; she wanted what she wanted ... *immediately*. It affronted her to be forced to tolerate the present somewhat invidious position.

Digby hailed her, coming from the dining-room.

'Small world.' He sat down beside her, finding that a certain curiosity gripped him as he met her blue eyes; eyes which though cold were nevertheless inviting.

'Very.'

'Thanks for phoning me,' he said briefly.

'Since the poor lamb's world's crashed... I thought you were just the right person to mend the broken toy.'

'I'd like to think so.'

'Ever heard of the word "rebound"?'

'Yes, without caring for the sound of it much.' He paused. 'I'm not quite the tame friend, hang-dog, and all that – the type conveniently turning up in novels.'

'I'm perfectly aware of that, my dear man. I know a little about men.'

'More than a little I should say.'

'Digby!' She grinned and looked pleased. 'I'd like to see Vicki happy,' she said smoothly. 'And you – well! It's obvious that you would achieve that objective for me.'

Digby studied her.

'And just where does Guy fit into this jig-

194

saw puzzle of yours.'

'Guy?' She looked incredibly innocent.

'Yes, Guy! I was at the party the other night, if you remember, and witnessed your touching little reunion!'

'Oh – *that!*' She laughed. 'Here now, don't jump to the wrong conclusions.'

'The words are yours not mine,' he said coolly.

'Raymond and I met Guy in Sweden. At the time he was very much involved in an affair of the heart.'

Digby found that his curiosity overwhelmed him; his love for Vicki made every word of vital importance since Guy was out of the picture and while the sentiments he had uttered to Vicki were sincere regarding his attitude, now, facing Brinda, who might well know the truth, silence was impossible. He said tensely:

'Could that have caught up with him to bring about this somewhat dramatic change?' He eyed her with suspicion. 'Isn't it asking rather a lot to dissociate you from it all?'

Brinda stared him out.

'If your sister, to whom you were devoted, were about to marry someone whom you knew to be entangled elsewhere, would *you* remain silent?' she asked frankly, disarmingly. Adding: 'Although I do not feel that it is fair to Vicki to discuss the matter.'

Digby said rather startlingly:

'You know, I liked Evans – even though I detested him for being my rival. I could understand his having an affair – who hasn't had one – before Vicki's advent ... but I should have judged him to be the type who would finish one thing before starting another. You surprise me.'

Brinda looked convincingly grave.

'It has been a pretty ghastly shock, Digby. Shall we leave it there?' How confident she felt in her trust of Vicki whom she knew would never betray her, even to Digby! Principle was an excellent thing when indulged by the other person, she thought cynically; it made one's own position so much more secure.

He gave her a steady scrutiny.

'You're an enigma, Brinda. I've known you for years but there's always something missing in the continuity.'

'That charm which gathers power through its own elusiveness,' she mocked.

'No,' he said shortly. 'I'm afraid I didn't mean it that way. On the surface you add up; everything would appear quite perfect ... but your eyes belie that which your lips utter. Don't try fooling me, or meddling in my relationship with Vicki.'

'Digby! Is that nice?'

'No; but it is, I feel, a language you understand, my child.'

'True. Don't worry; I'm far too selfish to concern myself with the affairs of others. By the way, I've taken Swinley View. Charming place.'

Digby nodded. His thoughts were with Vicki. If what Brinda had told him really had any bearing on the broken engagement, then he could well appreciate the unbearable disillusionment to anyone of Vicki's temperament. Guy, he thought swiftly, must have been mad. His heart lightened. In time Vicki would forget. Fate had a strange way of moving her puppets.

Digby asked casually:

'Did you see Major and Mrs Riddel?'

'No.' Brinda smiled. 'But I saw some photographs of a singularly handsome man about the place.'

'That's Charles,' Digby said.

'And his wife? Is she attractive?'

'Very.' Digby felt that Brinda was disappointed. 'You'll meet her, of course, before you take over.'

'It won't break my heart if I do not... I never, somehow, get on with my own sex, Digby. Women are so jealous.'

'And discerning,' he countered, his smile provocative.

'Discerning to be so jealous of me,' she suggested.

'That wasn't,' he assured her, 'quite what I meant but ... it doesn't matter. And now I must be going.' He eyed her coolly.

She met his gaze with interest. It struck her that Digby was really rather attractive and while not to be compared with Guy might have been a most satisfactory string – second string. A vicious thought chased through her mind... Should Guy ever fail her... Digby was just the kind who might prove weak, given a certain amount of temptation. Rather amusing to spoil Vicki's chances twice. But the only important thing now was to get Vicki married to Digby; that was an essential factor to her progress. The rest didn't matter.

CHAPTER 11

Vicki dressed slowly and apathetically on the night of the thirtieth, wishing fervently that she might avoid going to the ball yet knowing that, to withdraw at the last moment, would be very ungracious and ungrateful to Digby who, during the past week, had proved a staunch ally, ever at her side, consoling in his silent sympathy, unquestioning and understanding. He had thus further endeared himself to her and she was conscious of the debt she owed him: alone during that time, and she might well have plunged to her own doom, she argued.

She had secured a receptionist's post with Dr Adamson and worked without thought of weariness or hours, undertaking many tasks outside her province and proving her worth to the delight of a thankful employer. Financially, she was better off because, where before she had the expense of the daily journey to London, now there was only a modest bus fare.

Brinda strolled arrogantly into her room, jealously realizing that Vicki presented a glorious picture in her tiered silk chiffon gown, exquisitely sequined and off the shoulder.

'So *you're* wearing black,' she said pointedly.

Vicki retorted, without looking round from the dressing-table:

'Is there any law against it?'

Brinda frowned; she had hoped for and expected a meek, docile Vicki who recognized her master when she found him. She, Brinda, being the master.

'None; except that I wanted to wear my Worth model which happens also to be black.'

Vicki screwed a diamond ear-ring into her ear.

'One of these days you will learn that you cannot have everything your own way,' she said smoothly.

Brinda's expression became darkly spiteful.

'I haven't done too badly up to now,' she exclaimed. 'And my white Dior is, after all, far more glamorous. Black can be aging; *you* most certainly do not look *your* best in it.'

Vicki shook her head.

'There are times when you are quite pathetic, Brinda.'

Brinda shrieked, outraged:

'When I'm – *what?*'

'Pathetic,' Vicki repeated patiently. 'Like a greedy child terrified lest any other child might also have some sweets and wanting to hog them all for herself. There will be some very beautiful women at the ball tonight *and* most beautifully dressed, irrespective of what you think or hope.'

Brinda scoffed:

'I am accustomed to being the most glamorous woman at any gathering.'

Vicki was not going tamely to accept such nauseating conceit.

'I've heard it said that Englishwomen abroad have a hundred times less competition than in their native land. You will find you have very much more to live up to here... Men are not two a penny in England.'

Brinda gasped.

'Why – you–'

'Don't waste your energy,' Vicki said

coolly. 'You'll need every ounce of it to compete with the lovelies there tonight.'

'And have I never *been* to any functions here before?'

Vicki looked unruffled.

'Many; but you have a conveniently short memory ... if you don't hurry up you will not be ready when Digby calls.'

Brinda rapped out:

'Then he can wait.'

Vicki smiled.

'He would not consider that a privilege.'

'You're so sure of Digby – aren't you?' Brinda's anger was like a dagger, she wasn't balanced when it came to her emotions towards Vicki.

Vicki, irritation rising, said sardonically:

'I am quite sure that *he* isn't in love with you, Brinda – if that is what you had in mind.' As she spoke Vicki picked up her white, fox cape and moved to the door.

'And what do you know about love,' Brinda cried sneeringly. 'Beyond the nursery rhyme variety?'

'That is something,' Vicki said with a quiet dignity, 'which not even you can assess.'

For a second there was a tense silence, then Brinda rapped out:

'I'll take that smug, satisfied look off your face, my dear, before this evening is out – believe me.' She added as she saw the utter distaste on Vicki's face. 'And I know what you're thinking. I haven't any of the scruples or the niceties of the Waynes... That my upbringing is not reflected in my behaviour. True. I'm a throwback. I seem to remember Daddy talking about a rebellious grand-mother... I can't stand the stuffy atmos-phere of your world; you sicken me.' She stopped. This was not the mood she had intended to sustain on this particular night.

Vicki swept past her; she didn't speak, but went gracefully down the stairs, Brinda glaring after her.

For all that, Vicki was trembling; were it not for the fact that in a matter of days Brinda was moving to Swinley View she would have been forced to leave White Cottage finding the whole situation there, as it involved Brinda, wholly untenable.

Nadia said lovingly:

'You look very beautiful, Vicki. I hope you enjoy it, darling.'

'I shall try,' Vicki assured her, feeling that her heart was leaden and that carefree gaiety was barred for ever more – lost in the mists of a precious yesterday.

Digby arrived just as Brinda was descend-ing the narrow staircase – a dazzling figure in sleek white crêpe that clung to her figure and revealed its every line. Digby said:

'May I introduce Martin Gaunt... Mrs Wells.'

Vicki – who had already smiled and

offered her welcome, had previously met Martin Gaunt and dismissed him as a pleasant egotist whose chief concern was Martin Gaunt – thought that he and Brinda should find a great deal in common.

The Majestic Hotel lay in the seclusion of pine woods, between Ascot and Windsor and, as they approached it that evening, it seemed to bring back all the splendour of the Arabian Nights. Its vast grounds, flooded and festooned with myriad lights, whispered of romance and a magic unreality as though, for a few hours, the hands of time had been stopped to allow the enchantment of swift desire respite from the shadow of tomorrow. The evening was warm, but without humidity and a soft breeze, laden with the aromatic fragrance of earth and many flowers, hung in the air like incense.

Vicki caught at her breath. This was the one place to which she had not been with Guy and only his name had any significance as she gazed at the scene around her, feeling the swift, tearing pain of longing that was physical as well as mental.

She said swiftly:

'Digby, let's stay out here for a while; it's too heavenly to go indoors.'

Brinda had scanned the wide forecourt already packed with cars and felt her heart almost stop beating as, even in that second, she saw Guy's gleaming Jaguar sweep into the gates. She hastened:

'We'll see you later, then.' She hustled Martin Gaunt into a position where he blocked Vicki's view of any approaching car.

'Very well.' Digby slipped his arm through Vicki's and they moved to the back of the Regency building, with its deep-bowed front and stately pillars that looked over some fifty acres of parkland in which a miniature lake gleamed like sapphire.

'A perfect night for it all,' Digby began tritely.

Vicki wasn't listening, except to the noisy beating of her heart which seemed to throb in an empty void. She said mechanically:

'Perfect.'

He could not stay the question:

'I hope this doesn't awaken any painful memories.'

'None,' she assured him.

He looked down at her.

'You know what I'm going to say, Vicki – don't you?'

She didn't prevaricate.

'Yes.'

His gaze held hers.

'And do you know your answer.'

She cried:

'Oh, Digby; I *want* to know it but–'

He hastened:

'I can't go on like this, darling; I'm not the

204

tame pet at heart and I've kept quiet during these past weeks for your sake–'

'I know – you've been wonderful.'

'Does that merit no reward?' he asked humbly.

'It is because it merits such great reward that I hesitate now,' she said honestly.

'Marry me, Vicki; I'll take you away from here; we'll travel, darling, and the things that have hurt you will, in time, seem never to have been. Oh, I know that isn't easy to believe, but unless it were true, people would never be able to go on.'

Vicki raised her gaze to his.

'I must not put the burden of all this upon your shoulders,' she said gravely. 'Allow all your generous plans for me to blind me to the fact that it is a wife – loving, loyal – that you seek. How far short must I almost inevitably fall, Digby, since I cannot, in all honesty, tell you that I am *in* love with you?'

He persisted:

'You can tell me that you love me and, I hope, respect me.' There was a quiet impressiveness about him as he spoke. 'That is enough to begin with, particularly as I am by no means convinced you really know quite what you do feel about anyone at this moment.'

'Then surely that is the very worst possible time to make a decision,' she argued. 'I *couldn't* cheat you, Digby.'

'My dear, this is no new love on my part and *you* could not cheat anyone. I'm quite aware that the past still holds its flame, but to me it is no more than that. I do not believe that you have loved so deeply, so irrevocably, as to make all hope of building a new life fantastic. It is up to me to prove to you that the heart was never more steadfast than when it finds faith renewed after bitter disillusionment.' He added, and there was a strange and almost prophetic ring to his words: 'I'd rather die than bring you misery, my dearest.'

'You have been so good,' she whispered tremulously.

'But I cannot remain now just the placid friend,' he warned her. 'And quite apart from *my* angle, it is not in itself kind to you since it merely enables you to drift.'

'I know that,' she admitted. 'I'm so mixed up inside–'

'Poor sweet,' he said softly. 'You need me to take care of you, you know.' He changed his mood. 'Giving you days, weeks in which to ponder all this,' he said shortly, 'will get us nowhere, either. I'd like my answer tomorrow, darling.' A wry smile twisted his mouth. 'Since this proposal of mine is nothing new to you and I rather feel that you have already assessed my character ... although don't overlook what I might yet achieve with the incentive of ... my wife.'

Vicki studied him very earnestly.

'You shall have your answer, Digby – perhaps even before tomorrow morning.'

'Soft lights and sweet music – may they be my allies,' he said. 'Now suppose we go inside.'

They went into a hydrangea-filled palm court, through which a cool, perfumed breeze stole from the open windows of a terrace at the end of the ballroom; the strains of lilting music came hauntingly. She moved forward on Digby's arm.

'We must dance,' he said smiling into her eyes, 'and perhaps I can mesmerize you into saying: "yes".'

Idly, as they took the floor, Vicki's gaze wandered, meeting smiles of recognition no matter in what direction she looked and then suddenly, she saw Brinda dancing in Guy's arms... Brinda – face raised invitingly, lips parted and Guy...

A dagger stabbed and stabbing seemed to deal a mortal blow at what had been her love for Guy; she could not divorce it from the searing contempt that surged upon her. And suddenly, so that Digby gasped as one hardly daring to believe her words, she said swiftly:

'You do not need to mesmerize me, Digby... I will marry you any time you wish, my dear, and if *wanting* to love you as you love me, can achieve that end–' She rested her gaze in his.

'My darling,' he said thickly. His face was suddenly gay and boyish. 'I'd like to leap up on to that chandelier and broadcast the fact to the world.'

She nerved herself to respond to his mood; her laughter seeming natural, but to her so remote as to be utterly foreign.

'Don't give the gossipers too much food at once,' she said lightly. 'Just think of all they have had and will have to digest as a result of all this! Sudden engagement of Victoria Wayne to purchaser of Old Meadows; abrupt ending of same. Equally sudden engagement of Victoria Wayne to Digby Graves – old friend of the family. Just how they will fill in the gaps!' She felt that she was playing her part exceedingly well, as she knew she must continue to play it. This was the test of her courage, her pride, her loyalty to Digby. Obviously she would have to speak to Guy, or else unleash a spate of vicious gossip, thus creating the loathsome impression that neither was civilized enough to acknowledge the other, even in public. She knew that Digby had not seen Guy and Brinda and, above all, she realized that he would have no reason to assume that she *had*, once *she* drew his attention to them, which she now did saying as if startled:

'Digby! Look over there. No! By the first window leading to the terrace...'

Digby looked, then:

'Guy,' he said fiercely. 'With *Brinda!* What the devil's he doing here.' A pause. 'Sorry, darling, but–'

'This *is* a public affair, you know.'

'I don't care what it is, if he'd any taste he wouldn't turn up in a place where he might be almost certain to–' He stopped: 'Perhaps that's his game or... Would you like to go?' he finished abruptly.

Vicki squared her shoulders. She did not doubt, but that Brinda had engineered this and, obviously, Guy was only too ready to fall in with her plans.

'On the contrary,' she said firmly. 'That would cause even more gossip and probably of a less pleasant nature. I should hate to run away and give the matter undue importance by so doing.' She caught at her breath. 'Particularly now I'm engaged to *you.*'

Digby beamed.

'For a moment,' he said absurdly, 'I was so scared of losing you, that I'd forgotten you'd just promised to marry me!'

'Suppose we go over to them,' Vicki suggested; 'the music is stopping anyway.'

'With the greatest of pleasure,' Digby said, preening himself for his conquest.

Guy had decided to visit The Majestic as a last resort. Determined to talk to Vicki, if not there, then to arrange another meeting.

The necessity for dancing with Brinda had anything but pleased him but, so adroitly had she contrived it, no alternative was left to him. He watched Vicki come towards him and it was as though his heart were being torn from his body in an effort to reach her. And, at last, they stood face to face, with Brinda, smirking in a fashion that only Vicki could understand, at his elbow. Vicki said:

'Good evening, Guy; you are quite a stranger to this district.'

He inclined his head and she was conscious of the fact that, in his evening clothes, he looked fine, distinguished and, to her, by far the most attractive man there.

'It could be that you also are a stranger to London.'

'Definitely a stranger,' she said calmly, averting her gaze as he sought to draw it to his, and aware of the fierce, indestructible power he still exercised over her.

Digby said in his pleasant fashion:

'This is no night for discussions, or for anything serious... I demand to be congratulated; Vicki has just promised to be my wife.'

Every word seemed to fall with that deadly significance as though nothing could ever again approximate the drama of the utterance. Brinda spoke first, aware that Guy had paled visibly, while the set of his jaw had tightened as obviously he sought fiercely to maintain control.

'Digby, how wonderful ... you see how inevitable your boy and girl romance was... Guy, you were the merest interlude,' she said smoothly, 'but since no harm has been done... Vicki darling ... all the happiness you deserve.'

Vicki looked at Guy, praying that her eyes might not betray her. He said, and the low, resonant tones of his voice echoed with a curious intensity:

'I hope you'll be very happy.' He glanced at Digby: 'Congratulations.' Then: 'And now I'm going to claim the privilege of an ex-fiancé,' he said deliberately, 'and ask if I may have the pleasure of this next dance.' Before either Digby or Vicki could protest, he had swept her into his arms and so to the dance floor.

For a second the impact robbed them of all power of speech. Then, slowly, bitterly, her pride, jealousy and contempt crystallized into a burning rebellion; it was as though Guy, through his association with Brinda, was now smeared and tainted with her own dislike and distaste *for* Brinda ... the fact that there was neither logic nor reason in the emotion – only the pitiful weakness of human nature – did nothing to lessen it. The dead past, she thought violently, when at a word from Brinda he was there, dancing with her... Obviously

Brinda and he were in touch… On, on her brain raced until Guy said:

'This is a case of "off with the old love and on with the new" – very swiftly, Vicki.'

She retorted:

'An arrangement no one, surely, could be better fitted to appreciate than you. I didn't expect to see you here tonight.'

'I came only to see you,' he said quietly.

'How very convenient that I happen to be Brinda's sister,' she flashed.

'From my point of view,' he corrected her, 'how damnable.'

Vicki's taut nerves relaxed slightly; a strange sensation of unreality surged upon her. She felt helpless against the swirling emotions now tearing at her heart.

'I'm quite sure you will overcome the handicap,' she said.

He drew her gaze to his.

'Oh, my darling,' he said hoarsely, 'if you could but know the insensate folly of all this – the pitiable folly, the *waste*.'

She started and her heart seemed to be trying to escape from her breast so violent was its beat.

'I'm afraid, Guy,' she said remorsefully, 'I am not impressed by such dramatics.'

He looked down at her, his dark eyes burning with a fervour almost frightening.

'Were those months of happiness, of love – dramatics?' he demanded fiercely. 'And for *what* have they been discarded?'

'Substance that is the past; shadow that is both today and tomorrow,' she said and her voice shook. 'Do you imagine that I could have spent my *life* within that shadow?'

He continued to hold her gaze, trying to fathom the working of her mind.

'Great love would not have seen the shadow and ... would have forgiven the substance,' he said quietly, painfully. A sigh escaped him. 'One day you will understand that Brinda is not, and never could be, so much as a name to me now... It is because you have lived so far from the frailties of human experience that you have allowed the past to assume such importance, my darling. Had this not been so and no matter what Brinda might have said to you – and I in no way overlook the possibility of her efforts to make trouble in that respect – it just would not have mattered. Nothing could have touched us–'

Vicki cried out:

'No purpose can be served by all this, Guy. I am going to marry Digby and, for all your protestations, I do not doubt but that you will marry Brinda–'

He gasped:

'Are you *mad?*'

She started at the vehemence of his tone.

'No; why should I be?'

'Do you seriously imagine that if I had

cared for Brinda sufficiently to want to marry her now, I should *ever* have left her without a fight, or without seeking her out during the year of her widowhood?'

'But–'

He said gently:

'You don't understand ... but when you lie in your husband's arms and long for mine, for my lips, you will remember what I am saying now, my dearest, and prove for yourself that physical intimacy, without intimacy of the soul and spirit, is as empty as my life will be without you and yours without mine... It's all right: I'm taking you back to your fiancé; there's nothing more I can do, because until you know love – know it fiercely, destructively, in all its moods and phases, its desires and despairs, you belong neither to him nor to me. I've shattered your *dream* of love, Vicki; killed many of your illusions and for that, I'm desperately sorry. But one day you will find the eternal truth of a love that is a law unto itself. Pray God that when that day comes – for your sake – it will be your husband who inspires it.' He pressed his lips against the top of her head. Then, passionately, he whispered: 'Although with the worst that is in me, I'd give my soul that it should prove to be ... *me*.'

Vicki shivered, his words breaking, so it seemed, into a hundred fragments of sound that stabbed at her brain and heart. It would have been so easy to respond to his fierce attractiveness, to tell herself that Brinda really had no significance and that her continual presence in the future would be of no consequence ... but even as she caught sight of Brinda's confident, almost triumphant glance, the old horror and disgust crept back. Never would she escape from her evil scheming, never would she walk in the sunlight, proudly, knowing that nothing menaced her life with Guy ... that menace was there and damnably real in a way that not even Guy, himself, could see. A strange remoteness crept upon her; emotion died; she was caught up in the web of fear that paralysed response. She said, her voice low, but steady:

'Words are very cheap, Guy, and I think I'm too weary of all this, even to stress my own point of view. But in all fairness to myself, I would emphasize the fact that a dead past is one thing – forgotten, obliterated. This case is vastly different and always would be.'

Guy looked down at her.

'A past is only rendered "dead", my darling, when its memory is erased from the *heart*. The physical *presence* of a person does not bring that past to life, if anything it but serves to destroy the last remnants of emotion.' He drew himself up, resolutely: 'And now I will return you to your fiancé ...

good-bye, Vicki. I have an idea that it will be a very long while before we meet again.'

With that, and as the music stopped, he guided her back to where Digby and Brinda were standing.

'Thank you,' he said formally then, with a swift glance at the others. 'I have to get back to town, so I will say good night.'

Brinda, instantly conscious of the possible effect of those words upon Vicki, said with a quiet possessiveness:

'I'll wander out to the car with you ... it's been terribly short, Guy, but–' She stopped, aware of the steel-like glance he gave her and not wishing for complications.

Vicki turned away. She had only to see him with Brinda to be fortified in the rightness of her decision. Could any woman in the world – sophisticated or otherwise – be expected to accept such a distasteful situation? She would, she told herself, be thankful to be married to Digby and escape from Brinda's hateful presence and sordid reminders.

She watched Guy go without knowing just what she felt about him; there was chaos and conflict, love and hatred, jealousy and fear all mixed into an impossible medley of emotion. Fiercely she shut her ears against the remembrance of his words to her... She had said that words were cheap... Her gaze followed his tall figure as he walked across

216

the ballroom and she watched Brinda slip her arm through his ... doubtless he had some very pretty speech for *her*, too! She drew back sharply, horrified by her own attitude.

Brinda was saying:

'I'm so terribly sorry it didn't work out, Guy.'

He looked down at her and even as they reached the seclusion of the grounds, flung off her restraining arm.

'That,' he said incisively, 'I find extremely difficult to believe.'

She looked wide-eyed and innocent.

'But, for heaven's sake – why? Didn't I take the trouble to write to you and–'

'I'm fast coming to the conclusion, Brinda, that you are the type always to have an ulterior motive.'

She said with telling emphasis:

'Aren't you being rather unfair? Can *I* help it if my sister happens to be a glorified Snow White? I really don't see why I should be banished from all home contacts because she isn't broad-minded enough to wipe out the past; or I should say sufficiently in love with you to trust you in my presence! I would gladly have gone away had I felt it would have changed her attitude in the slightest.' She shrugged her shoulders. 'I've done my best and you don't have to hold it against me merely because you once wished to be, and were, my lover.'

Guy sighed. What she said was, of course, perfectly true; but so bound up was his misery with the very name of 'Brinda' that she had become anathema to him; a symbol of all he had lost.

'I'm sorry,' he said roughly.

She raised her gaze to his.

'That's all right, Guy. I understand,' she said softly. 'And if ever you should happen to be driving past Swinley View – I've taken it furnished for a year, by the way – look in.' She added swiftly: 'And don't part with Old Meadows – please.'

He said grimly:

'I've no intention of parting with it.' He said sombrely: 'So you're moving out of White Cottage.'

'Yes.' A sigh escaped her. 'Vicki hasn't been exactly pleasant. But I can't blame her; she just has never lived and cannot be expected to hold other than the very narrowest of views. So ... to preserve the peace... It will make it easier for Mummie, too. And, quite honestly, apart from that, I want my own home again.'

He studied her intently.

'And just where are you going from here – figuratively?'

She flashed him a provocative glance.

'Where are you?'

'I've no idea,' he said almost curtly.

'Neither have I.' She paused hopefully, but he said briefly:

'It's getting chilly out here – go back into the ballroom. Good night, Brinda.'

'Good night, Guy.' She simulated a calm she was far from feeling, but knew instinctively that this was not the moment in which to attempt either to entice, or attract, him and not without bitterness and chagrin, she realized that his gaze was cold and impersonal.

Deliberately, she lingered a few moments longer in the hall of the hotel. Vicki would naturally assume that she was still with him. Then, a smile on her lips and conveying an air of breathless gaiety, she rejoined them, saying coyly to Martin Gaunt:

'Do forgive me for deserting you ... have you heard the news that we've an engagement to celebrate?' She looked triumphantly at Vicki as she spoke, as if to say: 'Now, my victory is complete'.

The evening, for Vicki, seemed interminable; gradually they were drawn into the circle of their more intimate friends, of which James and Gloria Morris formed the nucleus and while the scene was one of richness and splendour, of jewels blazing on soft, white throats and gowns lending an enchantment with their vivid colour, their exquisite materials, to enhance the beauty of the wearers, to Vicki it had neither life nor gaiety... Was it possible that, only the previous year, she had attended a similar function, while standing tiptoe and breathless on the very rooftop of life? Her heart, gay and carefree, her emotions, romantic yet secure. Then she had danced without thought of tomorrow, conscious of no problem more significant than the long and attractive list of engagements that lay ahead. She was young, untouched by life, unspoiled by luxury ... and the very stars themselves seemed to be reflected in her eyes. Digby had been her escort, his proposal part of the sequence of events of the evening. She had respected his devotion, without taking it seriously and without wanting to be tied, or drawn into the more sober of life's relationships, while yet dreaming of that lover who should whirl her into the glorious, ecstatic mystery of marriage that was, in her imagination, fashioned by the beauty and devotion of Nadia and her father. It had all been so *simple*. Old Meadows had lain still and serene in the moonlight as she and Digby returned to it; a citadel of happiness and permanence, of dignity and well-being ... a world unto itself, of which she was an integral part.

And now, only a year later, her father was dead... Old Meadows had gone; she had found and lost love, disillusioned by the sharpness of its sting, the astringency of its bitter lesson and ... she was going to marry Digby.

To marry Digby... She told herself fiercely that before she had been but a foolish romantic, building an altar to a love which existed not... With Digby she would be safe, cherished; could she in the circumstances, ask for more than that measure of happiness? Suppose she had ignored Brinda's threats, gone on with Guy to ultimate destruction... His bold theories about her regard, or lack of it, were but a sop to his own conscience. Was it love she still felt for him – this mixture of pain, longing, disgust, tainted by Brinda?

Digby said:

'Darling, come back; you're miles away.'

Instantly she countered:

'I was thinking of last year–'

Brinda said insinuatingly:

'A very great deal can happen in a year.' She added confidently, 'We must all gather here next year and compare notes.'

Gloria Morris felt a certain antipathy towards Brinda and said slowly:

'The most important things in our lives can never be discussed or compared ... the secrets of the soul.'

Brinda's laugh was metallic.

'Gloria darling, you're so intense – like Vicki, although I think that she is beginning to learn that it doesn't pay – aren't you, Vicki?'

Digby saw Vicki's expression change and a certain dark shadow creep into her eyes. He said swiftly:

'This is where I whisk Vicki away from you all and if you shouldn't see us again tonight … good night everyone!'

They escaped and Digby said:

'Did I do right, darling, to get you out of there?'

'Yes.'

'That sister of yours can be a little irritating.'

Vicki glanced up at him.

'And also very fascinating, I should imagine – to your sex.'

The suspicion that had flashed through Digby's mind earlier on, returned to gather impetus. He said honestly:

'True; but I doubt if we should cherish any illusions about her, darling.'

'Why?' It was a sharp, inquiring sound.

Digby said quietly:

'Brinda is hard, Vicki; men dislike that intensely.'

She looked bewildered:

'Then why is it that–' She broke off. 'Never mind.'

He said, watching her reactions closely:

'Physical and mental instincts are not always compatible and the physical is all too often the Achilles heel of man.'

Vicki didn't speak; but she was trembling. Would she ever have convinced herself that Brinda was not *still* Guy's Achilles heel?

Digby said:

'What is it, darling? You look so grave.'

'Nothing.' She said, forcing a note of gaiety: 'Let's go home and tell Nadia about – us, Digby. I'd hate her to hear from anyone but us.'

He smiled:

'That isn't likely!'

'News travels incredibly fast in this district,' she said lightly.

'Vicki?' He drew her gaze to his.

'Yes.' She held her breath as one fearful of the question about to be asked.

'I couldn't stand the tension of a long engagement. Marry me almost at once.'

She hesitated only a second.

'Any time,' she agreed.

'Next month,' he said, earnestly.

'September!' She murmured hastily: 'Yes.' Had she not been going to marry Guy in November.

'Darling.' His gaze caressed her and she found herself reaching out mentally towards him as one seeking balm for a gaping wound. 'You must,' he insisted, 'give up your job with Adamson. I–'

She shook her head.

'No, Digby; I must keep on if only to help

him out.' She added ruefully: 'I seem destined to leave the only jobs I've ever had, almost at a minute's notice.'

'*I* shall be your job from now on,' he said softly. 'Thank heaven I can, at least, give you all the things you deserve. Where do we live, my sweet?'

She wanted to say: 'As far away from Brinda as possible' but instead, exclaimed:

'Sussex – somewhere; not so far away that Nadia would be cut off.'

'We must buy and house and furnish it … won't my family be thrilled? They'll say that you'll make a man of me! Oh, yes,' he admitted honestly, 'They have never been very flattering, you know. I suppose I *have* idled my life away. But industry appalls me. Farming would appeal more.'

Long afterwards Vicki remembered, poignantly, their conversation.

'Then why don't we buy a farm?' she suggested, whipping herself into a mode of eagerness. 'I'd like that and I'd like to see you prove your worth … *incentive*, you said … let me be that, Digby.'

He stared at her.

'By jove, why not. A farm. I could put a manager in and learn as I go along. It's an idea, darling. I'll talk to father about it.'

She said:

'And we must become self-supporting. I've learned so much about money, about living–' She caught at her breath at the mention of that word 'living'; hadn't she been accused of not knowing anything whatsoever about that...?

'You are not going to lack anything,' he said sharply. 'I am a director of the old firm, you know. And I have money left to me by my grandfather. It's only father's advice I want. He's shrewd. He'd smell out the *wrong* farm!'

Vicki told herself that anything would be better than idleness and that with productive interest, as the focal point of their lives, she and Digby would be building something for the future, instead merely of living to extract every ounce of amusement from each day.

Thus comforted, she whispered, as Digby took her in his arms for the first time:

'I want your happiness, Digby.'

'And I yours, my darling.' His kiss was eager and unintentionally demanding and she tried to respond, clinging to him in a fervour of emotion which was compounded of gratitude and deep affection. This was the beginning of a new chapter in her life and she must give to it all the devotion, loyalty and love of which she was capable, shutting the door on the past and erasing Guy completely from her mind. And in that moment, the mere desire to achieve this success appeared to be all that was necessary and she relaxed in the comfortable assurance that, in Digby, she had a man whom she could both respect and trust and with whom, even though she might not reach the heights, she would equally never be plunged to the depths. That must suffice.

CHAPTER 12

Digby and Vicki were married a month later. The wedding taking place, at her special request, quietly at a register office in the district. No reception of any kind followed and Nadia made no attempt to influence her in this direction. Only Brinda said:

'You could at least have allowed *me* to provide a reception at a local hotel. This whole things looks–'

Vicki said quietly:

'My sense of humour would not allow of your defraying the cost of my wedding reception, Brinda. And the idea of being exhibit A after the ceremony, makes no appeal to me whatsoever.'

Brinda mocked her.

'And would that have been your attitude had it been Guy instead of Digby?'

Vicki maintained a pose of extreme calm,

schooling herself to meet Brinda's eyes levelly:

'I do not waste my time thinking in terms of the past, and I propose, in future, to please myself. That is reason enough, since Digby is in complete agreement.'

Brinda was finding Vicki's composure slightly infuriating. It might well have seemed that by smashing her engagement to Guy, she had, in truth, brought her to a state of contentment and happiness – the very last thing she, Brinda, desired. Now she found that she even resented the fact of her marrying so wealthy a man as Digby who obviously adored her. Her twisted brain could not endure a picture other than of Vicki's complete ruin and humiliation, almost as though she craved it as a drug for her diseased brain.

Nadia accepted the position without comment of any kind. But she was not deceived by Vicki's bright smile and rather too high-pitched laughter. She knew, full well, that Digby might well be the man she loved, but certainly not the man with whom she was *in* love. And as she kissed her just before Digby and she left for their honeymoon which was to be spent in the West Country, beginning at Carylon Bay, Cornwall, she murmured:

'All my thoughts go with you, darling. Be happy,' she added in a breath.

Vicki felt perilously near to tears. The day

had for her been an ordeal far beyond her power to envisage at the time of her engagement to Digby. The irrevocability of the step she had taken weighed upon her with sudden, almost terrifying force. She managed to say shakenly, and Nadia felt her slender body shaking violently:

'You'll come to stay with us, won't you, Nadia – just as soon as we get settled into our own home?'

'Try to keep me away!'

Digby said proudly:

'I not only get the most adorable wife, but a mother-in-law who could never be equalled.'

Brinda said spitefully.

'Nadia is only Vicki's stepmother – you seem to overlook that small, but vital, detail.'

Digby rose to that.

'I forget it because no one, except you, ever does remember the fact, my dear sister,' he said mockingly.

Brinda bit her lip in mortification. One day, she vowed, she would be revenged upon Digby for that remark.

Digby led Vicki from the cottage, saw her into his gleaming Rolls coupé, waved a last farewell to Nadia – who stood beside Vicki's door, feeling that part of her was being torn in two – and then glided swiftly away.

'Now, *Mrs Graves.*' He relaxed, and looked at her adoringly. 'How do you feel?'

'Rather like a jelly that hasn't quite set,' she admitted.

'Me too! How I've blessed you today for cutting out all the trimmings. The only important thing is that you are my wife, darling, and I cannot quite believe *that* just yet. I'm afraid I'll wake up and find that you've vanished, or something.'

Vicki clung to the lighter implication of the remark, as she said:

'I'm far too solid to vanish!'

He looked at her.

'For all that, I want to see you a little fatter; just wait until we get our farm going and I can feed you up on cream and–' He paused. 'I'm looking forward to that farm, darling; it's like suddenly belonging in the world after having drifted through it ... and with you beside me ... I'll be the idler no more.'

Vicki heard all that he said, but every word seemed to flow over her head; she sat there in a strange vacuum, detached from her surroundings, while staring almost unbelievingly at the slender, platinum wedding ring that now lay beneath the exquisite square cut solitaire that gleamed on her left hand. Digby's wife... *Digby*... Not Guy's... She wrenched her thoughts away. The last person about whom she must think was Guy... She said:

'It will be a great interest, Digby, and we

couldn't have found a more heavenly spot –
a Sussex farm lying at the foot of the downs
between Pulborough and Storrington!' She
forced herself to add: 'Never did I think I
should be a farmer's wife!'

He laughed at what seemed the absurdity.
'We'll make it another Old Meadows,' he
said helpfully. 'I mean, of course,' he
hastened, 'in so far as the atmosphere within
is concerned. That happiness and serenity,
Vicki.'

Old Meadows… And Guy beside her. The
haunting memory of words once uttered
came back to torture her: *'I refuse to believe
that any woman has ever loved any man just as
I love you.'* And: *'I could not live without trust;
it would degrade me. To be jealous without cause
is surely an unforgivable vice; to be jealous with
cause must, equally, be a living hell.'* She shut
her ears against the strident sound that beat
within her brain and then, again,
remembered words she had quoted as he
looked up at the façade of Old Meadows on
the very last occasion when she and Guy
were there together: Keats's words: *'If I am
destined to be happy with you here – how short
is the longest life. I wish to believe in immortality
– I wish to live with you – forever.'* It seemed
that her body were on fire, even as she sat
beside Digby; that her cheeks were aflame
for him to see and yet she shivered, shivered
as from the impact of some deadly mistake;

230

some fantastic error. For an instant she closed her eyes as if to shut out all vision while she gained equilibrium. Yet ... could she be the same person who once spoke those sentiments ... could they have been true, or was the heart so false that she must shrink from the measure of its falsehood?

Fiercely, resolutely, she fought the mocking voices; throughout all these weeks she had lived without recourse to this feeble analysis; she had, since her engagement, deliberately told herself that Guy was dead ... dead; that her every thought and allegiance was to Digby. And with Brinda ever there to remind her of the past, her task had seemed the simpler... Now ... she panicked; she must not, could not, begin to look back; to see things that were not there; she must allow sweet reason to cancel out impetuosity and fear.

The car, moving like a silken thread across velvet, purred on ... through the Wiltshire downs ... Exeter, Tavistock, Okehampton, Liskeard, and, climbing out of Lostwithiel to St Blazey, came the first glimpse of St Austell Bay lying like a crescent moon in a sapphire sea.

'Almost there, darling,' Digby said triumphantly.

'Carylon Bay Hotel,' she murmured. She was going to stay there with Digby. Her heart thudded, her body quivered, her mind darted like a minnow in a pond. There was no continuity in her thoughts, nothing but ghostly shadows and hollow, mocking echoes from the past. She pulled herself up sharply. In a minute, she and Digby would reach their destination. Was she going to fail him so ignominiously and in so short a while?

They turned off beyond the Britannia, left on the Fowey road, then branched right and so came upon the hotel standing gleaming like a little white palace in the sun against the almost Indian sky and deep blue of the Cornish sea... Hydrangeas lined the drive, and below, far below on the beach, myriad-coloured umbrellas still remained testimony of a summer that had blazed into autumn, merging with the magic and stillness of a September glory.

Into the spacious entrance hall, standing while Digby signed the register ... *Mr and Mrs Digby Graves.* And feeling suddenly that both staff and the few guests idling by, were aware that they were newly married. And so to their suite ... overlooking the shimmering bay that rolled into infinity, star-spangled as a dancer's dress, where the sun caught the faint ripples of the waves...

And Digby saying hoarsely as his arms went around her:

'Oh, Vicki; it's been so long, my darling.'

With all her strength, then, she struggled to return his caress; to wipe out all thought beyond the emotion of the moment; to remember she was his wife and that he loved her ... he loved *her*... Oh, God, she prayed, let me love him, too...

But her heart beat no faster, her lips felt dry and cold, her mouth incapable of parting for his kiss. He drew back sharply:

'You're tired, darling; I'm an impatient beggar ... look–' He put his arm protectingly around her shoulders – 'isn't that a sight for the gods ... that ship in the distance – far on the horizon; that yacht lying in the bay ... and those dun sails against the blue–'

'A Mediterranean blue,' she said, grateful almost to the point of tears, for his understanding.

'We'll travel later on,' he said quietly, 'when we've mastered the intricacies of farm and married life.'

And her thoughts were saying:

Guy loved Cornwall ... he knew this hotel ... he knew me... No; he didn't understand anything; his ideas were wrong; everything he said was wrong. He and Brinda ... strange how far away Brinda suddenly seemed – almost like a phantom that had inhabited her mind and then – vanished.

'Yes,' she whispered, 'travel. I want to go to Rio, Digby. Gloria says it's wonderful... I must unpack; yes, I'd rather unpack myself than have it done for me. Most independent these days.' She glanced around her at the beautifully appointed room with its adjoining, spacious bathroom. 'And even flowers massed to welcome us–'

'I ordered them, my darling,' came the quiet reply.

'Oh, Digby!' She looked at him, feeling distracted and nervous. 'You are so terribly good to me.'

'That's not difficult,' he said hoarsely.

Methodically she unpacked, leaving out a slipper satin *négligé* and magnificently embroidered georgette nightdress, praying that Digby might not notice, or be aware of, her feelings. Then:

'Shall I bath first … I shall have that much longer for my face,' she said fighting to sound gay, natural.

'You'd better; you women take such a time over your make-up and hairdos.'

'That sounds experienced!' She stopped as though her heart had ceased to beat.

He looked at her.

'I have no past that could ever hurt us today,' he said quietly, 'without claiming to be any degree whiter than the next man.'

'I didn't mean it that way – only jokingly,' she hastened somewhat nervously.

She bathed, leaving the door open, striving to establish an intimacy which was, in itself, an agony to her. After a few minutes, Digby said:

234

'Am I allowed in to shave, my sweet?'

'Of course.' She lay like alabaster under the perfumed water, her firm, round breasts gleaming, rose tipped; her long slender body and small waist the very poetry of physical beauty. Her gaze met his and she willed that gaze to be steady and encouraging, without a false modesty which she had ever been taught to despise as cheap and vulgar.

'You are,' he said gently, 'so perfectly lovely, Vicki.'

It seemed a little easier then; she was caught up in the impulse of an emotion welling from the generosity that was characteristic of her nature, but, for all that, she knew there was nothing of herself in the scene; nothing that was passion or desire or ecstasy either of mind or body; she, Vicki, was the stranger looking on, seeing, yet blind … hearing, yet deaf; aware only of the necessity for creating the right impression, striving valiantly to live up to the vows so newly made.

Dinner offered her a welcome respite, despite the fact that she was not in the least hungry though she concealed the truth from Digby. It struck her, as she looked at him, that he seemed strangely boyish; the gay, debonair type – not the distinguished, magnetic male. She would not allow her thoughts to concentrate further upon those lines… Guy had so definitely been the latter.

Interested glances were cast in their direction from nearby tables for they made a glamorous pair. Vicki, breath-takingly beautiful in white chiffon, pearl-embroidered, Digby immaculate in evening dress. Vicki's only jewellery was a magnificent necklace, fragile in design and executed in diamonds, which adorned her throat and which had been Digby's wedding gift; with it were matching ear-rings which completed a picture perfect in its understatement.

Vicki tried to keep the conversation gay and inconsequential, never to allow those dangerous pauses, or to reveal the agitated state of her mind. The night was perfect, the setting everything to be desired, with the magnificent view of the bay hung as a glorious tapestry no matter in what direction the eye might roam.

'September,' Digby said, 'is a good month.'

'I think my favourite,' she said honestly. 'Autumn ... perhaps I like the faint tinge of sadness that steals into the word – sharpening its beauty.'

'You're a fanciful darling – aren't you? I think I'm almost afraid of you, Vicki,' he said quietly.

'Nonsense! You used to pull my hair when I wore long pigtails,' she insisted, not wishing to talk personalities.

'That was different. Now I am conscious of my mental clumsiness,' he said painfully. 'Oh, I know myself only too well. I'm no intellectual, Vicki.'

She made a wry face.

'Which certainly gives us one tremendous thing in common.'

'Ah,' he went on swiftly, 'but I'd like to be.' He held her gaze. 'You have a great appreciation of it – of the arts, music, poetry, too.'

'That proves nothing,' she persisted.

'I've wasted the years, Vicki – oh, I have! I've been weak and vacillating. Loving you has been the only worthwhile thing in my twenty-eight years.' He looked at her with great earnestness. 'But now it's going to be very different.'

'Just so long as you are not different. I don't want any "new" Digby – except in the sense of an ambition to understand farming!'

'You'd make excuses for anyone.'

She caught at her breath. Had she made them for Guy... Swiftly, she beat down the thought and sipped her champagne. Yesterday was dead – dead...

After dinner they sat looking out over the channel, watching the sun dipping the magic of fire into the sea in sharp crimson rays that gradually diffused upon the still waters the rose-tinted glow that caught at every ripple, every wave, edging it with gold that finally merged into the heathery-pink of a sunset that left the earth quivering from its impact, hushed as from a splendour indescribable. And now the sky was a vast dome of light in which a single star gleamed like a frozen tear ... a tear shed for sheer love of the beauty that surrounded it.

Vicki felt the muscles of her throat contract as she gazed, awe-struck at the scene... The sun slipped over the horizon – a flame that was no more. And night stealthily obliterated the gold and crimson, amber and mauve, with the serenity of its cool, deep blue, negativing all but its own majesty, as the moon rose and, rising, turned the bay into molten silver that lapped the shore in soft, sibilant caress.

Later, Vicki stood at the windows of their room and gazed out to sea... September, and the harvest moon shaming the garish ghost of day.

She felt the sudden warmth of Digby's body close behind her; the sudden clasp of his arms as, silently, he lifted her and gently laid her on the bed. Her heart was thudding, not with passion, but with sharp and sudden fear for which she despised herself. Where, now, was the ecstasy, the yearning to turn this moment into purest bliss; to quicken her pulses and heat the blood in her veins...

'Vicki ... *darling.*'

She tried to speak, but no words came and, in panic lest he might read in her eyes that which she would not have him see, she reached up and ... now only the moonlight illuminated that silent room.

With every thought, every instinct, she tried to respond to his caress, while yet knowing that her body might suddenly have been carved from wood, her heart drained of its blood, her mind and spirit of all ecstasy. Finally, a tenderness, almost maternal, welled within her ... this man beside her was her husband; he loved her ... his *happiness*... Brave words that turned to ashes in her mouth. Was *this* physical intimacy – this barren waste of experience which left her untouched by emotion, while yet burning with the desire for a passion she knew, instinctively, that Digby could never awaken?

In that moment Victoria Wayne, elfin spirit of romantic illusion, tiptoed away, leaving a woman suddenly alive to the fierce reality of love and all it embraced.

CHAPTER 13

The honeymoon last three weeks, during which time they toured most of Cornwall and, on their return, a good deal of Somerset. To Vicki they were weeks of violent adjustment, when she dared hardly think because the present clarity of her brain, her ability to see past, present and future, without illusion or romantic tinge, meant, of necessity, a painful studying of problems she had considered no longer menacing.

It was on their last night – breaking their journey at Exeter and staying at a hotel in the Cathedral close – that Digby said:

'Have I made you happy, Vicki?'

It was only then that the dark secret crept mockingly from its hiding place and all her strength, her fidelity was defied that it might proclaim the truth... *Happy!* She knew that every moment had been an ordeal and that, with all her heart, soul and body, she was in love with Guy not as before but ... in love with him so deeply that every word he had ever uttered seemed carved into her heart. *'When you lie in your husband's arms and long for mine, for my lips, you will remember what I am saying now, my dearest, and prove for yourself that physical intimacy, without intimacy of the soul and spirit, is as empty as my life will be without you and as yours without mine.'*

How bitterly she had learned the lesson of those words; how far, not in time, or distance, but in human experience, had she come, to learn their tragic truth. Was it only three weeks, or three centuries? Guy had been so right when he had said that *she was in love with love and called it – Guy.* Then, she had seen in Brinda menace against which she was powerless; now she knew that a great love would have risen in revolt, defying any power on earth to part her from him. Experience had taught her that. Before, she had been too close to the immediate problem to see it in true perspective, while the slow poison of Brinda's mocking, challenging presence had seeped slowly within her, killing faith, tainting love and awakening a jealousy that burned to destroy the adolescent flame of an untutored, inexperienced regard. Yet out of that immature emotion had grown the love, fierce, indestructible, that now surged into her aching heart. Understanding, now, the significance of the physical act, she realized that these weeks with Digby had taken nothing from her passionate fidelity to Guy and that *Life,* in its worldly sense, must inevitably be bound up with meeting as a stranger someone in whose arms you might once have lain ... knowing that the past was neither honoured nor recalled, merely erased. Thus had it been with Guy, so far as Brinda was concerned. Calmly now she could contemplate that episode in Sweden. A physical attraction ... satiation ... forgetfulness. Strange how there welled within her this sudden burning awareness of the truth; how intimacy, in all its phases, had taught her that only the mind and spirit could magnetize it to produce any enduring, or divine, spark. But she was Digby's wife and there could be no going back because she had learned a bitter lesson and been too far removed from life to appreciate the insensate folly, even tragedy, of such a marriage.

She became aware of Digby's appealing gaze upon her and remembered his question as though it had come back to her over years of contemplation, so that startled, aware once more of her surroundings, she hastened:

'Have you made me happy, Digby?' She caught at her breath. 'As happy, my dear, as it is possible for me to be.' Her smile embraced him as she spoke, so that the inner meaning of her words, their attempt at honesty, was lost completely on him.

'Then life is good, Vicki,' he said humbly.

'I never knew until now just how good.'

That night, as she lay beside him in the darkness, his hand clasping hers as he slept, a terrible calm was upon her as she visualized the road ahead; a road which, while paved with duty, gratitude and affection, could, nevertheless, be lit only by the love locked forever in her heart for Guy... Guy whom she had wronged so shamefully and, in her ignorance, her inexperience, discarded. She recoiled from the hurt she had inflicted, suffering with him now the torments and agony of their parting. The thoughts of Brinda came like a shadow, ghostly, impermanent; no tremor passed over her... Brinda had become merely a pathetic figure; a woman wantonly destroying happiness in others without ever finding it for herself.

Swiftly, then it seemed as if the hand of tragedy brushed her cheek; silently the tears began to roll unchecked down her face as the enormity of the situation, and of the havoc wrought, was borne upon her. Weakly, she found herself murmuring Guy's name and sending out a prayer for his forgiveness.

Then at last, exhausted, she fell asleep.

CHAPTER 14

To Guy those weeks had been an ordeal such as he had never before experienced. The announcement of Vicki's marriage in *The Times* had smashed his last, frail hope that, finally, she might relent. Yet how well he understood her attitude and it was this very understanding which had mocked his every plan, his every belief in ultimate success. He worked longer hours and withdrew unto himself, clinging to the illusion that time would dim the memory, but as summer came again to Old Meadows in which he was now installed, so the anguish increased. There were moments when, as memory stabbed, he would say roughly to himself: 'I'll get rid of the place – clear out, sell up and leave England' and then, as if the very atmosphere were impregnated with yesterday, he was drawn back and held as one mesmerized. The structural alterations had followed the precise plan designed by Vicki herself ... the furniture – mellow and steeped in the tradition of the past – had been set out even as he knew *she* would have set it out... The grounds spread their magic as of old to the far-flung hills... On just such a June day as this had he first met her... Her voice came back to him through the silence of his study: *'You've been very lucky today'.*

He lit a cigarette, the hand holding the match unsteady; his vision blurred, his heart thudding. And it was at that moment he saw Brinda standing, pertly, even arrogantly, upon the threshold of the room, having walked in unannounced, through the french windows.

'Hallo, Guy,' she said brightly. 'You're such a stranger that I thought I really ought to do something about it. My dear man, you've been here for ages now – without so much as coming to see me.'

'Is there any reason why I should see you? I should have thought it to be the very last thing you expected.'

She smiled, and glanced around her.

'You know, this looks almost as it did in the old days ... was that intentional?'

'Since I didn't know it in those days, I can hardly say.' He felt irritated by her presence.

'Then your imagination has served you well ... you *could* ask me to sit down.'

'I'm sorry.' He indicated a chair into which she sank gracefully. He remained standing.

'Heard from Vicki?' she asked softly.

'No.' He loathed the sound of Vicki's name on her lips and yet longed for news which

245

she might well supply.

'You know they have a farm in Sussex, Moat Farm. Digby's thrilled to bits with it. Vicki, too; they're very happy,' she added smoothly. 'No children expected as far as I know, but they want a family.' She put a hand up and smoothed her hair. 'I go down there occasionally, but I can't say that it appeals to me very much... You can't drag *Vicki* away from it, though. Very much the adoring housewife.' A pause. 'You know this is a lovely old house, Guy. I suppose I never really saw it when I lived here. That's the way of things.'

'With some people,' he said uncompromisingly... *'They're very happy ... no children expected as far as I know ... can't drag Vicki away from it.'* Bitter, stabbing words that went to his heart tearing it asunder.

Brinda had known a blind, insensate fury on account of Guy's treatment of her. Once Vicki was out of the picture, she had insisted to herself, that it would be easy to entice Guy back, but at every turn, he had been elusive, refusing her invitations, offering her no more than politeness when casually they met.

'Are you going to the races this week?' she asked, her gaze raised to his, her eyes appealing. 'I was told that you were on holiday.'

'I am on holiday,' he agreed; 'but I am not

246

going to the races.'

'Not even if I asked you very nicely to take me?' Brinda was seeking to set the stage for Vicki's visit to Nadia – her first to the district since her marriage. And if on the very day of her arrival *she* could be going out with Guy...

'No, Brinda.' He studied her intently.

'Oh – Guy darling,' she said softly. 'Why can't we be – different? We're both alone and there is so much–'

Guy was in no mood to mince matters.

'There is nothing that we could ever have in common, Brinda. Just as there is nothing quite so dead as a dead past. As a woman of the world, you should realize that and not force me to be so ungallant.'

Brinda clenched her teeth; a flame of anger, thwarted desire, flashed into her blue eyes.

'And I suppose you are still in love with Vicki?' she said contemptuously.

For a second he stared down at her. Then:

'Even though that is none of your business I have no objection whatsoever to telling you that I am ... that I always shall be in love with her and that no other woman will ever share my life here.'

His words, ringing with conviction, produced a shattering effect upon Brinda who, for the first time in her life, saw that which she most wanted disappear out of reach… This was a moment when she could no longer delude herself; when, having carefully played a waiting game, she saw her plans come to naught and realized that, with the past, she, too, was dead to this man now standing before her, for whom she felt the only real regard she had ever experienced for any human being; a man she desired above all others, her unbalanced nature craving the bliss of his caress and, denied it, plunged into a mood of reckless defiance and desperation. She persisted, rising slowly to her feet:

'Aren't you just a little too confident, my dear man? Your emotions were not always so stable.' As she spoke she moved closer so that her perfume was wafted to him in what was to him a sickening wave. Even though she knew herself defeated, she could not, dared not, wholly submit to the horror of that realization.

'Love is the one thing on earth about which there is absolute confidence,' he said firmly, and even as he spoke stepped away from her.

Again her eyes blazed their disappointment, chagrin and fury.

'Too bad,' she said mockingly, 'Vicki did not share your idyllic view.'

His gaze rested upon her, his expression coolly contemptuous; a contempt that stung far more than his anger might have done.

'One day,' he said promptingly, 'life will catch up with you, Brinda. When that day comes – God help you.'

She retorted, her eyes blazing with an almost murderous gleam:

'The devil always looks after his own, Guy, and if ever I should go down then, believe me, I shall make sure that my enemies join me!' She added: 'Yes, a melodramatic little speech, but not idle words, I assure you.' She moved towards the windows through which she had come: 'And don't be too sure of living here alone...' Her voice was heavy, warning. Despite himself Guy jerked his head up. 'Ah! I see you are interested! Well! The days of my inactivity are over, my dear man. I'm bored, to be frank ... too bad, you couldn't see things my way. But you will,' she added overbearingly, 'you will.'

Guy saw her go and muttered to himself: 'The woman's an egomaniac and sex starved – a deadly combination.' With that he dismissed her completely from his mind.

Vicki arrived at White Cottage the following day, going to Nadia's welcoming arms like a homing pigeon and crying:

'Oh, darling, it's so wonderful to be back.'

Nadia hugged her.

'More wonderful to have you... Emma will bring your case in; just come into the sitting-room and let me look at you. How are you – honestly?'

'Very well.' Vicki averted her gaze.

'Everything—'

'Perfectly all right. Digby's really interested in the farm. It was the best idea ever.'

Nadia was not deceived by the brightness of the smile, or the inflection of the voice, but she said:

'I'm so glad, darling… I knew, of course, how terribly fond Digby was of you but—'

'I know – the streak of irresponsibility born of idleness—' She stopped. 'All I want is his happiness, Nadia.' It was an urgent sound.

'And are you not sure of that?'

Vicki spoke in a low, tense whisper.

'No. Oh, in so many ways – yes. We're good companions; we both love the farm and Digby's so good to me, so thoughtful—'

'Are you not that to him, too, my darling?'

'Yes, but—'

'Marriage doesn't end with those things.' Nadia spoke gravely.

'No,' Vicki echoed, 'marriage does not end with those things.' She leaned forward. 'Nadia, do you understand. I've worried, bottled all this up—'

'My darling, I know; it isn't easy to live with one man and love another.'

'Nadia!' It was a gasp.

'Do you seriously imagine I didn't know? At the time of the wedding I believe that your feelings for Guy were so uncertain that

I prayed Digby might come to inspire in you what obviously Guy had failed to do ... but time has passed and I've seen you in your own home. There's a passive kindliness about a wife who feels affection and gratitude towards her husband–'

Vicki's voice broke:

'A passive kindliness! Oh, Nadia! The bitter truth of that.' She added fiercely: 'I want to give more ... but it isn't there to give. I didn't deceive Digby about my feelings for him and the subject has never been mentioned between us, but every time he leaves my arms I know I've failed him, no matter how desperately hard I try not to... Our nerves...' She sighed. 'I didn't mean this to be a tale of woe and above all, I mustn't build it up until it is one. Digby isn't the introspective kind, which helps, and he's somehow gained what he believes to be his self-respect.'

'It would break him if you left him, Vicki.' The words came slowly and with gravity.

'Left him!' Vicki's eyes widened. 'I could never leave him while he wanted me,' she said quietly. 'I know that even if I cannot give him all, he would rather by far have *less* and keep me with him. But that does not prevent my own feeling of failing him.'

'And your own happiness–'

Vicki's smile was wistful.

'I threw that away, Nadia; one can never

expect to get back what one has – discarded. I deserve no sympathy on that score,' she added fiercely. 'And if I still cannot explain the past–'

'My dear ... explanations between us – no!' Nadia looked at her steadily. 'I've watched you become a woman, Vicki; before–'

'I was an adolescent bathing in moonlight,' Vicki said remorsefully.

'Perhaps your father and I might be blamed for that,' Nadia said ruefully. 'Our life at Old Meadows was so far removed from harsh reality.'

Vicki didn't speak for a second, then:

'Is *he* living there, Nadia?'

'Yes.'

'Do you ever see him?'

'I have once – just before he moved in. Very little was said.'

Vicki sighed. Then:

'And Brinda? How is she?'

'Well ... and was supposed to be having diner with us tomorrow night; but when she called earlier today she seemed indefinite about her plans and, I thought, decidedly strung up.'

Vicki nodded. Brinda had become a matter of indifference.

The following evening Vicki said:

'I'm going for a little walk, Nadia... It's weak, I know but I want just to go past Old

252

Meadows ... and for a few minutes, at least, allow my thoughts freedom ... at home I'm always terrified lest they might be noisy.'

Nadia said gently:

'I shall go to bed, darling – perhaps before you come in.' A pause. 'Didn't you think Brinda's behaviour strange tonight – just coming in for a second?'

Vicki met Nadia's worried gaze.

'Isn't it always impossible to fathom Brinda's actions?'

'I suppose so; you were very tolerant of her attitude.'

Vicki smiled.

'I'm sorry for her, Nadia. Whatever it is that she is allowing to rust into her soul will, in the end, destroy her if she is not careful.' She hastened: 'But don't you worry! Brinda knows how to look after herself!'

Vicki went out into the silence of the June evening. Around her the familiar pine woods threw into relief the laciness of silver birch and beech that intermingled in a tapestry of variegated greens. The sky was still blue and against it, in the distance, the gentle rise and fall of hills was a dark frieze, creating a scene of richness and splendour. She walked slowly, idly; the luxury of solitude seeping into her restless, troubled soul. She thought of Digby with a rush of tenderness such as she might have felt towards a child ... he would be missing her, yet had insisted that she had these few days on her own with Nadia – their first parting, he reminded her as she left, since their wedding day.

But there was only one name that throbbed in her *heart* – Guy. With every step the need of him increased and the memories crowded back... Here at the pillar box in Coronation Road she had taken the bus to the station when she worked for him... From that moment she walked, as by instinct and unseeingly, to Old Meadows ... coming upon its wide, white gate leading to the rhododendron-lined drive that was flanked, also, with giant firs and beeches ... through the trees she could trace the outline of the house, see a light glowing from a lower window...

'*Vicki!*'

The sound came on the breeze like a passionate sigh and she heard it as if in her imagination until again, and this time more insistently, the awareness of a presence made her turn. Then:

'*Guy!*'

For a second they stood uncertainly, eyes meeting eyes in a glance that held them spellbound; a glance which told its own story.

'What,' he asked hoarsely, 'are you doing here?'

'Staying with Nadia for a day or so and–'

She paused in confusion, her heart thudding, her body shaking. 'I wanted to – to have a look at Old Meadows and–'

'Will you come in and see it, now that it is finished?' he asked.

A power stronger than reason, or her will to resist it, impelled her forward.

'Very well,' she whispered.

They walked in silence to the house where once inside Vicki gazed about her saying:

'You–'

'Kept it just as you wished it to be. I believe,' he said slowly, 'I have more or less accurately placed the furniture so that the former tradition is preserved.'

Vicki found herself saying, half bitterly:

'I wonder you had any wish to preserve that.'

He studied her, his pulses quickening, his love for her sweeping the thought of all else before it so that, as they walked into the deep silence of his study and he faced her, the words were torn from him, involuntarily:

'I was right, my darling – wasn't I?'

For a second her gaze was lost in his then her voice, low and shaken, came on the breath of a sigh.

'So right and I so wrong … and there is so *much* that must be said between us.'

'*Vicki.*' It was an urgent call rather than the mere utterance of her name, and passion

255

leapt between them mocking their resistance, reminding them of the frail thread between them and surrender. 'Oh, my dear, I understand,' he murmured. 'Anything seems bearable now that I have you here like this and can find in your eyes the message that is so plainly there for me to see.'

'You once said that I should have to know love fiercely, destructively, in all its moods ... well, now I know it that way, Guy; know it in my love for you, my longing for you, my need of you and as I have known it for the last long months. These are the things that must be said if I am ever to know any peace... I was so ignorant, so wrong, so ready to judge and–' she paused, 'so pitifully jealous because my love for you, then, was not *great* enough to cast out fear.'

For a second they stood; two people held by a magnetism that nothing could destroy. Then, swiftly, he took her in his arms, his lips seeking hers with a hunger matched by her own and now the lips he kissed were those of a woman; a woman awakened, desirous, aware of the fierce tumult of emotion that surged, drawing them into its forgetfulness, its intoxication. Her mouth, soft and warm, pleaded for a caress beyond that of mere momentary rapture, giving him all the strength of a love transcending anything she had dreamed before, or of which she had imagined herself capable.

Wildly, desperately, she pressed against him, her arms tightening around his neck, feeling his lips upon her eyes, her throat and again her lips. And only when, exhausted, suffocated, resting limply against him, her head on his shoulder, her cheek against his chin, did she manage to whisper:

'Now you know how true were those last words you spoke to me, my darling.' She added passionately: 'Oh Guy, if these hours ahead were all that were left to us of life how simple it would be.'

He released her as he said heavily, striving to maintain an iron control:

'But they are not all, my dearest.'

'No.' It was a whisper.

He looked at her.

'Don't speak; don't bring to this moment anything of yesterday ... let it be ours ... poised in time; our time,' he murmured.

'Our time.' She didn't take her gaze from his and the one seemed to dissolve into the other, drawing them so spiritually close as to reach beyond the soul.

He held her, then, tenderly, gently, drawing her down beside him on the deep cushioned settee, keeping his arms about her shoulders and cradling her head in the crook of his arm.

'I love you,' he whispered as if repeating words that might well be for the last time, 'as I have always loved you and shall love you until I die, Vicki. There never has been anyone in my heart but you – you know that now, don't you?'

'Yes – beyond all doubting.' She looked up at him. 'How you must have despised me for my lack of faith, of love.'

He shook his head.

'My dear darling, you could not have known those things which experience has now taught you ... and with Brinda–' He broke off.

'She was so *close*, Guy; so suffocatingly close, so determined to ruin our love; she dragged everything down to such a sordid level that it seemed the only thing I *could* do was to say good-bye.'

'Which was what she wanted' – grimly.

'Yes ... now it all seems so far away, but at the time also there was the fact that she had been married and that Raymond had been deceived...'

Guy became instantly alert.

'So that was what she made you believe! Fool,' he cried, 'fool that I was to overlook the possibility that she would not tell you she posed to me as a single woman during those weeks–'

'Oh, *Guy!*'

'And when I learned the truth, I walked out,' he said sharply.

Vicki's eyes met his adoringly.

'If love is *great* enough, nothing can

menace it. If I'd felt for you as I do now, all that Brinda could have told me, all that she could threaten, sordid though it all was ... of what account so long as *we* understood.' She drew in her breath sharply. 'Physical ties, to me then, seemed to have some strange power; I could not dismiss them, because I could not imagine them ever being unimportant–'

'And – now?' His voice held an arrested note of pleading.

'Now I know that were I to live with any other man for the rest of my life, the physical bond would take nothing from you, either physically or mentally,' she said in a low voice.

'Darling...' His lips touched her forehead. Then: 'If only I'd realized just *what* Brinda was saying ... but she was so plausible in her assurance that she would be perfectly ready to go out of our lives if she felt it would alter your decision.'

Vicki gasped:

'And she swore that if I married you she would haunt you, never allow me respite from jealousy and fear... You saw her that night after I – I left Wimpole Street – didn't you?'

'Yes; I took her out to dinner. She made capital–'

'Naturally and to me, then–'

'Poor sweet.' It was a caressing sound.

Then he added: 'She called here two days ago, wanting me to take her out ... until this moment she has merely been dead to me; now, my blood boils when I think of all the misery for which she has been responsible.'

'The blame is not all hers... I was found wanting,' Vicki whispered remorsefully. 'Just as she knew I should be.'

'And – now?' His gaze held hers and the tragedy of what might have been and of an inevitable future, suddenly loomed like a hideous phantom, mocking, inescapable.

'Oh, Guy,' she cried fearfully, 'what have I *done?*'

Gently, firmly, he released her and got slowly to his feet, lighting a cigarette to steady his nerves. Looking down at her he said very quietly:

'You have married a man who loves you, my darling.'

In that moment, Vicki gained strength as though some invisible power had lit a lamp within her.

'Yes,' she murmured, 'I have married a man who loves me and were I ever to fail him ... then the love I bear you would for ever be discredited, my darling. Is that what you mean?'

'What I know to be right ... not what my heart pleads for,' he said roughly.

They had not noticed the darkening room, nor the reflection of the sunset filling it with a ghostly radiance. She knew that this was the end; that somehow she must leave that house which held for her everything she held dear in life...

'To have been here like this, talked to you,' she said suddenly. 'I've longed for it; there's been no peace, Guy, and the thought that you might hate me–'

He made a gesture to silence her.

'Your heart told you that was not so–'

'Sometimes the heart is mocked by the brain.' Her voice broke.

'It never will be again, my dearest.'

'Never.' She got up and stood beside him, taking in every detail of the features she knew so well, feeling the surge of passion rising as their glances met and desire was a mirror reflecting their every mood.

'*Vicki.*' He held her suffocatingly, almost hurting her with the fierce pressure of his arms and yet was she triumphant in that same hurt, which merged with the ecstasy, the rapture of his kiss that held within it the agony of parting and of surrender denied. 'I adore you,' he breathed. 'Remember that – always.'

'And I you ... keep me here in your heart, Guy; don't think of me *there*–'

'I know,' he said, 'that torture... I, too, have learned what jealousy can mean; but now–'

'Give me courage,' she whispered

261

brokenly, 'and know that only your arms... Guy–' Wildly she clung to him, her mouth bruised by his kisses, her cheeks aflame, her body trembling so fiercely that, as he released her, she swayed and he caught her to lend support. 'I must go,' she said fearfully ... 'don't come with me – please... I couldn't bear it if you did–'

'My darling–' It was a hoarse cry that seemed to break in his throat.

But ... he heard her footsteps across the hall; the front door open and close and felt the stillness as of death upon the house.

Outside, Vicki beat down the sobs that choked her. She must control herself, but somehow it was as though she could not bear the protracted agony of walking down that long, familiar drive now on fire from the light of the afterglow. She began to run, her hair flying in the breeze, her cheeks cooling with its impact... Blindly almost she reached the gate and heard a car starting up. Then, fighting for strength to walk normally upon legs that refused to support her, she moved slowly to the road.

And Brinda's voice said hatefully:

'Can I give you a lift, Mrs Graves? I hope you've enjoyed your tête-à-tête with Guy ... rather indiscreet – what?'

Vicki's first instinctive fear vanished. Now that she was strong in the knowledge of Guy's love, Brinda could never touch her again. She said politely:

'I prefer to walk, thank you all the same. And whom I choose to visit is no concern of yours. Good night, Brinda.'

Brinda sat stiffly in her driving seat, while fury swept upon her like an avalanche. Vicki and Guy ... why had she been to see him? Did it mean that she could no longer resist the temptation of a love she had once dismissed? Was that it? Would Vicki *dare*...? A malevolent gleam came into her steel-blue eyes; a sudden plan took diabolical shape. Well! So be it! Now, at last, she knew precisely where she was going. Guy had talked of living at Old Meadows alone and no doubt Vicki was now cherishing fond illusions regarding his fidelity. Well, she'd soon alter that ... and if she failed she should not be the only one to suffer – even as she had warned Guy. It was all very simple...

CHAPTER 15

Digby switched off the radio with an impatient gesture, lit a cigarette, picked up the evening paper and made an unsuccessful attempt to read it. How still the house was without Vicki, almost as though she had taken with her the music of familiar sounds, just as for him she had taken also the light which her presence spread, as from some invisible lamp. He glanced out of the wide open, lattice windows. Thunder storm brewing ... damned hot still; been hot all day. He stubbed out his cigarette with nervous movements and flung aside the paper. Nothing in the rag, anyway, he thought fiercely. Seemed that Vicki had been gone for two months instead of two days and there was still another two to go before her return. He paused, resisting the thought that leapt to his mind destructively: would she see Guy while she was at Ascot and, if so... Why should she see the fellow...? Trouble with him was that his nerves were getting out of hand and it was time he did something about it. He'd everything any man could ask of life and the farm had proved a great interest... Would Vicki ever love him as he loved her? The question stabbed like a stiletto plunged into his heart. One thing, she had never pretended and he could find no fault in her as a wife. He stopped abruptly; she could not give to him a passion such as he felt for her. He drew in his breath sharply: why think of all that now? They were happy together, ideally happy, and few married people could say that.

The sound of voices in the hall attracted

his attention and he went swiftly to the door of the lounge and flung it open.

'Good heavens, Brinda!' He stared at her aghast. 'Where on earth did you spring from?'

Brinda handed her light coat to the maid who had admitted her and then turned her attention to Digby:

'I've been visiting friends nearby and thought I might look in on you – even cadge a bed for the night,' she added coolly. 'There's a terrific storm coming up and I'm not particularly fond of driving in thunder.' She gave him an innocent stare. 'Should I be putting the household out very much if I were to stay?'

Digby said instanatly:

'Norah, tell Mrs Holt that my sister-in-law will be remaining.' He added: 'Nice to see you. I was not particularly looking forward to my own company.' He walked beside her into the large, chimney-cornered lounge that was bright with chintz and plain, dusty pink carpet. 'Drink?'

'By all means. I think – a pink gin. What does the hour matter?' She sat down opposite the chair she knew to be his, crossing her slender legs, aware that in the half-light prematurely produced by the elements outside, her natural charm was enhanced.

Digby mixed her drink, handed it to her, sat down immediately opposite her and before raising his glass, apologized:

'Sorry about my get-up. Had I known you were coming I'd have been more presentable.'

She smiled.

'On the contrary, I like the informality and that deep tan against your cream shirt – most attractive.'

He smiled. Then:

'You've seen Vicki.'

'Oh yes, my dear man; I've seen Vicki.'

Digby frowned.

'Why the sarcastic tone?'

'No reason ... you know this is a charming room – low and long and the oak beams give it importance. You were lucky to find this place.'

'Don't I know it.'

Brinda paused.

'You're – happy?'

Instantly he was alert and distrustful.

'Why do you ask? Isn't that obvious?'

'I'm not interested in the obvious, Digby. I've not seen much of you since your marriage, I must admit, but your nerves–' She paused, adding insinuatingly: 'I was married to a passionless, under-sexed man and I know the strain of it.'

Digby said indignantly:

'I have no wish and no intention, Brinda, of discussing my–'

She caught and held his gaze.

266

'Don't be absurd, Digby,' she said softly. 'I'm not quite a fool.' She sighed. 'Queer business life – the way some people attract one and the way others just – don't.'

Digby felt suddenly tense.

'Inevitable,' he said shortly.

'True... You don't mind my coming here like this?'

He looked at her.

'Why should I?'

She shrugged her shoulders and asked him for a cigarette which he gave her. He lit it, aware of her gaze intently upon him as he did so. Then:

'No reason ... we've a great deal in common really – temperamentally. Or should I say – physically? In the emotional sense.'

'Oh I don't know, Brinda–'

She rested her head back against the cushions of the chair.

'It's restful here ... ah, now for the storm; I like storms when I'm safely tucked up inside ... just listen to the rain.'

Digby switched on a desk lamp.

'It's damned hot,' he said jerkily.

'I love the heat, too.' A pause. 'In fact I really have all the right animal instincts.'

'But not a great deal of heart,' he said slowly.

'That rather depends on what you mean by "heart". Most certainly I'm not the passive, loving type ... but what man wants

267

a passive woman, after all?' She sighed. 'How does it feel to be here on your own – or how did it, until I dropped in?'

'Pretty awful,' he admitted. 'I miss Vicki like hell; the place's a morgue without her. Did she knew you were coming to see me?'

'No.' Brinda looked at her glass. 'And I don't think she would have been very interested, anyway.'

'Why not?' He felt that the room was suddenly stifling; that some invisible hand had a grip at his throat.

Brinda rose from her chair, building up the drama by her lazy, seductive manner as she walked to the windows, saying:

'Digby … just look out there over the downs! Vast mountains of black clouds – split with lightning… What did you say?'

'I asked you,' he repeated, 'just why Vicki wouldn't have been interested in knowing you were coming here.'

She sat down again.

'You are either very stupid or very blind, because you *want* to be blind, my dear Digby. You should know that all Vicki's thoughts are diverted to a very different channel.'

At that Digby thundered:

'What the devil do you mean?'

She raised her eyebrows.

'Now, now! Don't rave at me… I'll say no more.'

268

'Oh yes, you will,' he said harshly.

'Very well, although you must know the real reason why Vicki has gone to Ascot.'

'She's gone to see Nadia,' came the instant retort.

'A convenient alibi only.' Brinda leaned forward: 'Listen, Digby, I'm not condemning, or criticizing Vicki for doing something that I'd do myself, but your ostrich-like attitude baffles me completely.' She was measuring the effect of her every word as she moved slowly, cunningly, towards the climax she had already determined upon.

Digby's body seemed to sag in his chair; his expression changed.

'You mean – Evans?'

'Who else?'

He half shouted:

'I won't listen to your hateful insinuations. You've never behaved like a sister to Vicki. There's always been *something* that I can't put my finger on–'

'Just the difference between the worldly and the unworldly – although Vicki has managed to use the latter pretty successfully as a cloak.'

'That's a lie and you know it.'

She smiled. Digby was no match for her; unlike Guy, he was apprehensive, fundamentally weak, while striving to be strong. She knew that and had made all allowances for the fact.

'All I know is,' she said and now her voice was deadly in its calm, 'that I saw Vicki going into Old Meadows at a very late hour last night … and although I waited a very considerable time I did not see her come out.'

Digby went very white.

'And still I do not believe you.'

'Very well; I'll wait here, if you like, until Vicki gets back just to prove my point.' She made a little gesture of appeal. 'Come now, Digby, do you suppose I'd be such a *fool* as to make a statement of that kind unless I could substantiate it?'

He struggled to maintain both loyalty and dignity.

'And are you suggesting that Nadia would be a party–'

She cut in, half-pityingly:

'My dear man, Nadia goes to bed very early. Vicki would need only to say that she was going for a walk … the hour of her return would never be noticed.'

Digby protested:

'The mere fact of her visiting Old Meadows proves nothing.'

Brinda blew a tiny cloud of smoke into the air.

'Oh – true; but why should she be visiting Guy alone and at a very late hour and secretly, too.'

'I'll not listen to your vile insinuations; it's an insult and you should be damned well ashamed of yourself. Your own *sister—*'

Brinda didn't flinch; she smiled.

'There isn't a great deal of love lost between Vicki and me, my dear man. I owe her no allegiance and I'm not condemning her, or building up any case against her; but I do think that for your own good you should stop this idealistic nonsense and begin to live a more human life yourself. Far better for you both – in the end.'

She saw him start.

'If you mean what I think you do then the idea is monstrous.' He added stiffly: 'And I'll thank you not to discuss my wife further.'

She laughed softly.

'*Digby!* You don't know how foolish that sounds. For heaven's sake, don't strangle yourself with your old school tie! You don't have to defend Vicki to me. I don't *profess* to have any morals!' She held his gaze with a fascinating directness: 'You despise me – don't you?'

'Yes.' It was a curt sound.

'But not half so much as you … desire me.'

A dull flush crept to his cheeks. He swung from his chair and stood, his back to her, staring out upon a scene of magnificence as the now almost black sky was rent with lightning, and the downs themselves became mere smudges in the distance.

She followed him and stood by his side.

'This pompous self-righteousness won't get us anywhere, my dear man.'

He turned away from her, poured out another drink and gulped it.

'You're–'

'I know; I'm not at all a nice person. But' – her moist red lips gleamed invitingly in the subdued light of the room – 'for all that, I know you; all you're starved of now; there's not one breath of emotion, of passion, in this whole magnificent edifice that you call your marriage. No abandon, Digby, to–'

'You'd better go,' he said through clenched teeth.

'Afraid?' It was a slow, provocative sound.

'Damn you.'

'The truth is never palatable.' She sighed. 'Why you need to put up all this pretence–'

'I love Vicki; for the first time in my life I'm interested in a job of work,' he thundered. 'You wouldn't understand that *or* the self-respect that comes with it.'

She said softly:

'You don't have to build up a picture unless it is to fortify yourself against me.'

Digby's brain was reeling. The thought of Vicki and Guy came insidiously to mock him. Brinda wouldn't, even as she had said, be such a fool as to make a statement she

272

could not substantiate about Vicki's visit to Old Meadows. Was *that* why Vicki had gone to Ascot?... Nadia could, far more easily, have come to them. Vicki, of all people – whom he would have trusted with his life. His heart raced, his temples throbbed. He felt like a man incapable of making any considered judgment, a man crazed by his own fears, his jealousies.

'Against you–' He spoke jeeringly. 'Why I–'

She moved and as he flung himself again in his chair, perched on the arm of it.

Instantly, he got to his feet and went to the cocktail cabinet, pouring out his third drink.

'I'll have another,' she said deliberately and held out her glass.

He half snatched it from her; he was like a man wrestling with imaginary demons.

Thunder, violent, destructive, volleyed and reverberated around the countryside; rain fell torrentially. Brinda's eyes gleamed as she held his gaze while he returned her glass to her.

'This is what I'd like life to be – emotionally,' she said. 'Thunder and storm and fire... Beyond that mood, you can have your wishy-washy feelings towards humanity.' She added: 'I wonder if Vicki could ever be roused to this passion–' She added tauntingly: 'That is something you will never know about her, Digby. But Guy–'

He swung round them and gripped her shoulders.

'You she-devil!'

At his touch she quivered and he felt the fierce, magnetic force of her desire almost mesmerizingly upon him.

'Go on,' she whispered. 'I like that... Digby, don't be such a *fool*.' Her body pressed with sudden violence against him, her head went back, her lips parted, and her eyes looked into his passionately, invitingly and in triumph.

CHAPTER 16

Vicki returned to the farm two days later, driving up to the sixteenth-century house, and nerving herself for the ordeal of Digby's welcome and endeavouring to meet it with the same measure of enthusiasm. But even as he came towards her she was aware, with a sense of shock, that he looked drawn, even ill, so that instantly solicitous, she cried:

'Digby, my dear – you're not well! Why didn't you let me know?'

Digby reached out and caught her in his arms.

'It's been hell without you, Vicki,' he said with a kind of desperate betrayal.

274

'A few days–' She stared up at him. Then, trying to infuse a lighter note: 'If this is how you're going to behave when I'm away–'

He looked down at her with a burning intensity:

'Don't go again,' he said. And even as he held her there came the loathsome, insidious memory of Brinda… *Brinda.*

'I most certainly won't,' she promised. She studied him thoughtfully, her heart contracting; he looked so different and yet… Was that because she, herself, was so different? Because her whole horizon had changed? 'Come in and let's have coffee together. I came early because I thought you might prefer the morning to the afternoon.'

'Bless you.' Was it possible that those clear, honest eyes could gaze upon him so innocently and yet be guilty of his own perfidy… Sickening jealousy rose again. Suppose– He said jerkily: 'I want to hear all about Ascot, where you've been–' An imperceptible pause. 'Whom you've seen–'

To Vicki the scene held all the unreality of a stage set. She and Digby might have been characters in a play, conforming to all the rules set out with which to present a picture of a happy marriage. She walked, her arm through Digby's, with him into the coolness of the lounge which, even after an absence of a matter of days, seemed different in her eyes, even unfamiliar.

'Ah,' she said as she sat down. 'Home.'

(Brinda had sat in that chair, raced Digby's thoughts.)

He handed her a coffee cup which stood on a nearby tray and held out the sugar to which she helped herself. She smiled her thanks.

'Service,' he said lamely.

'Perfect... Nadia sent her love. I've lazed, Digby; seen nobody.'

Instantly, suspicion leapt to life.

'Surely that is hardly possible unless you've been an absolute hermit.'

Vicki's heart began to race. She wanted Digby to know that she had seen Guy, because she loathed the idea of any kind of evasion or secrecy; yet how to phrase her words as not to make an issue of it. She corrected:

'Well, I have been a hermit ... but I did see Guy.' She stirred her coffee as she spoke and then met Digby's gaze with clear eyes. 'I wandered past Old Meadows one evening just before bedtime and we met at the gate.'

'Did you – go in?' Digby fought to keep his voice steady.

'Yes; he wanted me to see all that had been done. It looks very much like the old home again,' she said casually. 'The only person, by the way, I haven't *really* seen is Brinda, although I did run into her as I came out of Old Meadows. She made some unpleasant remark and I preferred to walk home! Why do you look at me like that?'

'So you didn't know that she'd been down here?' he said nerving himself to speak as naturally as was possible.

'No, of course not.' She shook her head. 'Whatever made her come here when she knew I was away?'

Digby busied himself with emptying a new packet of cigarettes into the silver box. Then, lighting one and looking at her through a faint haze of smoke, he managed to say:

'The storm; she'd been to see friends in the district. Did you have it at Ascot? It was terrific down this way.' He added swiftly: 'I could only ask her to stay the night.'

(Stay the night ... stay the night, mocked his thoughts.)

Vicki, alert now, alive to every trick of cunning of which Brinda was capable, said:

'Now I think I know why you were so anxious to find out whether, or not, I'd seen her.'

Instantly he started; his own guilt rising like an enemy to attack him.

'What do you mean?'

'You wondered if I'd told you about seeing Guy merely because I had considered the possibility of Brinda already having done so.'

Digby's hands shook.

'Yes,' he said in abject apology.

'And, of course, she told you about seeing me at Old Meadows, no doubt adding a few untruths to give point to her words.'

'Yes, but, Vicki–'

Vicki said gently:

'It doesn't matter, my dear. Only don't' – her voice was suddenly very calm and very strong with infinite power and purpose behind it – 'ever listen to Brinda again, Digby. If ever I betrayed you, believe me, *I* should be the one to tell you ... until that day comes. I deserve your trust, my dear.'

Digby felt that something within him was curling into a hideous shape of bitter self-reproach; his very soul recoiled from the picture upon which he was forced to gaze. Should he tell her ... could he dare take the chance of losing her...? Later, whispered a voice of self-preservation, when it is all so much further away ... it is always so much easier to forgive something that happened a long time ago, but never to forgive that which happened yesterday...

He got to his feet and moved to the arm of her chair, looking down at her with an almost frightening urgency and earnestness:

'I don't deserve you, Vicki, but if I lost you–' His voice broke. 'Darling – forgive me.'

She suffered his caress and her arms went round him almost as in protection. There

278

was something almost pathetic in his frenzied appeal, his humility. She looked at him.

'And now all that is put to rights,' she said softly. 'I think some demon must inhabit Brinda.' She shivered. 'One almost comes to fear where next she may strike.'

Digby didn't speak … he could not.

It was some weeks later that Brinda called at Old Meadows and Guy, crossing the hall even as the door was opened to her, was forced through sheer courtesy to invite her in. Then, when alone in the lounge, he demanded:

'And just what brings you here. I'm not in a particularly patient mood and–'

She sat down confidently.

'That's just too bad, darling; you will need your patience before I've said all I have to say.' As she spoke, she peeled off her grey suede gloves and smoothed them as she might have smoothed the edge of a dagger, to make quite sure it was sharp enough for her purpose.

Guy's heart missed a beat.

'Vicki–' The cry came involuntarily.

Jealousy blazed into Brinda's eyes.

'This hasn't anything to do with Vicki – at the moment.'

He relaxed.

'Suppose you come to the point.'

279

'Very well … it so happens that I am going to have a child, Guy–' She paused before adding while she stared him out: '*Your* child.'

'Now,' he said as one taken beyond the bounds of credulity, 'I know you are mad.'

She looked at him and her expression was in deadly earnest.

'Can you prove that it *isn't* your child?' she asked and there was a low note of cunning in her voice.

Instantly, he became alert.

'So,' he said and a great wave of disgust encompassed him.

'I hope you are not going to waste words with a series of ejaculations,' she said impatiently. 'The point is, just what are you going to do about it?'

Guy sat down and studied her. Never in his life had he met a more perfect specimen of calculated, concentrated evil. What was more, she had no qualms, no desire, whatsoever, to conceal her rottenness. The egomaniac plunging to her own doom and, in the process, dragging whomsoever she chose with her. He said with a quiet, indomitable strength:

'Firstly, you may, or may not, be going to have a child; secondly, if you are, we both know that it has nothing whatever to do with me; thirdly, I am exceedingly busy and have no more time to spare you.' He added:

280

'Whatever damnable scheme you have in your mind—'

'I merely intend that you shall marry me,' she said coolly.

He laughed outright.

'The stage has lost a great actress in you, Brinda.'

'I have no wish to contradict you,' she said smoothly. 'But I repeat what I just said, for all that.'

Despite her air of assurance, Brinda was experiencing an agony of suspense in that moment. She had staked all on a last throw, determined, since she had failed in one way to entice Guy back, that she should succeed in another – and far more desperate – measure.

He looked at her steadily, remorselessly:

'If you were the last woman left in the world I would not marry you.' His voice was cutting in its contempt.

Brinda winced. Guy aloof, attractive, whipped to life every emotion of which she was capable, mentally as well as physically and his complete disinterest in her awakened a frustration that nothing could assuage.

'Guy—' It was a breathless, pleading sound.

'Suppose we bring this fantastic scene to an end.'

She looked at him as she said urgently:

'And have you thought of all this from my mother's and – and Vicki's point of view? To say nothing of your own, once I make the facts public.'

'If,' he said contemptuously, 'you are gambling on blackmailing me through your mother for whom I have a great affection and Vicki whom I love ... do not waste your time. They would be the last two people in the world to wish me to be the burnt offering in so unworthy a cause.'

'And what of your reputation – your unblemished reputation? Once I choose to make this whole thing public, the past dragged out of its convenient hiding place to give strength to my charges?'

'I will,' he said forcefully, 'meet those charges when they are brought. But don't overlook your own position in this. For all your bravado, your boasting, you are a coward at heart. You'd loathe the publicity, particularly that,' he said scathingly, 'associated with so hackneyed and sordid a story. For a woman of your experience–' He paused significantly.

Colour flamed into her cheeks.

'I'll–'

He cut in:

'You shrank from the divorce court ... this would merely make you look *ridiculous*.'

Brinda, thwarted and now sick with fear, flung at him:

'Then I shall not be the only one to look ridiculous: Vicki's position will not exactly be—'

'What,' Guy thundered, 'has Vicki to do with it?'

She sighed.

'Only that it just so happens that Digby and I—'

'*Digby!*' It was a low, horrified sound. Then: 'I don't believe you.'

'No? What purpose would I have to lie over that?... And there is always the possibility that Vicki might be getting fond of him to make the situation more intriguing.' She added: 'It could, of course, be most unsavoury.'

Guy closed his eyes for a second as if to shut out the horrific picture taking shape. Then:

'Is there nothing to which you would not stoop!' he said lifelessly. 'But Digby ... it's—' Words failed him and he flung out his hands in a gesture of despair.

'I thought that might throw a different light upon the subject,' she said, gaining confidence.

And suddenly, Guy became alert, his attitude changing.

'It has,' he said and his tone filled her with sudden fear. 'You've gone your destructive way through life, hurting all those with whom you've come in contact but, just this once, you've been too clever and' – he paused – 'too stupid; you've overlooked one thing–'

'And that–' Despite her arrogance she hung on his words.

'That anything you might do at this stage, so far as Digby was concerned would, automatically, provide Vicki with grounds for divorce.'

At that Brinda laughed – a gloating, sardonic laugh.

'Do you seriously imagine that I should be such a fool, to let her know the truth *at this stage!* Oh no! I've only to tell her, now, that *you* are responsible... The very last person she would suspect is Digby and, somehow, I cannot see you sneaking around corners to impart this sordid little item of news. So you are quite wrong, my dear man; it isn't as simple as you imagined.' She added cunningly. 'Whichever way it goes, and *in my own time,* I can stir up a very, very great deal of mud ... that is, unless, of course, you choose to see reason and simplify every-thing.' She added curtly: 'Think it over.'

Guy walked to the door:

'I have nothing to think over,' he said.

'But–' She stared at him aghast.

'If you imagined that your lying to Vicki about me would add further weight to your blackmailing efforts,' he said icily, 'then you are very much mistaken. She would not, for one second, believe you.'

Brinda paled.

'We shall see about that.'

'Do, by all means,' he rang the bell as he spoke, then said to the maid: 'Show Mrs Wells out.'

Brinda hesitated and, knowing herself defeated, went.

Guy poured himself out a stiff whisky. Now what? Had he been right...? It seemed to him, then, that Brinda was like a snake, leaving a trail of misery wherever she went... His head reeled with the facts placed before him. Digby... Anger seethed and then subsided. What devil's method had Brinda used to encompass *his* ruin...? For the prejudice of mere jealousy in no way convinced him that, but for Brinda's diabolical scheming, Digby would ever have betrayed Vicki... But now that he had... Infinite possibilities crowded into Guy's mind; possibilities that one moment changed the very face of heaven and the next, plunged him back into darkest despair.

One thing only was certain. *His* resistance of Brinda. He knew, deep within his heart, that Vicki would the more easily suffer any torment than that which embraced his association in any degree whatsoever with the woman responsible for their present suffering... And the thought struck him that in the tenseness and strain of the moment, he had omitted all mention of the past. But of what avail mere words of vituperation.

He sank down into his chair... Outside, all was peace. Old Meadows lay within the hush of evening. September's glory was upon its mellow grounds; the radiance of the afterglow bathing it in the magic of soft, crimson light. The thought of Vicki was visual; his longing for her anguished. His heart seemed to stop as he thought of Brinda's accusation. Suppose she should so present the situation as to make Vicki believe her. The very idea was a little death, his own helplessness a prison from which there was no escape.

He bowed his head in his hands. And words came back mockingly from the past:

'The Moving Finger writes.'... He found the words haunting him in a desperate frustration: 'Nor all thy Tears wash out a Word of it.'

The relentless hands of time would move on ... and nothing he could do, or say, would change the pattern of tomorrow.

CHAPTER 17

Brinda prepared for her scene with Vicki as an actress might prepare for a mighty climax in a dramatic play. The fears that haunted her must not be allowed to obtrude, or weaken her. It was true that, at this stage, Guy had refused to marry her, but she had a very long way to go before that decision became absolute. And, whatever happened, so long as she could wound Vicki, be revenged upon her for Guy's defect in spurning her, Brinda, then nothing she had suffered, personally, would be in vain. The knowledge of Guy's implacable resolve seared her. And what she conceived to be her love for him increased with the measure of his contempt.

She dressed in black on the morning she decided to visit the farm. Sombre black that threw into relief the pallor of her cheeks and so cleverly was she made up that her face appeared haggard and strained, her eyes dull and lifeless. She knew Vicki; her heart was a sponge that absorbed the other person's suffering... Oh, this time little Brinda was going to be very *very* clever...

When Vicki saw her standing on the

threshold as a maid admitted her she gasped:

'*Brinda!*' Then instinctively: 'You're – ill.'

The maid retreated. Vicki took over.

Brinda said slowly:

'I'm all right, Vicki; but I had to see you.'

Vicki said quietly, fighting down the memory of the past, her sympathy aroused, all that was impulsive and generous in her nature surging in an upward rush as she told herself that, after all, Brinda was her relative.

'Come in; you look frozen.'

Coffee was ordered and brought and when they were settled over the fire, Brinda asked:

'Digby–'

'He won't be in just yet... Oh, Brinda what *is* it?'

Brinda's thoughts raced: how she hated Vicki for her flabby soft-heartedness. Was that what had won Guy; made him so revoltingly faithful to her...? She began subtly:

'I've behaved rottenly to you – oh, yes, I know it. I was jealous and bitter and all twisted inside ... but that's all over and I cannot undo any of the wrong, Vicki–'

Vicki stared at her aghast. *Brinda* apologizing! She said swiftly:

'Looking back is never profitable. Suppose we agree on that.'

Brinda nodded and sighed, sipped her

coffee, nervously folded and unfolded her wisp of lace handkerchief and then said:

'There's no one else I can turn to in all this.' She added as though the words were torn from her. 'Vicki, I'm going to have a child.'

Vicki caught at her breath, staggered, stunned into a terrified disbelief. Then:

'Brinda!' The name and her utterance of it, seemed all her brain would allow.

'You're – shocked?'

Vicki hastened.

'I'm not thinking of *that,* but of you. I mean–'

'I deserve it, I suppose; but somehow one panics and–'

'But the man... I mean–'

Brinda struck:

'He refuses to marry me... Oh, Vicki, what shall I *do?*'

Vicki cried:

'But he – he can't just–' She stopped.

Brinda lowered her gaze.

'He can be very brutal...'

Vicki's thoughts were in tumult. Then:

'Do I know him?'

'Yes ... although I hate having to tell you his name.'

'But – why?'

Brinda looked pathetic:

'I've hurt you enough and–' Then as Vicki's eyes widened in startled, perplexed inquiry, she added: 'You see it's Guy.'

The name came softly, insinuatingly; it fell with a deadly precision and, for a moment, robbed Vicki of strength, fortitude and courage.

'*Guy!*' It was a horrified gasp.

'I don't want,' Brinda hastened, 'to blacken him in your eyes – truly I don't.' She experienced a thrill of surging, unqualified triumph as she realized just how subtly she could move from that point of vantage further to shatter Vicki's trust and awaken her jealousy. 'Perhaps, despite all that has happened between us he still cares for you ... and I wondered if you–' She made a little, desperate sound: 'I know how ironical all this is ... but I thought if *you* could persuade him – use your influence–'

And Vicki said suddenly, her voice coming like a pistol shot:

'I don't believe you.'

Brinda started, but held herself in check.

'What do you mean – don't believe me? Oh, I know you've every reason to distrust me but, over a thing like this–'

Vicki's eyes were alight with a strange, unconquerable fire:

'This is the very last thing about which I should be likely to believe you.'

In that moment Vicki felt the power of Guy's love for her rising like some magnetic force, indestructible, irrevocable. Nothing could shake her faith in him; nothing destroy the spiritual fusion of those sacred moments at Old Meadows when understanding had taken the place of distrust, and devotion cast out fear. This was her ultimate and supreme test and a great calm was upon her as she faced Brinda's arrogant, defiant and challenging stare.

'You daren't believe me – that is it; because you are still so madly in love with Guy yourself that you cannot endure the thought of his making love to any other woman.'

Vicki answered impressively:

'This I know: that if and when Guy chooses any other woman that woman will never be you, Brinda.' She caught at her breath because the very contemplation of such a thing was wounding. 'You're not dealing with the Vicki of old, you know – although I was, I freely admit, fully prepared just now to shut the door on yesterday and help you if I could–'

Brinda, furious, afraid, cut in violently:

'But your charity doesn't extend beyond your own interests, and because it happens to be Guy, I'm condemned.'

Vicki did not raise her voice as she interrupted:

'If it *were* Guy then you know, in your *heart,* what my attitude would be. As it is, there is nothing you could say or do, Brinda, that would even awaken doubt within my mind. So suppose we do not argue the point further.'

Brinda stared at her, mouth agape.

Vicki went on:

'I was no match for you, before; you built up a sordid, revolting picture knowing what its effect would be upon me. And the past strengthened your threats for the future. I wasn't experienced enough to treat those threats with the contempt they deserved. Conveniently, too, you omitted to tell me that even during your association with Guy, you posed as a single woman, therefore neither treachery nor deceit was involved from his point of view. A vastly different matter.'

Brinda smirked.

'A likely story.'

'One I believe implicitly,' came the implacable reply.

'And now you are so wise, so smug, such a loathsome little prig that–'

'Ah,' said Vicki, 'the cloak falls from your shoulders and you drop back into character again.' She added tensely: 'If you knew how I *despise* you–'

Brinda, goaded to fury the greater because of her own folly, cried vehemently:

'I'll ruin Guy.' Her teeth were clenched. 'If you two think you can get away with your pathetic, clandestine little affair while I– Ah, you pale at the thought, don't you? It wouldn't be in keeping with your precious ideal of him were he to be dragged through the courts in a breach of promise action. My word is every bit as good as his and the child—' A hateful gleam came into her eyes. 'To say nothing of the past – which he could not deny – to lend strength to any accusation I might care to make. A pretty little story when embellished with newspaper trimmings.'

Vicki's heart seemed to drop.

'You wouldn't *dare* – the scandal and publicity from your own point of view—'

Brinda snapped her fingers in the air.

'I should have sweet revenge,' she said triumphantly.

Vicki stared at her as though she could hardly believe any woman could sink to such depths of degradation.

'"Hell hath no fury"' ... she murmured. And got to her feet. 'I see no purpose in prolonging this distasteful scene.'

Brinda gazed around her with a predatory air.

'You're all very cosy here – aren't you?' she said hatefully.

'Very.'

'And – happy, too.' She looked at Vicki searchingly, aware that there was a new strength about her, even a serenity in her expression that added to the beauty of her face. 'Mrs Digby Graves! All nicely tucked up in blue ribbons; no worries; an adoring husband' – sneeringly – 'to say nothing of a convenient lover. A little too perfect.'

Vicki said quietly:

'It must be a source of great annoyance that you can find no flaws here. As for your remarks about Guy – they do not need contradiction because they are beneath contempt.'

Brinda gave a mocking little laugh.

'No flaws! You poor, deluded fool!'

'I think,' Vicki said swiftly, 'you must be mad.'

Brinda gave her stare for stare.

'The kind of madness from which one recovers...' She moved to the door. 'I shall be seeing you,' she said threateningly.

'I hope not,' Vicki said with a compelling firmness. 'You and I have nothing what-soever to say to each other now, or at any future time.'

'That,' said Brinda, 'is for me to decide.'

And with that she went from the house.

Driving back and deciding to call upon Nadia, after having stopped to put some colour on her cheeks, Brinda wrestled with the immediate problems that confronted her. Her temper was frayed, her nerves on edge and when she reached White Cottage and saw Nadia's smile in greeting she said:

'I'm in a bad mood, Mummie. Am I too

late for lunch?'

'Of course not.' Nadia studied her in alarm. 'But what's the matter? You look–'

'How do I look?' – defiantly.

'Drawn–'

Brinda averted her eyes.

'Nothing,' she said lightly. But a hateful wave of faintness surged upon her frighteningly so that she clutched at a chair for support.

'You're *ill*–'

Brinda snapped:

'It's nothing ... too many late nights.' She hardly knew what she was saying and when lunch was served the very sight of the food nauseated her, so that she left it untouched, to Nadia's consternation.

And suddenly, as one coming out of the mists of unreality, Brinda was forced to face the facts... Already Nadia said she looked ill and she felt ill; the sickness revolted her; the waves of faintness increased... How long before everyone would be making the same comment and when *that* phase was over... The colour drained from her cheeks as sanity returned after what, then, seemed a period of madness. In her insensate jealousy of Vicki, her desire for Guy, she had accomplished what might well be her own doom. And suppose she did have her revenge even as she had threatened...? Wasn't Vicki right? Could she bear to appear in a court as the mother of... Her brain felt that some furnace had been lit within it. All this in the belief that she might blackmail Guy into marrying her .... deluded fool that she'd been. *Fool!* A hand went up to her cheeks as a shiver of horror passed over her ... the fierce tumult of jealousy, desire, revenge died down and she saw only the grim truth about her own immediate position. Didn't all people make that one, fatal mistake when trying to wreck the happiness of others...? Was this hers? She recoiled, rebellious against the idea. If Guy had... *If* Guy had... She'd been mad to take the risk, confident that in the event of repercussions, she could sail triumphantly to victory, not only through blackmailing Guy, but appealing to him, through his devotion to Vicki, to spare the family disgrace. It wasn't, she realized, even as she dwelt upon the facts, the behaviour of an experienced, sane woman ... but of one more in need of psychiatric treatment. The deep-rooted hatred of Vicki, inherent since childhood, had turned like a dagger in her own heart; her professed love for Guy ... and just how deep was that love should Vicki not menace it? Colour crept back into her cheeks, and the blood heated in her veins ... that love, that passion for Guy had been no more than the fire of her own frustration, her jealousy. She panicked. Something would have to be done ... she couldn't face the consequences of her blind, imbecile folly. In the cold, harsh light of fact the whole thing seemed like some fantastic play, conceived in a nightmare. And, then, suddenly, she knew the answer. Now her own self-preservation was uppermost; to acquire the protection of marriage, to escape from the horror of her present position – these more than outweighed any former objectives. And suddenly it became simple. Digby would have to get his freedom and marry her. It could be done discreetly and, expedited, the case would be over in order that their marriage could take place before the advent of the child ... the very thought of that child maddened her. She, Brinda, the woman of the world, lowering herself, demeaning herself for revenge and jealousy, frustration and desire ... what a commentary! She had approached the whole thing with a vulgar clumsiness worthy only of inexperience and feeble-mindedness. And seeing the picture in true perspective, she writhed at the impact of her own self-contempt. No remorse, no spark of penitence coloured her reflections; her crime, her unspeakable folly, in her own estimation, was the failure to achieve her objective through the stupidity of the methods chosen.

Now, harsh circumstance demanded

compromise and it was useless shrinking from the unpalatable truth. She must, in future, gamble only on a certainty, discarding her more ambitious hopes and unable longer to afford the luxury of revenge.

Vicki would, she thought bitterly, be thankful to divorce Digby and marry Guy. How ironical that, in the end, she, Brinda, would have helped her to achieve her heart's desire.

CHAPTER 18

It was late that same evening, just before dinner, that Vicki phoned Guy. From the moment of Brinda's leaving, she had argued with herself as to the rights or wrongs of such an action, deciding, finally, that since their life was so barren of comfort they might at least be spared the agony of suspense.

He answered the phone to her. Then:

'Vicki!'

'I had to let you know,' she said and her voice was like a caress: 'Brinda came here today; I didn't for one second believe any of the lies she told me.'

'Darling... I told her you wouldn't believe

her; but, for all that, one can torture oneself and that I've been doing ever since.'

Vicki cried:

'Nothing could ever make me doubt you; but I'm afraid; she's in an ugly mood and *her* word–'

He laughed softly and confidently.

'Don't worry. It isn't pleasant to have to say this, but Brinda is, like all her kind, a coward at heart. Once she is faced with the penalty of her own folly she'll go to pieces. I'm not afraid of any one of her empty threats – and neither must you be, my darling.'

'It is for you I'm worried.'

'Don't be... Oh, my beloved, to hear your voice–'

'And *yours*–'

'The days are years,' he said hoarsely.

'You know my heart,' she answered.

'Yes; and I am always near you.'

'And I, you.'

She replaced the receiver and sat looking down at it as though it had ceased to be inanimate. Her longing mounted in a fierce wave of passionate need that became a desperate hunger. She heard Digby's footsteps in the hall ... dashed a hand across her eyes because they were suspiciously bright, and went forward to greet him at the same time deciding that no good purpose could be served by mentioning Brinda's visit and that no deceit was entailed by the omission.

It was two days later when, sitting quietly together in the softly shaded lamp-light after the day's work was done, Vicki said suddenly:

'You've really come to love all this – this life, haven't you, Digby?'

He looked down at his strong, firm hands that bore traces of work.

'I marvel, my darling, at the miracle you've achieved. I could no more idle my time away as I used to do–'

She said urgently:

'And I've not really failed you–'

A knife twisted in his head. She fail him! For weeks after the episode with Brinda he had lived in the deepest abyss of misery and despair, alternating between confession and silence – the silence of self-preservation. He had nothing but contempt for Brinda and while, at the time overwhelmed by the enormity of what he had done, the passage of time had produced a merciful analgesia. The normality of everything around him and Brinda's absence fostered the illusion that his defect was something lost in the mists of time, to be both forgotten and ignored.

'How could you ever fail me?' he said and stopped, recalling Brinda's savage ridicule of Vicki's emotional response, aware that having endured the sharp agony of fear, as a result of his own infidelity, all other issues had been eradicated, lending to his existence with Vicki a seeming perfection it might well otherwise not wholly have achieved.

'In many ways,' she said earnestly.

He smiled, not wishing to discuss personalities too closely; conscious of that thin danger line between uneasy remembrances and blissful forgetfulness.

'Never could you fail anyone ... we're a most remarkable couple!' He laughed softly, reached for a cigarette and sat down on the edge of her chair, his arm around her shoulders. 'This is the time I love most,' he said. 'Wind whistling outside; a storm brewing and here in this quiet old room – just us and peace.'

And even as he spoke he turned at the sound of the latch of the door clicking into place and, every scrap of colour draining from his face, gasped:

'Brinda.'

'I said I would announce myself... I'm so terribly sorry to butt into that most charming little domestic scene and to destroy the peace but–'

Vicki, too, had risen to her feet.

'What do you want?' she asked coldly and authoritatively.

Digby looked from face to face, alarmed by Vicki's tone and Brinda quick to grasp the situation said:

'Didn't Vicki tell you that I called here two days ago? Somehow I rather thought she wouldn't... Do we have to stand here in a semi-circle as if about to start a prayer meeting? ... Digby don't look so uncomfortable.' She sat down as she spoke, as did Vicki. Digby remained standing. Then:

'What was it you came about?' he said fearfully.

'A little matter which I chose to state concerning myself and Guy,' she said slowly. 'Only Vicki refuses to believe one word, one breath of scandal associated with him.'

'Look here, I–'

Brinda sat back comfortably in her chair, and looked up at him: it pleased her to think that, if nothing more, she was causing him acute suspense and fear. So long as *someone* was being hurt...

'I wonder if your wife will extend the same magnanimous faith and infinite trust to you, Digby.'

Vicki became almost mesmerized; it was like being in the presence of evil and helpless to combat its ruthless force.

She said:

'There is nothing you could say, Brinda, that I should be disposed to believe about anyone unless I had irrefutable proof. Is this unpleasantness necessary? Haven't you done enough–'

'I thought you were supposed to be so very *just?* Everyone surely, is entitled to a hearing ... so you'd want irrefutable proof of anything further I might say? That's fair enough. I think, this time, I can furnish that too.'

Vicki lost a little of her strength as she asked in a scared undertone:

'What do you mean?'

'That now I am prepared to tell you the name of the man whose identity you questioned when last I was here.'

Vicki felt that a load had been lifted from her shoulders.

'So you do admit, now, the grave injustice–'

'Freely!' Brinda spoke lightly. 'My gamble just didn't come off.' She glanced up at Digby. 'Vicki's faith in Guy is, of course, quite disgusting ... but–'

'Leave Vicki and Guy out of this. Nothing you've said so far makes sense to me but–' He floundered and stopped, arrested by the expression of malicious cunning in her eyes.

'Don't be pompous, Digby,' she said briefly. 'You cannot afford to be.'

Vicki spoke sharply:

'And just why have you suddenly thought it necessary to correct your statement and confide in me?' Her voice was cold. 'I'm sorry, Brinda; I'm not concerned any more; your affairs are your own and–'

'My affairs are yours, my dear child.' She looked up at Digby. 'Isn't that so?'

Digby felt that the blood was slowly draining painfully from his heart. He sat down on the edge of an upright chair, staring transfixed at Brinda, not daring to speak lest his words betray the agony of fear and suspense that gripped him. With difficulty he managed to say:

'If I knew what you were talking about–'

'Oh, of course.' Brinda looked smug. 'But Vicki knows… And it so happens, my dear trusting little soul, that the man is your own husband.'

Vicki glanced distractedly about her, caught up in the hideous drama that seemed to come upon them with paralysing effect. Her voice was cracked, hollow as she answered:

'I don't believe you. I would never believe you – get out of my house.'

Brinda didn't move beyond turning her gaze towards Digby and saying slowly:

'I think if you study your husband's face you will appreciate that for once in my life I am not lying. And that he has been unfaithful to you – with me.'

Vicki closed her eyes for a second, hardly daring to look in Digby's direction and yet knowing by the instinctive shudder that passed over her body that the accusation was true.

And before she could speak, Digby burst out, his voice low, dead, his body seeming to sag lifelessly in his chair:

'What Brinda said is true … that night you were away. If loathing myself and her could have wiped out the horror–'

Vicki said brokenly:

'Oh – *Digby.*'

He looked at her.

'I could never hope to make you understand and all my words can only sound empty and hypocritical.'

'Did you know about the – child?' Vicki spoke as though the words burned her tongue.

'*Child!* What do you mean?' He turned almost savagely to Brinda. 'What devil's trick is this?' he demanded.

'A little trick of nature's,' she said coarsely. 'And suppose we cut out all this squeamishness and face the facts. At least I've established the truth.' She looked at Vicki: 'Much against my inclinations, although not unmindful of certain benefits in the situation, I'm going to be instrumental in your getting your freedom. You now have grounds for divorce and, in the circumstances, Digby, being a gentleman, can do no other than marry me afterwards.' She paused. 'Digby need have no qualms about *your* feelings, since he must know how madly you are in love with Guy, anyway.'

Vicki went very white. Digby said:

'Damn you, Brinda, if–'

'Save your breath, my dear man,' she said coolly. 'There's nothing you can do about it.' She glared at Vicki: 'Well, why don't you say something?'

'Because,' said Vicki, very calmly, 'I am not ready to say anything.'

Brinda started.

'But the situation is simple enough–'

'All situations are simple enough,' Vicki rapped out, 'according to you, because they revolve simply and solely around what you most want.'

Brinda smiled hatefully.

'Never did I think the day would come when I should enable *you* to have what you want... But, quite frankly, I couldn't care less about Guy now. It is always foolish to try to pick up old threads again. The lover of yesterday–'

Digby said in a hushed whisper:

'So you were at the bottom of all the trouble–'

Brinda smirked.

'Yes, I was.' A sigh. 'But by some miraculous process Vicki has had her faith in Guy completely restored lately – haven't you, darling? You should have seen her defending him! Too sweet. Ah well, I'll be going.' She got to her feet. 'Thank heaven, that's over.'

Vicki's gaze unnerved her slightly.

'Now I know the facts I'll come up to Ascot tomorrow,' she said in a business-like tone.

Brinda nodded.

'There isn't all that time to waste... Don't glare, Digby; we're two of a kind, you know, and once the nine-day wonder has subsided... We don't after all, have to stay in England.'

He stared at her, speechless; every muscle in his body seeming to ache in unison with his heart. In a matter of half an hour he had been stripped of honour, of manhood and of all hope. He could not meet Vicki's gaze and the thought of having to face her alone appalled him.

Vicki said:

'Your plans are not of the least importance at this stage, Brinda ... good night.'

'Very well. You certainly have learned restraint, my dear! It isn't every day that a woman manages so effortlessly to get free of a husband she doesn't want in order to—' Something in Vicki's expression froze the words on her lips, then with a: 'Oh, very *well*... I'll expect you tomorrow. I'm still at Swinley View... What time will you come?'

'I'm not sure—'

Brinda said arrogantly:

'I don't want to be kept in all day and—'

'You will,' said Vicki sternly, 'wait my time.'

307

Brinda stared at her, somewhat deflated.

'We shall have to break the news to Nadia. I'll be thankful to get the whole thing settled; it's become rather a bore.' She looked at Digby. 'You look scared to death,' she said scornfully. 'Just like a man – no moral courage when it comes to it.'

The silence during those moments when her car raced down the drive was shattering and so tense that every sound had the impact of thunder. Then Digby burst out, his voice suddenly seeming old, his face pain-wracked:

'Vicki, I won't insult you by excuses, but if you could bear to listen–'

Vicki felt that her head had become curiously light. Digby and Brinda … freedom. No more anguish, fighting, longing … only escape… She and Guy… She and Guy. But behind that ecstatic thought lay a shadow half-formed. She said:

'How long, Digby–' Her voice was subdued and without criticism.

'Long!' He uttered a little sound that seemed more like a groan. 'That one occasion. Vicki, *Vicki,* if only I could make you understand without expecting, or even asking your forgiveness–'

Her gaze rested for a moment in his.

'I'd like to understand,' she said and it seemed as though she were reaching out and finding a wisdom transcending all else as she added: 'I think I could help you–'

He shook his head.

'I had paradise and threw it away; you cannot discard a thing and get it back–'

She heard those words as from a great distance – the echo of her own to Nadia.

Digby went on, almost lifelessly as one who had ceased to hope; one who, in all fairness, could not plead his own cause:

'Brinda came here unexpectedly that night.'

Vicki murmured as he paused:

'She built up the picture of my having seen Guy–'

'Yes,' Digby said with a curious dignity, 'but that fact offers neither excuse, nor do I plead it in extenuation. All I know is that there was about her that night some force, evil, paralysing–' He flung out his hands. 'I couldn't explain, Vicki, and even if I could, my action stands to kill everything you may have felt for me.'

Vicki said honestly:

'I don't know what I feel, Digby. One never can know – just at first–'

'But you, even now, have no words of contempt or condemnation,' he said brokenly.

She looked at him almost pityingly.

'That is not my mood.'

He burst out almost bitterly:

'Because I do not mean enough to you–'

She stirred.

'No – not that, either. I've got to sort this thing out, Digby – for both our sakes; know my own strength and my own weakness.'

He lit a cigarette, his hand shaking violently:

'The door of your cage has been opened, my darling,' he said softly. 'Here lies, for you, freedom.'

'What,' she asked, 'is freedom?'

'For you divorce and … re-marriage. I know that yours is not the nature to change and that, deep in your heart, Guy Evans–' He added: 'Just as I know that, but for all this, and even despite Guy, I had found a greater happiness than I'd ever believed it possible to know…'

'Was it ever enough, Digby?' She leaned forward earnestly. 'Oh, let there be truth between us, now, if nothing else.'

'Yes; enough because I knew that it was the very limit you had to give,' he said. 'And because I could contemplate anything rather than – losing you, Vicki. Just at first I craved more … and, then, after that damnable night … nothing mattered except that you were still beside me; it seemed to increase my need and my happiness once the first tor- ments of conscience had died down. In my desire to atone – I suppose to reinstate myself in my own eyes, if you like – all things between us had a new meaning … and your

310

smile, just your *glance* held a significance that counted beyond measure. And as the months passed we were so happy... I felt that we belonged – always, and I defied life to take you from me.' He paused. 'Quite a speech.'

'And if you knew that you could never have more than we've had together ... my love, my friendship, my fidelity–'

'Don't–' He winced.

'I don't mean the word to be given point,' she hastened. 'And I ask this in no idle fashion.'

'I should consider that some kindly Fate had given me Paradise,' he said solemnly, 'which I in no way deserved. In the same way that, in this minute, I know that I have lost everything – everything,' he said desperately, 'that makes life worth living.'

'Oh – Digby.'

'It's true ... and yet, you deserve–' He breathed heavily. 'I'm not magnanimous enough to endure the thought of your being with anyone else...' He held his head in his hands, elbows on his knees. 'I haven't your strength, Vicki, but from you I was beginning to–' He stopped. 'Words, words,' he murmured harshly. Then, fearfully: 'What do you want me to do?'

'Nothing,' she whispered.

'You will divorce me, of course.' He got to his feet. 'In which case,' he added, 'I shall be forced to marry that woman … but never to live with her.' A great sigh escaped him. He raised his eyes, hunted, pleading.

'Why don't you speak, Vicki?'

'I was thinking,' she said sombrely.

'Would you like me to leave here – tonight?'

She said suddenly:

'No… I shall go to Ascot tomorrow, think things over and let you know my decision–'

At that his eyes blazed with the light of hope; his body relaxed, his voice rose as he cried:

'You mean that you might even consider *not* divorcing me?'

His pitiful gratitude smote her.

'Would that mean so much?'

'The difference between life and death.' He paused: 'But if your decision should go against me … I shall never love you less than I do now, my dearest. No matter what I have done, nothing has touched that love – nothing. You must believe me; no part of my heart or soul or spirit was alive to betray you – only some vile treachery–'

'I know,' Vicki said in a tense whisper. 'And I believe you.'

'There couldn't be another woman as generous as you,' he said humbly. Then: 'When will you let me … know?'

'If I am not back here tomorrow night by dinner time,' she said solemnly. 'That I think is the best and simplest way for us both... We don't want protracted scenes, Digby, and neither do we want any possibility of collusion.'

'No; I appreciate that,' he said almost stiffly. 'By dinner time – seven-thirty tomorrow. Thank you for reducing the suspense to a minimum ... and for being – just you... Should this be good-bye ... may the future atone for all this, my darling. And Guy deserve you as I never have.'

And with that, abruptly, he turned and strode from the room.

She did not see him again before leaving the farm. A note was placed on her plate at breakfast which read:

I could not endure watching you go in case you should not return. Forgive me if you can.
                                        DIGBY

Vicki shivered. It seemed that life itself was held precariously by a breaking thread.

CHAPTER 19

Vicki reached Guy's London flat just after one o'clock that day, having phoned him and agreed on the hour and place of their meeting.

She watched him as he came into the room, bringing with him that dignity and strength from which, instinctively, she drew her own. Even in that moment of dramatic tension she was aware of his dark jacket and pin-striped trousers, the immaculate white shirt and collar, and the atmosphere of calm reassurance that was a part of his personality. Their eyes met, his searching, inquiring, hers pleading, bewildered.

'Vicki...'

She rushed to his arms while her love for him became a hurt that clawed at her heart until it seemed to bleed with its own anguish.

He held her with intensity, his kiss passionate, yet tender. Then:

'What is it, my darling?' He eyed her anxiously, aware of the strain, the indecision of her attitude, the almost pitiful appeal in her dark, troubled eyes.

'So much, Guy, that I don't know where to

314

begin.' She gave him her hands and drew him down beside her on the settee. 'You have so little time to spare just now that–'

'I have an hour and a half,' he said quietly. 'I was able to change an appointment...' He got to his feet and lit a cigarette. 'I can think more coherently,' he said hoarsely, 'when I am not so close to you.'

Vicki's heart thudded madly; nothing, then, seemed real but her own need. She loved Guy – a love that increased with the passing of time; a love deeper, truer because of all the hardship, the difficulties of the past. She began slowly:

'Did Brinda tell you about – Digby?'

Guy started, shocked.

'Yes.' He added almost as though the possibility were too distasteful to contemplate. 'You mean that she had told ... *you?*'

'Yes.' She looked down at her hands and back again to meet his gaze. 'Having failed to blackmail you she panicked and came to me last night, demanding that I divorce Digby so that he could marry her.'

'My God!' Guy said in a deadly whisper. 'If ever there was an *evil* woman–'

Vicki cried desperately:

'Only her own self-preservation goaded her, otherwise the very last thing she would have done was to give me the evidence by which I could be free.'

Guy stopped pacing the room, his expression transformed to a sudden, incredulous joy.

'Darling,' he said hoarsely, and again, this time with a passionate yearning: *'Darling.'*

She said huskily:

'Free, Guy ... to marry you; to end all this agony of separation, this nightmare of living apart.'

He moved to her side.

'Your lips speak those words – not your heart,' he murmured apprehensively. 'Why?'

She drew a hand across her forehead as though she would remove that which corroded her brain and made coherent thought impossible.

He put a finger beneath her chin and turned her face upward, forcing her to meet his gaze.

'Are you still in love with me?' he asked solemnly.

'So much,' she whispered, and her sigh was sick with the longing that consumed her, 'that nothing else is real – nothing.'

'Then what is it?' he asked gently, sitting down beside her now and taking her hand in his.

Her voice came with a terrible stillness, as though each word were a little death.

'The knowledge that if I didn't love you, want you so desperately,' a sob caught at her throat, 'I should not dream of divorcing

Digby for one isolated act, in which he was goaded beyond endurance by a woman whom we all know for what she is; the knowledge that, but for this aching need of you and my yearning for happiness, I should otherwise live up to the vows I made when I married.' She cried: 'Oh Guy, help me – *help* me.'

He studied her with great earnestness.

'What would you have me say, my dearest?'

'What your heart feels to be – honest,' she answered in a breath.

Guy looked at her long and with a lingering reflectiveness. His expression shaded from tenderness, to passion, resentment to the sudden fire of rebellion. Then:

'You want me to appreciate that, because we love each other, we are, in effect, using Digby's infidelity to suit our own purpose; condemning him in order to justify the happiness we crave ... and throwing him into the arms of the enemy.'

Vicki heard those words almost as a death knell.

'Yes,' she said dully. 'Oh, Guy, it isn't easy to see the right way out of a thing like this. There is so much to confuse the issue. I could argue that Digby betrayed me shamefully and no one is more conscious of the fact than he ... it was, on the surface, unforgivable. But knowing Brinda... I know, too, that it brings us back to all we thrashed out before and there is nothing in my heart that would not, in normal circumstances, allow me to wipe out that incident, close the door on it, without losing one scrap of faith in *him*. I've lain awake at night telling myself that my only allegiance is to you because I adore you; insisting that I have every right to divorce Digby without so much as a qualm.'

'But you cannot make it ring true?' he said heavily.

'No.' Her eyes searched his face for some betrayal of what must be his ultimate judgment. 'I may be wrong – if only you could tell me I *were* – but I don't feel that I really have any more justification for leaving Digby now than I had when last I saw you... Because he was wrong, weak ... am I to use that as a weapon with which to smash our marriage, merely to suit my own ends? Withhold forgiveness when I would so freely give it otherwise? Oh Guy, if our positions were reversed and you know the man as I know Brinda...'

He picked up her hand and held it against his cheek.

'I should argue as you are doing now,' he said shakenly, 'although I'd give half my life to deny the fact. Were this some protracted affair ... had there been any questions of clandestine meetings– No; then I would go through with it resolutely. But as things are–'

318

A tear splashed down from her eyes, falling upon his hand and swiftly, with a hoarse anguished cry he drew her into his arms, holding her as he might have held a child and feeling the agony of loss spreading over them in tragic inevitability. She said chokingly:

'I couldn't go on without knowing you understood; knowing that you felt as I. Your love, your faith is my strength; without that–' She turned her head into his shoulder and clung to him then, convulsively, raised her lips to meet his.

It was a matter of seconds later that Guy asked:

'Does Digby know – has he any idea – of your attitude?'

'He knows that I am to be in Ascot today to see Brinda and probably Nadia. I left it that, should I not be back by seven-thirty tonight, he would understand that I was not returning at all.'

Guy said ruefully:

'Poor devil; I can feel it in my heart to pity even him. I know what losing you means.'

Vicki gave a little pained cry.

'If only I'd understood *then* as I do now.'

'Now you are strong, mature and – wise, my darling,' he added softly. 'Wise to know that in order to be happy one must, of all things, be at peace with oneself. Better that we should live forever on our memories and *through* them, than live together with the shadow of Digby to stand between us.'

'I realize that,' she said remorsefully. 'The torture of wondering… You say I am strong; perhaps I am; but, also, there is a numbness, Guy; the days pass without meaning; the process of living is mechanical. Perhaps bearing all that makes one immune.' A sigh: 'Is that strength?'

He shook his head in dissent.

'No, my darling; and it isn't immunity; it is the consciousness of the power within one's own heart; the strength within one's own soul, born of that love we both know … and shall ever know.'

She pleaded:

'And there is no doubt in your mind?'

'Because of your decision?'

'Yes,' she breathed, her heart throbbing, her body aching.

'None. This isn't an issue between personalities, but – codes,' he said almost sharply. 'Destroy the one and you destroy the other. I honour you … no one in this world could have been quite so *fair*–'

'My feelings,' she hastened, 'haven't changed, Guy; they never could. Had I been in love with Digby, natural jealousy might have whipped me to some kind of emotion. As it is I feel only that deep sense of regret for all the misery he caused himself and of disgust that Brinda–' She stopped. 'I *had* to phone you that night,' she said irrelevantly.

'Hearing you was a reprieve,' he admitted.

'But you knew that my faith—'

'I knew; but the heart can fear even then,' he said tensely.

She glanced at the clock, nervously, distractedly.

'Oh Guy, it always comes back to this – this agony. I—' A pause: 'If only I could see you sometimes—'

He shook his head.

'We love too well for that, you and I, my darling. I couldn't bear it; neither could you. And I want you far too desperately ever to be with you and—' his voice died away significantly.

She felt his arms around her; his lips hard and demanding against hers, the pressure of his coat against her breast, the fierce passion of his caress that held a certain frenzy, a certain despair in its finality.

He raised his lips an inch from her own.

'I shall stay at Old Meadows,' he said hoarsely, 'because it is a part of you; and you know my life there; my work, too.'

'And you understand all this and know that it has nothing to do with my love for *you.*'

'I understand,' he said gravely. 'And I thank God, above all things, that you came to me.'

'I had to,' she whispered. 'You are so much

a part of me that to make this decision alone would have been like cutting my heart out ... and to have left you in any doubt as to my *motive*–'

They knew that this was good-bye; the final, agonizing parting from which there could be no retreat. She looked up at him, taking in every detail of his face, tracing a finger over the smooth line of his hair and then, suddenly, crumpling up almost piteously, like a child, in his arms.

He held her, pressing her head against his shoulder, feeling the shuddering of her body and then, suddenly as one who had drawn from him immeasurable strength, she said resolutely:

'I love you, my darling and never have denied, or will deny that love; it is yours – always.'

His dark eyes met hers.

'Bless you, my dearest...'

She said, her voice barely audible:

'Let me go first ... my spirit will haunt this room, be with you everywhere.'

'I adore you,' he said his voice rising on a note of anguish as the next second she was gone.

Guy's teeth were clenched; his heart pounding...

One-twenty ... and a patient at one-thirty. He squared his shoulders, fighting to maintain an iron control, not daring to think. The telephone rang shrilly. He picked it up mechanically.

The routine went on.

Vicki motored down to Ascot, without being aware of any of the journey; she drove as an automaton until, instinctively, she reached Swinley View. It didn't occur to her that she had not eaten since the previous evening and as she made her way to the front door, a faintness stole upon her so that, for a second, she stood uncertainly, praying for the strength to get through the ordeal that lay ahead.

Brinda, exquisitely gowned in powder blue moss crêpe, smiled a challenging welcome as she was shown into the room, saying:

'Sit down and make yourself comfortable. You know, there's a good plot for a play here – don't you think?'

'That rather depends on one's taste in plays,' Vicki said, feeling that deadly calm which follows in the wake of dislike.

'Well,' Brinda began. 'Have you seen your solicitor? I'm not very sure of the proceedings but–'

Vicki said, grateful to rest against the back of the chair:

'There are not going to be any "proceedings", Brinda.'

Brinda echoed the words incredulously, adding:

'But you must be mad. It is absolutely essential that I marry Digby.'

'Since I am his wife there can be no question of that.'

Brinda paled.

'You mean that you are not going to divorce him?' she said in a horrified whisper.

'Just that,' Vicki answered.

Brinda half shrieked.

'But you can't refuse; you must divorce him. What of my position—'

'You should,' Vicki cut in, 'have thought of that before.'

Brinda tried to fathom Vicki's attitude, to understand her mood.

'But you're in love with Guy. This was the perfect opportunity for you to get your freedom.'

Vicki said coolly:

'I don't have to account to you for my motives, Brinda. And I have no intention whatsoever of discussing Guy with you.'

Brinda felt the panic of fear as she sat there; before Vicki's advent she had built up the numerous advantages of being Mrs Digby Graves and had made comprehensive plans for the future. But now—

'This is fantastic,' she gasped.

'Everything is fantastic that doesn't work according to your wishes,' said Vicki. 'You've had your own way so long now, smashed I don't know how many people's lives, that you take it as a right that everyone should do your bidding. Well, there always comes that reckoning day, Brinda. This is yours. You set out deliberately to wreck the lives of those around you and, in the end, it is yours that will be ruined. In fact you dug a pit for others and have fallen in it yourself. That, after all, is poetic justice.'

Brinda gasped.

'You don't mean all this. You can't. I'm your sister. I–'

Vicki's lips twisted into an ironic smile.

'My *half*sister, Brinda. Now you wish to trade on a relationship which you have previously scorned, trade on it when, *as* my sister, you smashed my happiness with Guy and, not content with that, deliberately, foully, contrived to make my own husband betray me. No, I don't think I owe you any thought, or consideration – none whatsoever.'

Brinda, feverish now, terrified as she contemplated what lay ahead, insisted:

'But you still love Guy; you can't just out of spite–'

Vicki shook her head.

'Do you seriously believe that spite could possibly enter into this decision of mine?'

'Then – what is it? Tell me that.'

'Justice,' said Vicki quietly. 'Do you think I could place Digby at your mercy; condemn him to the kind of life inevitable with you, knowing that he hasn't one spark of regard for you and only the utmost contempt? No, Brinda … you engineered these circumstances, deliberately and wilfully; there was no chance about any of it… My only regret is that you have brought your life to *this*.'

Brinda might not have heard a word of that as she rushed out:

'But don't you realize what this would mean to you and Guy? You are supposed to be so madly in love with each other. Well! In a few months you and he could be married. Why care about Digby? Why should *you* consider *him* of all people? If he were my husband–'

'Exactly! What an intolerable position for any man.'

'How dare you!'

Vicki dragged herself to her feet.

'There is nothing more we have to say to each other.'

Brinda made a final effort.

'And the child? What of that? You're supposed to be so tender-hearted, so–'

Vicki's gaze turned slowly, steadily upon her as she said, her voice low, implacable;

'Have you spared it any thought?'

'But Digby – after all, it is his liability and–'

Vicki caught her breath:

'Is it? Are you quite certain of that?' Her

words came with a compelling force.

Colour flamed into Brinda's cheeks.

'What do you mean by that?' It was a sharp, almost fearful sound.

'Am I to be blamed if, now, I have no faith whatsoever left in you?' Vicki said regretfully.

'You're brutal.'

'Even you must see the irony of that remark. And you know – beyond all doubting, that had you loved Digby – had this been a case of overwhelming emotion – I should not have been found wanting when it came to helping you. As it is–'

'I'll go back to my original intention,' Brinda cried. 'I'll drag Guy into this. If I've got to bear the disgrace I might just as well go the whole hog and have done with it. Wait and see; you won't have been so clever, after all. Of course... Guy... Ah, that worries you.'

Vicki moved to the door.

'Good-bye Brinda–'

'It won't be good-bye, my dear girl, don't worry. I shall call you as a witness, seeing that I took the trouble to enlist your aid in the hope that you might persuade Guy to marry me ... and I don't think that you would like the idea of dragging Digby's guilt into it... You're really not so very smart, darling. I'll give Ascot something to talk about! Just you *wait!* I said I would bring you all down with me and … I will,' Brinda regained her lost confidence. 'For a little while, I'll admit, I got panicky. Now! I just don't *care;* I shall have the sympathy of all the people I know … and I doubt very much if Guy allows the case to come into court.' A hateful chuckle. 'You will probably be dancing at my wedding before you know where you are … good-bye, Mrs Digby Graves,' she said with a sneer.

Vicki left and Brinda sat sullenly staring into the fire. What was to stop her bringing the action; it might be amusing to be centre-stage, her name and photographs blazoned in the newspapers. She'd been in a back-water long enough. Her past relationship with Guy … the breaking of his engagement to Vicki *because he was still in love with her, Brinda* – it would all fit very neatly into the pattern of things. She'd surprise them all… And why shouldn't Guy, mindful of Nadia's and Vicki's feelings – when it really came to dragging the case to court – relent and marry her…

She would go to see her solicitor tomorrow.

CHAPTER 20

Vicki reached Moat Farm at four-thirty. Digby was out and she was grateful for the respite. She changed into a soft, iris blue woollen frock, taking her time and gazing about her, after the manner of one who says: 'This is where I must live for the rest of my life.' The anti-climax of the past twenty-four hours had cut violently across the stability of her previous decisions, throwing her back into a state of anguish, sharpened by the memory of all that had been said between her and Guy only that afternoon. It was not that she had loved him less the day before, but that she had, by then, made friends with her grief; now, it was aggressively, torturingly her enemy again and it would take many weary weeks of unmitigated struggle to reach any kind of peace.

She turned her gaze to the panoramic view that embraced the rich, verdant lands of the farm. September mists were rising, shrouding valleys and floating gently to soften the ridge of the far flung downs. But even as she gazed, super-imposed upon it all was a vision of Guy ... Guy for whom she hungered until it was like death.

Five o'clock … the last patients would be leaving. If she could but transport herself in that second to Wimpole Street he would be there, calm, reassuring, masterly. Once she had been able to walk into his room after the day's work was done, knowing herself beloved, dreaming of a future bright as the stars. Bitter, agonizing memory and now, here she was – a stranger in her own home. Even the large room in which she stood appeared wholly unfamiliar; she might never before have lived there… She caught a glimpse of her face in the mirror. How pale she looked. Feverishly she added some rouge. Everything hinged upon the manner in which she handled this scene with Digby, for what availed her sacrifice unless she could convince him of the sincerity of her decision?

It was just before six when he returned home and, having seen her car parked in the drive, rushed forward into the lounge and then stood, tongue-tied, almost unbelieving, upon the threshold.

'You've come back,' he said thickly. And again: 'You've come back.'

Vicki moved towards him.

'Yes, my dear,' she said gently.

He looked at her uncertainly, his face at first solemn and then pitiful in its thankfulness and joy.

'Oh, Vicki,' he said brokenly. 'What can I *say?*'

'Is it necessary to say anything?' she suggested helpfully.

He drew her gaze to his:

'Yes, and yet nothing is adequate. I didn't dare to hope and I didn't dare *not* to.' His voice dropped to a hoarse whisper. 'Why, Vicki – why?'

Vicki said softly:

'I'm your wife, Digby; we promised each other a very great deal and–'

'I broke those promises.'

'One fault doesn't wipe out all the other virtues,' she answered simply. 'Marriage should be made of sterner stuff than that.' She fought to keep her voice both steady and resolute.

He caught her hands and held them.

'But what of you – your happiness?'

'There could,' she murmured, striving to frame the words so as to embrace the truth, 'be no happiness for me in leaving you now. None, my dear.'

He gave a cry.

'I can't believe it. Even now that you are here–' His eyes burned with the fervour of his devotion. Then his defences down, his arms went round her and she felt his lips against her neck as he held her almost as a man might cling to save himself from drowning; a man desperate, bewildered and humbled. She stood there her arms about him comfortingly as she whispered: 'The past is dead; I shall not spare it a thought; that you must believe.'

He breathed deeply and drew back from her.

'You mean that – that things will be the same as – as before? No – conditions?'

'Digby – *no.*'

'It's seemed centuries since last night,' he said thickly. 'I don't think I've been quite sane. Without you I'm nothing, Vicki – it's true. You are my strength – everything.'

She was trembling before the impact of his emotion; aware of her responsibility, of the nature of the task ahead which seemed now to be a hundred-fold more difficult, not on account of his defect, but because, having seen Guy again, the wound was gaping and raw in her heart.

'Then,' she said, trying to force a note of lightness into her tone without resorting to flippancy: 'It is just as well I came back, isn't it?' She smiled into his eyes: 'I flattered myself that you might need me, after all.'

He stood there, trembling before her, shaken, conscious of a devotion almost terrifying.

'You're the most beautiful, the most wonderful woman in the world, Vicki. God knows I don't deserve you; but I can, in future, try to do so... Will you ever trust me again?'

She looked at him very levelly:

'Just as truly as I did before; I know your heart and I know the truth that is in it.'

He closed his eyes for a second then, opening them, said thickly:

'I've tortured myself, Vicki, because I didn't *tell* you; it wasn't meant as deceit–' He paused. 'That sounds ridiculous and yet, loathing myself and *her* seemed somehow to justify my silence. Can you understand that?'

'I think so.'

'What did she say?' It was a harsh utterance as if he realized the inevitability of facing up to all the facts.

'She reverted to her former threats.'

'Evans?'

'Yes.'

Digby looked suddenly alert, his expression changing to an almost business-like thoroughness.

'Am I right – you don't have to answer this unless you wish, my darling – in the belief that he and Brinda had known each other once – intimately? That first evening when they met–'

Vicki didn't flinch.

'They had been lovers, Digby.'

'And she built it all up and tortured you with future possibilities.'

'Yes.'

'I can just see her,' he said grimly. 'And now she cherishes the illusion that the past would lend strength to any false charge she might bring against Evans at this stage.'

'What are you thinking?' Vicki said breathlessly.

Digby relaxed for the first time.

'You're not altogether happy that she will not still make trouble – are you?'

'She has it in her power to do so, since lies mean absolutely nothing to her. And ... mud sticks even if she lost her case.' Vicki shivered. 'It is all so horrible.'

'Was there anything else she threatened?'

'To call me as a witness to the fact that she came to me to beg me to persuade Guy to marry her. I could not deny the truth of that,' Vicki said, the whole horrific picture gaining strength even as she spoke.

'But you *didn't* believe her, or that Evans was in any way associated with her?'

'No ... but my *opinion*–' She caught her breath. 'Oh, Digby, a case like that would be–'

Digby put his arm round her shoulders.

'It will never be a case, my darling. Believe me.'

She asked fearfully:

'Are you sure?'

'Perfectly sure. What happened years ago does not constitute evidence to support a charge brought today.'

Vicki brightened.

Digby watched her carefully. Then:

'To be sitting here with you ... talking as though–'

'Nothing had happened,' she insisted.

'Am I really forgiven?'

'I don't like that word "forgiveness" – it seems to confer an unctuous self-righteousness upon the person who forgives. I am not without fault, Digby; you have shown me more kindness and consideration than I could ever repay, my dear. And since we are life-partners let's begin again – all square, shall we?'

'You could have behaved so differently,' he said with a wondering incredulity, 'and yet here you are, beside me.' He bent and kissed her cheek with a restraint that brought a sob to her throat. Why wasn't he the man with whom she was in love, the man for whose caresses she ached? Then, swiftly, almost abruptly, he exclaimed: 'Would you think me quite mad if I asked you to come down to Cornwall with me for a day or two... I want to feel that we're quite alone; not even share you with the domestic problems,' he added and there was a certain sombreness beneath the banter.

Vicki said in a breath:

'If that is your wish – yes, I'd like it.' Cornwall, anywhere on earth, it did not matter to her so long as he was content. She added, in order that he might not sense any indifference: 'Why not Carlyon Bay?'

A light of happiness flashed into his eyes.

'Would you like that?'

'More than anything.'

He crossed the room, picked up the receiver and a matter of seconds later had booked their rooms.

Vicki smiled.

'As simple as that.'

The clock struck seven.

Digby crossed to her side.

'The hour I love best – the hour that marks the beginning of evening and the end of the day,' he said softly. 'And never has this moment been so – so sacred as now. You shall never regret your decision,' he said solemnly. 'That I swear.'

Vicki got up from her chair. The strength of a great love was upon her; its vital force supporting her in the rightness of the cause for which she had fought. There must be no martyred self-sacrifice, no condescension to humiliate and sear the man whose soul had been laid bare for her to see... No gentle kindliness, passive and tormenting, in its patronage.

'I know that,' she said and her voice throbbed with conviction, 'beyond all doubting.' And, with that, she lifted her lips for his kiss, feeling the sudden tensing of his body against hers as the dam of a fierce restraint burst and his arms crushed her as though fearful she might be wrested from his grasp.

And in that moment she knew that her victory had been won and there was peace in her soul.

They went to Cornwall and while, to Vicki, the gloss of unreality lay upon each hour, it seemed that to Digby those days were etched in gold and that his happiness and delight in her presence held the fervour and intensity of a devotion transcending anything Vicki had hitherto experienced with him. They motored the length and breadth of the county, stopping at quaint fishing villages dotted like birds' nests poised precariously on the cliff edges; down to Falmouth still warm and glowing in the autumn light; to Fowey, glittering like a jewel at the water's edge, its narrow, cobbled streets breathing romance and a charm all its own.

'This,' said Digby, 'is my spiritual home, darling.' He parked the car and they sat looking across the water lazy in their contemplation of the richness of the scene, the river craft at their moorings, the yachts heaving gently at anchor; the ships moving out into the open sea; and around them the ancient square, the fishing nets and the peace...

Vicki's heart missed a beat. The longing for Guy surged unbidden, shooting like a pain through her body, seeming to paralyse her limbs; the sensation of utter emptiness that was upon her, part of an illness from which she had no hope of recovery. But she said fondly:

'Mine, too. It is said that people always return to Cornwall as though drawn by a magnet.'

'So shall I return,' Digby said and added abruptly: 'We might live here later on.'

Vicki started, arrested by a certain faraway expression in his eyes.

'Would you really like that?'

He reached out and took her hand.

'Just so long as you were there,' he said humbly, 'the place wouldn't be important, darling.'

There was a certain poignancy about the utterance; she felt the tug of it at her heart, coupled with the fierce desire to respond, not merely with words framed sincerely to please.

'What lovelier thing could any wife hear?' she whispered softly.

'*Wife*.' He echoed in a gentle lingering tone. 'How nobly you've lived up to the word, my dearest.'

'Don't,' she pleaded. 'You make me want to cry.'

Instantly his mood changed.

'Then we must alter that,' he said blithely. 'Back to the hotel and ... champagne cocktails.'

It was after three days that he said:

'I think we should get back now, Vicki. There are things to be seen to on the farm–' He paused: 'Why not get Nadia down for a week or so–'

Vicki's eyes glowed.

'I'd love that.'

'She'd be company while I was busy. How much does she know, darling?'

'Nothing that I'm aware of and I *can't* tell her.'

'Don't attempt to,' he suggested with an air of confidence. 'It is not your concern any longer. If she should mention it to you–' He stopped: 'I value Nadia's good opinion,' he said significantly.

'And will never lose it,' came the swift reply.

They returned to Moat Farm in the dusk of the September evening when a fine drizzle hung like a grey cloak upon the landscape, shrouding the farm in mystery and damping the bonfires so that their sharp pungent smell became more insistent.

'Home,' Digby said as they felt the rush of warmth from the hall and caught a glimpse, through the open door of the lounge, of the massive log fire leaping in a wall of flame half way up the chimney. 'The perfect holiday and the perfect return! Just as I wanted it.'

Later, upstairs in the silence of their familiar room he placed his hands on Vicki's shoulders and said with great earnestness:

'Thank you, my darling.'

'It's been wonderful, Digby.' Her voice was a trifle unsteady. Every nerve in her body was taut; the effort of keeping up almost more than her strength could stand; yet she knew that she had maintained a mood, as far as was humanly possible, attuned to his own, and that such a limit must in her case suffice.

'I love you.' He looked deeply into her eyes.

She leaned forward swiftly and kissed him. He held her closely for a second and then let her go. She said, aware of a certain tension:

'I must get everything unpacked and put away. One never feels home otherwise.'

He said swiftly:

'Let Martha do it... She loves playing lady's maid.'

Her gaze was questioning.

'I want you with me,' he said with a smile. 'A whisky and soda alone.' He shook his head.

'Very well.' They went down the stairs together. She gave her order and then passed with Digby into the lounge. 'Satisfied?' she asked.

'Perfectly.' He handed her a sherry. 'I know your taste; I know your every whim, mood—' He paused.

'Understanding,' she said uncertainly, 'is a

rare and precious thing.'

The grandfather clock struck seven.

'Seven o'clock on the evening of September 29th,' he said slowly. 'I wonder just how many years that clock has struck that hour on this important day—'

'And how many more it will go on striking while we listen in this very room,' she murmured and though her voice was gentle, content, her heart reached out in longing for the touch of a hand, the soft caress of lips … for the sound of that voice to be heard only in her imagination and her dreams.

Digby sipped his drink.

'I've never given very much thought to the serious things of life, Vicki. Until we were married I thought only in terms of pleasure, of sport. I could well have been described as having very little soul.' He paused: 'Would it sound sentimental if I were to say that now I feel that I've moved closer into that circle bound by – by more spiritual things?'

Vicki tried not to betray the surprise she felt and was yet conscious of the immense change that had taken place in Digby during these past days.

'You have,' she said, 'been different.'

'I did a great deal of thinking when I was in danger of losing you … do you mind my talking like this?'

'No.' Her gaze was intently upon him. 'I'm

interested and we are not afraid to speak of yesterday, even though the door is closed upon it.'

'Perhaps it is that I want you to realize all you've done for me, Vicki,' he said with a deepening earnestness, 'never to forget just what it has meant to me.'

She studied him thoughtfully.

'You are very generous, my dear. I cannot feel that I deserve such praise.'

'That is a point on which we must agree to differ.' He smiled down into her eyes, holding her gaze with an intensity that almost unnerved her. A strange sensation stole upon her that had nothing to do with the senses, but an emotion inspired by a certain consciousness of his great sincerity. She put out her hand to him and he grasped it eagerly.

'I love you very much, Digby,' she said gently.

'I know, my darling,' he said huskily. 'I know your heart.'

They sat there lazily throughout the rest of the evening which was interrupted only by dinner eaten by candlelight in the oak-panelled dining-room. The fire made them drowsy and as Vicki yawned, he said:

'Bed for you; you're tired.'

'Not really; just gloriously sleepy. The moment I move from here I shall be wide awake.'

He smiled at her indulgently, and helped her to her feet. Then arm in arm they went up the wide staircase to their room.

It seemed to Vicki, looking back on that time, as if it had been a perfect cameo placed in the coarse-grained setting of life.

CHAPTER 21

Nadia arrived at the farm the following day, Vicki having fetched her from Ascot. Digby glanced at her swiftly and experienced an overwhelming relief as she greeted him with all the old warmth and affection, testimony of the fact that she was still ignorant of past upheavals.

'I'm spoilt,' she said. 'And I love it. Are you sure, Digby, that it won't be a case of too much mother-in-law?'

'Never.' He smiled into her eyes. 'I want us all to be together just to celebrate—'

'What?'

'The fact that we *are* together,' he announced absurdly.

They laughed and, later on that afternoon, while seated around the fire, Nadia began:

'Have you heard anything of Brinda lately?'

Vicki started.

'I saw her some days ago. Why?' She was grateful that Digby had gone off on the farm.

'I'm worried, darling.' Nadia's face was clouded. 'She seems so strange; her whole manner ... she isn't well, either. Oh, Vicki there's *something*. I just know it. When I spoke to her yesterday she rambled on about my not being surprised if I heard of some case she was bringing against Guy.'

Vicki started; fear leapt back, the momentary peace vanishing as she said:

'Oh!' And felt her heart thud wildly.

'Can you throw any light on it all?'

Vicki replied evasively:

'Can anyone know the labyrinth of Brinda's mind, Nadia? She's like someone possessed.'

'And in love with Guy?'

Vicki didn't lower her gaze. Her answer came honestly:

'As far as she is capable of understanding the word – yes. But it isn't our kind of love, darling, and that isn't being smug. We could never destroy that which we loved but–'

'Brinda – could.'

'Yes; everything about her is violent, distorted. I hate saying this, but it is just as though she isn't of this family at all. Daddy – you – I mean–'

'If one could *help* her.'

'Ah! But if she were the type to respond to

344

such help she wouldn't be – Brinda ... do you remember how, even as a child at school, if she disliked anyone, or liked them too much, her possessiveness and jealousy wrecked everything.' Vicki was playing for time, uncertain what to say, how much to confide, aware of Nadia's gaze anxiously upon her and hating the necessity for any kind of deception, yet not daring to impart even a hint of the truth. Brinda ... how that name had come to stand for everything that was unhealthy, everything evil; a menace to contentment.

'I'm worried, Vicki – desperately worried.' A pause. 'Do you think there's anything she *could* bring against Guy?'

Vicki's reply came solemnly; her eyes were wide, honest.

'Nothing, Nadia. That I know and that I swear to you.' She paused. 'In the past she and Guy had known each other – you weren't deceived about any of that, were you?'

'No.'

'It wasn't a matter one could discuss and I just trusted you to understand – as you did and I thank God for it. Now, it is all so far away and so much else has crowded it out, that mentioning it harms no one. It was all over long before I met Guy and if only I'd been wiser, much of all that has happened since could have been avoided.' Vicki added remorsefully: 'Life allows us only to make *one* mistake. I didn't love enough, understand enough–' She caught at her breath. 'Now, I feel an old woman compared with the idealist of long ago.'

'Long ago … yet in time such a little while,' Nadia murmured.

'What is time?' Vicki asked. 'A moment can be a year; a second an eternity and with happiness, time is just the music of that happiness.'

Aware that Vicki preferred not to pursue the subject of Brinda, Nadia said:

'And you have made Digby very happy, darling.' A tender smile. 'He adores you.'

But Vicki's thoughts even as the conversation progressed were turbulent, speared with fear. Those words of Nadia's 'some case she was bringing against Guy'. A cold shiver went down her spine. But Digby had said that nothing could come of it. Why *worry?* Brinda's threats... Yet ought she to have divorced Digby to prevent all these possibilities. She thrust away the thought as a disloyalty. One thing was certain: she could not contact Guy to find out the truth... Never again must she see him … never *again.* Oh, anguished truth.

It was that night, alone in their room as they prepared for bed, that she expressed her fears to Digby.

'I'm worried; really worried.'

He turned abruptly, pausing in the act of tying his dressing-gown girdle.

'Why,' she asked breathlessly, 'do you look at me like that?'

'Because it is so sweet to me that I have your confidence; that you turn to *me*, even on this question,' he murmured thickly.

'My *dear!* To whom else should I turn if not my husband?'

'True, but–' He shook his head. 'Bless you for it, all the same.' Then, abruptly: 'You think she is going to bring this case?'

Vicki caught at her breath.

'Yes.' She looked at him levelly. 'And once the match has been put to the fire where will it end? It doesn't just revolve around Guy.'

'No,' said Digby tensely. 'It doesn't just revolve around Guy and if *you* are to be called even as she threatened.' He made a fierce sound of anger. 'Perhaps, my darling,' he said ruefully, 'you should have divorced me so that, once and for all, she could do no more harm.'

'Except to you.'

He held her gaze.

'If you had to make the choice again – would you do the same?'

She answered without hesitation and her voice rang with the strength of her convictions:

'Yes. Yes, Digby.'

He moved and stood looking down at her

very intently, his arms enfolding her as he said softly, reassuringly:

'Then don't worry, my sweet; don't *worry*. All this will work out – you see.'

Her eyes, faintly puzzled, questioning, sought an elaboration of the statement.

'Trust me,' he murmured. 'And tonight, shut the world out. Could you do that – for my sake?'

She trembled and then, aware of his need of her, drawn to him by that need, reminded of her promise to herself, her resolution for their future, relaxed as she whispered:

'Yes ... I can do that.'

It was breakfast that Digby announced brightly:

'I've business to attend to in London, you girls–' he smiled at Nadia, 'and may not be back until late. So! You can either toast your toes and have a really good woman's natter, or go off somewhere in the car.'

Vicki started. Was it possible that this 'business' had anything to do with Brinda? If so – what? She said smoothly:

'We shall probably toast our toes!'

'Splendid.' He threw aside his napkin. 'Must just see Morgan about that new herd–' He gave a short laugh. 'You see, Nadia! I'm fast becoming an expert! Now I can tell the difference between Friesians and Jerseys! All done by mirrors,' he added absurdly. 'I'll look in for coffee before I leave.'

He went out, stopping en route to implant a kiss on Vicki's forehead.

Vicki looked solemn.

'What is it?' Nadia asked.

'I don't quite know,' Vicki said shakenly. 'But it is just as if I were looking on a picture out of focus.'

'As fanciful as ever,' Nadia murmured indulgently.

(What could Digby do about Brinda?... Yet he had asked for her trust. She breathed deeply: so be it and trust didn't mean this conflict, confusion and worry.)

'We may grow wiser and more experienced, but the fundamental truths remain,' she said lightly.

Digby returned for coffee, stood back to the fireplace and drank it. There was something, Vicki thought, watchful in his eyes as they rested upon her, some unfathomable expression that deepened as the minutes passed. Then:

'I'm off,' he said blithely. He bent and kissed Nadia. 'Look after her for me–' He inclined his head in Vicki's direction as he spoke.

'I will, but she isn't likely to run away between now and dinner time!'

Digby put his arm round Vicki's shoulders.

'Come and see me off.'

'Don't I always?'

'Always … 'bye, Nadia,' he said again as he reached the door. 'Have a good day.'

Vicki went out with him into the drive. Only the faint rustling of the trees broke the almost uncanny silence. The crisp tang of autumn gave to the breeze a freshness that was fragrant with the smell of newly turned soil and dying bracken.

'Glorious,' Digby said, glancing up to a deep blue sky and then allowing his gaze to take in the panoramic view of the farm itself that lay, just below them – a vast mosaic set against the downs.

Vicki looked at him anxiously.

'I–' She stopped.

'What, my sweet?'

'Nothing … don't be late.'

'A wifely admonition!'

'Do you mind?'

'It positively inflates my ego!'

'Digby–'

'Remember what I asked you last night,' he said tensely.

'Yes.'

'Good.'

'Then this *has* something to do with Brinda?'

'Yes, my darling, it has.' His voice was grimly determined. His hands rested on her shoulders. 'Remember every word I have

350

ever spoken to you, beloved, as this day passes and that I adore you, more at this minute than ever before – if that were possible.' A pause. 'Promise.'

'I promise.'

He bent swiftly, kissed her and said briefly:

'Now, you go in, my sweet, or you'll catch cold.'

'And you'll not be late back?'

He slid into the driving seat and pulled his gloves on, talking to her through the open window.

'No, I'll not be late – for the second time!'

Vicki laughed. She stood, both hands clasping the top of the door. Then:

'Thank you, Digby, whatever it is you have in mind and whether or not it is successful.'

'You will know all about it later, my dearest.'

Her smile was loving and warm in its trust.

'Now in you *go*,' he said tensely. He picked up her left hand and kissed it. ''Bye, my darling.'

The car slid forward; he waved to her until he had reached the bend of the road and was lost to sight.

It was just after twelve when he reached Swinley View, gave his name to the maid and was shown into the lounge where, after a matter of seconds, Brinda joined him.

'Well! Well!' Her voice was mocking. 'Look

who's here.'

Digby nerved himself for the ordeal ahead, fighting down the loathing that sprang to life at the sight of her.

'A not too unwelcome visitor, I hope.'

Her eyes, blue, inscrutable, met his.

'That rather depends on your mood.'

'Should I be here in the *wrong* one, my dear?'

Her laugh was tinkling and confident.

'Hardly... Have you come to apologize for your neglect of me, or because you couldn't resist me any longer?' Her tone was challenging and arrogant.

'Both perhaps.'

She moved closer to him, her perfume stealing sickeningly to his nostrils.

'That's better ... you weren't made for the wishy-washy smug Victoria, my dear man.' Her arms stole up around his neck, her lips pressed against his.

Digby felt sick but tried to respond in order not to arouse her suspicions; at all costs he must keep to the formula upon which he had decided.

Brinda preened herself. Her confidence had been somewhat shaken by the failure of her schemes. A vindictive, triumphant gleam came back into her eyes. And Vicki imagined that she could hold Digby! The situation was as the breath of life to her.

Digby managed to escape her further

352

caress. They sat down and, thankfully, he was able to light a cigarette.

'Mine isn't an easy position,' he said tentatively. 'And what are you plans?'

Brinda's eyes narrowed.

'Since your dear wife flatly refuses to divorce you so that we can be married ... my plans are to stir up just as much trouble as is humanly possible and tip as much of it as I can into her lap,' she finished vehemently. 'And there is no better way in which I can achieve that than by dragging Guy's name into the mud.'

Digby's face remained immobile.

'So you still have that in mind!'

'Have it in mind! I've already seen my solicitor.'

Digby's nerves began to tingle.

'But, my dear girl, you haven't a hope of winning such a case–'

'No?' She showed her even white teeth in a greedy smile. 'That is where you are wrong!'

'But without evidence.'

'I have evidence,' she said. 'I may be dumb, but I happened to keep the little notes Guy wrote to me that time in Sweden. They are not all dated and there were several without any letter heading which could be just as applicable this year as when they were written. I also have a ring he gave me then ... equally useful when said to have been given me last year... My dear Digby, this will be *the* case–'

He was studying her intently:

'And you can contemplate all that publicity–'

'I can contemplate anything – now,' she said. 'And I can face the facts. At the eleventh hour Guy may find that his courage fails him when he realizes that Vicki will be called as a witness. Her testimony – and I have much to be thankful for that she is the truthful type–' she said sneeringly, 'will establish beyond doubt the paternity of the child– My dear man, you look uncomfortable. Don't! At the time of seeing Vicki I overlooked the importance of that visit as future evidence, because I was so intent upon damning Guy in her eyes... Of course, had Guy seen reason and married me, or had Vicki been like any normal woman and taken the freedom we both know she longs for–' A sigh. 'None of this need have happened. As it is–'

'But–'

'As it is,' she went on, ignoring his interruption, 'I cannot escape without *some* scandal, therefore much better to have a case people can get their teeth into. Like the man who steals five pounds and is damned as a "petty thief"; but the man who robs people of millions is an "unlucky financier". Oh, I've got it all taped and seeing that I was able to make out a perfect case for my own solicitor–'

'Have – have any papers been served?'

'No.' She smoothed her hands. 'I intend to see Guy just once more before I pull the trigger ... but this time he will know I mean business.' Her voice deepened. 'The kindest thing he ever did was to tell me that I was a coward at heart ... then, that was true, but he should have known that the challenge was dangerous. I'll prove to him whether or not I am a coward! He'll wish he'd never been born.'

'A strange kind of love, Brinda.'

'*My* kind,' she said and her eyes flashed almost with a light of madness. 'No one thwarts me, Digby. No one.'

Digby leaned back and surveyed her.

'So the case is all set – eh?'

'All set. The breach of promise case of the year. And even should I lose it – which I most certainly shall not do – Guy's name will stink! There is so *much*.'

'It will not be very pleasant for Vicki,' Digby said slowly.

Brinda laughed harshly.

'You don't imagine that fact worries me! Oh, no, my dear man, it won't be pleasant for Vicki; she was, after all, engaged to Guy and her breaking of that engagement immediately on *my* return will further strengthen my case that Guy still found

355

himself again attracted to *me,* but that we could hardly announce *our* engagement immediately. Clever don't you think?'

'You are,' said Digby, 'a diabolically clever woman.'

'Thank you.' She looked smug. 'At first, after Vicki refused to divorce you, I panicked, called myself all kinds of a fool ever to have taken the risk.'

'Was I a pawn in that game?'

Her teeth gleamed as she smiled.

'Shall we say *one* of the pawns, darling?' She added: 'I'm not the type to live a solitary, celibate life.'

Digby relaxed.

'And where do you imagine that *I* fit into this amazing picture?' A pause: 'Or have you forgotten that I do happen to be married to Vicki and that her discomfort must also be mine?'

'I shall not bring you into it,' she said. 'Obviously that would defeat my purpose entirely. And I don't see why you should worry about Vicki's suffering through *Guy!* As for our personal relationship—' She leaned forward. 'That is surely a matter of moods and our inclinations.'

'And should you marry Guy?'

Brinda sighed.

'I'm not the faithful type, Digby. And I do not profess to be – except in court!' She gave a light laugh. 'I ought to have lived in the days of the courtesan! I should have adored it all,' she said extravagantly. 'Funny, isn't it, how no one has the faintest suspicion of what I am like ... how we can live two lives–'

'Dual personality.'

'In a way – yes.' She looked at him. 'Aren't we wasting a great deal of time in talking?'

'Plenty of time ahead,' he said smoothly.

'Does Vicki suspect you might be with me?'

'Not in the sense that you mean.'

'I shall have to be very careful, of course,' she said with some importance.

'Naturally I'm the soul of discretion.'

'You weren't particularly charming on the occasion of our last meeting.'

Digby flung out his hands.

'What could I say? It wasn't particularly sporting of you to behave as you did.'

'Any port in a storm, my dear man.' A laugh. 'And this is much more cosy than ever our marriage would have been. We know too much about each other.'

He eyed her with a slow, smouldering contempt which she was too vain to see.

'I know much more about you than you know about me,' he said cryptically.

'Meaning just – what?'

'Nothing.'

She smiled.

'I'm not afraid of you, Digby. You couldn't

turn any evidence against me without implicating yourself and making the case twice as grim as it is already.'

'Good heavens,' he said lightly, 'I wasn't even thinking of the case.'

Her eyes met his.

'I like your suit. You're still attractive even if you do prefer my feeble-minded sister – at times,' she added hatefully.

'I thought,' he said, feeling that his collar was becoming many sizes too small for him and that his heart was hanging on a frail thread, 'we might go out to lunch somewhere. Then for a run this afternoon–'

'And return here for the evening?'

'If that is how you see it.'

'I do,' she said eagerly. 'And the wretched maid will be out then too.'

'Better tell her that we're going down to the farm,' Digby suggested. 'Otherwise my being here might give rise to suspicion. No use taking risks.'

Brinda smirked.

'You're learning, darling.' She paused and studied him. 'I'm so glad you came,' she added. 'I've loathed you for being able to resist me all this time.'

She moved to the door and spoke to the maid. Digby heard her conversation. That point at least was settled, he thought with relief. He waited, tensed, for her to return and when she did so, she looked at him with sudden curiosity and interest:

'You seem different,' she said breathlessly. 'I can't say you put up a very good show when I came to the farm and I went away contemptuous of you ... but I suppose we none of us behave so well in an emergency. I rather imagine that the virtues of this high-brow marriage are beginning to pall.'

'What do *you* think?' said Digby.

She laughed.

'I knew it would. The virtues are so dull; the vices so thrilling. I was just bored to extinction when I came back here first. Life without a lover is like an egg without salt,' she said.

'A state which hasn't troubled you for long, my dear.'

She flashed him a smile.

'How right you are!' She put her arm through his. 'You speak my language, Digby.'

'Think so?'

'Don't be so damned non-committal!'

'Merely wary.'

'Surely not with *me*.'

'Surely with you more than any other woman on earth,' he suggested tersely.

'Is that kind?'

'You don't want – kindness,' he retorted.

'How right you are. But you've nothing to worry about. Everything is neatly tied up in blue ribbons and if Guy prefers the scandal, so be it!'

Digby said slowly:

'As he will.'

Brinda instantly showed fight.

'Why should you say that?'

'Because nothing has altered — the material facts of the case haven't altered — therefore why should *he* alter now?'

Brinda looked defiant.

'I shall quite enjoy being in the public eye. Sell my story to one of the papers for a nice, fat sum,' she said. 'Money is always useful. I've got everything planned in my mind and arrangements made to allow for the minimum irritation. I'm moving to London — no place like London in an emergency — for the time being, by the way.'

'Really?'

'Yes, at the beginning of next month... Why do you look at me so strangely?'

'I wasn't aware of doing so.'

They went out to Digby's car. She settled herself comfortably in her seat, tucking the soft, fur rug around her legs.

'This is fun,' she said as he got in beside her. 'Now for lunch... I'm hungry.' She glanced at him. 'Where shall we go?'

'I've got it all planned,' he said quietly.

They drove in the direction of Hindhead and Brinda, noticing the fact said sharply:

'Why this way?'

'A whim of mine. I thought we could take in the Devil's Punch Bowl and—'

'Why? It will be frightfully late for lunch…
Digby, are you all right?'

'Perfectly.' He drove on at greater speed.

Brinda felt a sharp stab of alarm.

'Where are we going?… This is off the
beaten track altogether.'

'I'm going to show you a view that few
people have ever seen,' he said firmly. 'I
found the road by chance one day when I
was driving back to the farm.'

'I don't want to see the view,' she said
petulantly. 'I want my lunch and if this is a
sample of your taking me out–'

'You don't like it.'

'No.'

'Splendid.'

'Digby!' She gasped. 'You're ill – you're–'

'I'm not ill,' he said and his voice now was
deadly and menacing in its calm.

'Then what is it?' She put out a hand to
clasp his, but he shook her off, almost as
though she were a leper.

Instantly fear leapt into her eyes.

'Digby!'

'And you seriously believed that I came to
see you today in order to defile myself
further, betray Vicki once again?'

She stared at him.

'Why not?'

'Of course you wouldn't understand,' he
said contemptuously. 'Why not? And you
were perfectly prepared to go on, to

conspire with me—'

'You must be mad. Turn this car back instantly. If you think I'm going to sit here to be insulted, you're mistaken.'

'You couldn't be insulted because nothing that anyone could think of to say *to* you or *about* you could possibly be low enough to reach your true level...' He glanced at her, taking in every detail of the face that had become anathema to him. 'There's going to be no escape for you this time, Brinda – none,' he said tensely.

She uttered a cry:

'What do you mean?'

'I mean that you're not going to be allowed to carry out your vile schemes, to drag innocent people into the filth of your accusations—'

She laughed shrilly.

'And how do you propose to stop me?' Her glance was venomous. 'Nothing and no one can stop me and if you'd any sense you'd know that you have merely goaded me further.'

'You will see how I intend to stop you,' he said with a sudden calm. He added: 'Glance to your left – do you see that drop below, that view—'

She turned.

'What of it?'

He felt his heart almost stop beating as he said:

'That is our destination.'

She uttered a piercing shriek.

'You're mad... Digby, don't drive so fast.'

'I shall drive faster in a minute; but I've a few things I want to say first ... you've done all the harm you are ever going to do in this life. You smashed Vicki's happiness and now you propose to ruin Guy, drag your own family's name through the mire and filth of the courts for your wanton revenge... I *could* murder you, but that would merely create more scandal. Oh, I've thought of all this; worked it out carefully–'

'Digby!' It was a horrified gasp.

'You smashed my peace of mind, stripped from me my self-respect and then when I reached a stage of peace ... you struck again–'

'Vicki–' she gasped, 'there's Vicki–'

'Yes,' he said softly, 'there's Vicki ... who was ready to sacrifice her happiness – a lifetime of happiness – out of loyalty to me after I'd betrayed her... Do you think that I'd allow *you* to cause her one moment more of pain? Do you think I'd stand by after all she's done for me and watch her die a thousand deaths in some foul court, while she gave evidence to damn the man she loves, the man whom she would have married but for you,' he added fiercely.

Brinda rapped out:

'She could have divorced you. She could–'

363

'She was too fine for that; but you wouldn't even begin to understand why she refused.'

'To spite me – that was why. And because she could do so and keep Guy as–'

Digby's voice, thundering into the near-silence cut across her words:

'You're rotten, Brinda – rotten; you always have been and you always would be.' There was now an almost terrifying stillness about him. 'You've not one spark of real feeling, or of decency anywhere; you're a menace to the happiness of everyone around you.'

She felt the impact of his anger and fear, paralysing, petrifying, gripped her as she cried:

'I'll do anything – anything–'

'To save your filthy, squalid little life,' he finished for her.

'I'll drop the case; I'll–'

'And once the danger was over you'd strike again – somewhere. Oh, no. I'll not leave you behind to jeopardize all my hopes, my plans for Vicki's happiness and you can't unlock that door beside you, the lock's fixed.'

She cried shrilly:

'But you can't deliberately–'

He said softly:

'You wouldn't understand that Vicki has already given her life for me ... you've never known *love;* never known anything more

364

than your own sordid desires, your wretched little intrigues.'

'Listen, Digby!' Her voice rose in an agony of fear as the car gained terrifying momentum. 'Digby!' It was a blood-curdling shriek. 'Stop! *Stop!*'

But he didn't hear her; the picture before his mind was of Vicki ... Vicki turning to him and saying gently: 'I'm your wife, Digby'...

His *wife*... Now she could be free; honourably free, without torment of conscience, without self-reproach and as she never could be free any other way so long as he should live...

Brinda's shrieks and struggles seemed part of some fantastic drumming in his brain... The car, travelling now at maximum speed, swerved, somersaulted twice and, plunged headlong into the ravine below...

CHAPTER 22

The police brought Vicki the news just before seven o'clock that evening. She heard the story almost as if she could anticipate every word.

'Accident ... dangerous turn ... car out of hand ... both killed instantly... Mrs Wells had informed her maid that they were on their way here to you.'

Vicki sat there long after they had gone. There was no confusion in her mind, no doubt but that it had been deliberate and carefully planned. The past days came sharply into focus; every word that Digby had uttered had a new significance; the change in him; the quiet content ... *content*... And all the time he had *known*. It was as if, even during those days in Cornwall, his spirit had already gone on ahead of her and found – peace. His words to her only that morning: *'Remember every word I have spoken to you, beloved, as this day passes and that I adore you more at this minute than ever before – if that were possible.'*

And Brinda... How sure, how confident he had been about everything connected with her threats... *'Trust me and tonight shut the world out – could you do that – for my sake?'*

And now... *An accident ... both killed instantly... Mrs Wells had informed her maid that they were on their way here to you.* Nothing to cause suspicion because they were together; everything in order... *An accident...*

Nadia would never know the truth about Brinda's life; she would be spared that horror and the suffering attendant upon such knowledge; there would be no scandal...

366

And the name of Wayne remain forever untarnished.

Vicki's feelings were too deep even for tears; the magnitude of the act seemed to make all normal grief inadequate... He had not overlooked the need for Nadia to be beside her ... there was no flaw anywhere in his perfect sacrifice.

The newspaper reported the tragedy, building up the dramatic content; friends, acquaintances, even strangers, offered their sympathy.

And Guy wrote simply:

Vicki,
I am here when you need me and my thoughts are with you.

GUY.

Only then did the tears break through the dam of her restraint. *Guy...*

The weeks passed in a strange vacuum; nothing was real, not ever the awareness of her own freedom. Moat Farm and its contents and all Digby's fortune had been left to her with the exception of a legacy which went to Nadia giving her an income tax free income of four hundred a year for life. There was nothing untidy about the estate, nothing overlooked in the will that might be likely to cause controversy or confusion.

Nadia asked gently:

'Will you keep the farm, Vicki?'

'I don't know. He loved it.'

'And would wish you to do only what made you happy.'

'Happy … yes, that, above all else, he would wish me to be,' she said softly. 'It is all so unreal, Nadia. I can't grasp it–'

'Thus is it with the great sorrows or great joys of life–' A sigh escaped Nadia's lips. 'It is only afterwards–' She paused. 'You've lived under such a great strain, darling, don't forget; striving always–'

Vicki said thickly:

'If I could have loved him as he loved me.' She shivered.

Nadia hastened, her voice almost firm:

'It is not within our power to love to order. Were it so, what suffering we might be spared. You gave him all that was possible, Vicki – you know that.'

'Yes.' It was a whisper. 'I know that.' She added: 'It seems that, having lived under an iron restraint, I cannot now relax.'

'Only time,' Nadia murmured.

And that time passed… Autumn to winter… Winter to spring to summer, and Vicki left England during that time. She had to offer those months of solitude to the memory of the man who had given her tomorrow; as if, by doing so, nothing of his sacrifice was lost, or turned ignobly to greedy account. Nadia accompanied her and they went lazily from France to Italy and Italy to Spain, relaxing in the sun, until the day came when Vicki walked again up the drive of Old Meadows and found Guy, alone in his study as she tiptoed through the french windows.

'Vicki.'

'Guy.'

They stood there, their eyes meeting in passionate intensity; the time between slipping into the shadows, so that only the moment held any significance; a moment of magic, of breathless wonder. Then in a second she was in his arms, clinging to him feeling her heart come to life again, the whole enchantment of the future suddenly upon her.

'My darling,' he whispered, holding her with a tenderness as of reverence, even awe. 'To have you here after this – this *eternity*.'

She looked at him, her eyes darkly pleading. 'It had to be right and I dared not *see* you... I needed you, wanted you so desperately that only by going away–'

'I understood.'

'I love you so,' she murmured huskily.

Their lips met; their kiss hungry, seeking, as ecstasy touched them with the wonder of fulfilment. Her arms reached up and clasped his neck, her body supple, yielding and trembling at his touch.

'The hands of time go back,' he breathed.

'So much suffered; so much learned,' she added tensely.

'Oh darling, could I but have spared you it all.'

She rested against him.

'Now, I would not have suffered less,' she said with a curious gentleness in her voice. 'Never could I have imagined what it was to live without you; to want you so much that heart, mind and body ached with the longing… Now, being here like this–'

'Ecstasy is sharpened,' he murmured hoarsely.

She drew back a little from his grasp.

'There are things I'd like to say, to tell you, my dearest, and then–'

'And so much I want to hear.'

Simply she gave him all the facts as she knew them, finishing with:

'I couldn't write that, Guy, and–'

'I wondered,' he said heavily. 'The fact that Brinda was with him… I tortured myself with the idea that I ought to have married her and spared you–'

Vicki cried in protest:

'Oh *no*.' The idea was a horror to her. 'And the tragedy, then, might have been far greater. Brinda would have gone to her doom, Guy. That may sound dramatic, but somehow I knew it instinctively and that was what made me so afraid for *you*. She

370

was like one possessed. Death, I pray,' she added gently, 'may prove kinder than the Fate she would have chosen for herself.'

'It will,' he murmured.

Vicki gazed around her almost un-believingly.

'Home,' she said wonderingly.

'When will you marry me, beloved?'

'Next month?' Her gaze travelled over his face almost as if she found it difficult to believe that she was really seeing correctly and not still looking upon a vision. 'That was why I stayed away; I couldn't have endured any anti-climax; we've been through too much. Now, we can walk into the sunlight, Guy.'

He stooped and kissed her, a gentle, tender kiss.

The romantics saw in their marriage, a month later, a fitting climax. Guy had won approval in the district and was accepted as a man of stability and integrity. The tragedy of Digby's death was lamented, but the more discerning wondered among them-selves if in the end it might not after all open the door to a greater happiness for Vicki. They could not forget that, orginally, she had been engaged to Guy and that, since the breaking of their engagement, he had lived in solitude, obviously faithful to her memory. That Vicki, herself, should be back at Old Meadows occasioned great rejoicing among her intimate friends.

The wedding was quiet and took place at the ancient and picturesque church of St Michael's and All Angels at Sunninghill, and a small luncheon party was given by Nadia afterwards at the Berystede Hotel, its terraced gardens looking out over an encircling belt of pine trees that rose darkly to the vivid blue of the October sky.

Vicki, dressed in soft powder-blue seemed bewitched by her own happiness, her radiance almost poignant in its intensity. And when at last the moment came for farewells, as she and Guy set off for their honeymoon in Gloucester, Nadia held Vicki closely and whispered:

'Now, at last, darling, I am happy. There isn't a qualm or a doubt anywhere – you've found your happiness as I found mine.'

Vicki kissed her with a deep, intense devotion.

'Bless you for all you've been to me, Nadia, for all your help, your understanding throughout the years. You know all that my heart wants to say.'

'I know, darling.'

Vicki peered into the glass.

'Do I look all right?'

'Beautiful. Your eyes–'

Vicki flushed.

'They're not behaving very well – are they?'

'They betray you,' Nadia said softly, seeing in Vicki's passionate joy, the reflection of her own ecstasy on the day of her own marriage.

Downstairs, in the little hall of White Cottage the few friends assembled for last minute farewells. Gloria and James, delighted and thankful beyond measure that events had enabled Vicki and Guy to come together again – having firmly decided between themselves that they had always remained in love – said gaily:

'And when you get back, I'm going to give a party for you both.'

James chuckled.

'Now you know your fate.' He smiled into Vicki's eyes: 'You should, of course, be taken on a world tour for a honeymoon, my dear child, instead of ten days in the heart of the Cotswolds!'

Guy put in:

'Now don't you start that! I have to work for my living! And Vicki understands perfectly that I can't get away just at the moment – at least not for longer than ten days!'

Vicki laughed.

'The Cotswolds, Cumberland or Canada,' she said and her voice throbbed. 'Does it matter?'

'Not,' said James perversely, 'in the least.'

They left amid the usual hand waving and exclamations.

'James,' said Guy apologetically, 'is right, darling. I hate this—'

'*Don't,*' she breathed. 'Don't dare even to think like that. We're together – married,' she murmured tensely. 'And the heart of England somehow seems right to me ... the peace, the solitude and the knowledge that we haven't to – *part.*'

'*Dearest.*' He kissed her hand. 'You look so radiant, so utterly lovely.'

'I feel it,' she said with a childish delight; 'but only because I reflect my love for you.'

He glanced at her swiftly.

'There's no doubt in your mind, Vicki, about my continuing my work – is there? I mean, the fact of our financial in-dependence—'

'No doubt at all,' she said resolutely. 'I honour you for wanting to continue as you are and for giving so much of your time – as I know you do – free. Without that back-ground, even happiness might pall. Oh, yes, idleness breeds boredom, my sweet, and boredom is no companion for love. For these few magic days we want everything else shut out but our love for each other ... but ecstasy must be tempered with reality in the end.'

Guy felt that his heart was thudding audibly, so great was his joy in her answer.

They drove to an old country hotel just beyond Broadway; its grounds bronzed with the shimmer of autumn, the glow of the setting sun that poured liquid fire upon it even as they turned into the long, winding drive and, finally, in the sanctuary of their room, gazed out across the limitless countryside that rose darkly like a frieze of molten gold to the quivering, colour-splashed sky.

'Mrs Guy Evans,' he whispered, turning her towards him and gently removing her hat.

Their eyes met and now their defences were down as passion, so long denied, surged upon them in a hunger, a desire, that nothing could stem. Her lips were warm and inviting as she parted them to feel the fierce pressure of his own; her body relaxed, aching for his touch and quivering with the magic of surrender...

'I adore you,' she managed to whisper as, for a brief second she drew back for breath.

'I've dreamed of this moment, lived it a thousand times,' he said hoarsely, 'wanted you until–'

'And I–'

The room, then, was illuminated only by the soft light of the afterglow; a light that crept timorously upon them as they lay in each other's arms; a light that turned her body to alabaster revealing its beauty and the flawlessness of her skin, and only her sigh of ecstasy, broke the silence as she drew him ever closer, seeking and finding the answer to the passionate need that had mocked and tormented with its increasing desire.

And now there was nothing beyond that wild rapture; beyond the softness of his lips against lips, body against body and the surrender of mind, soul and spirit.

Nadia and Guy stood together in the silent lounge at Old Meadows. Guy was pacing the room, lighting and stubbing out cigarettes at an alarming speed; Nadia sitting quietly, hopefully, while dying a hundred deaths inside...

'What's that?' Guy raised his gaze instinctively to the room above.

'Just footsteps.'

'But, surely ... it's been hours... Nadia, suppose something—'

'Nothing will go wrong,' she insisted. She struggled to sound gay: 'And you, a medical man, too, expecting everything to be over in an hour or so!'

Guy turned and met her gaze; his face was pale, strained.

'If—'

'There are no "if's",' she said sharply.

'A fine specimen I'm proving to be,' he retorted.

'I know, my dear,' she said softly. 'I was told that *I* went through *nothing* when

Brinda was born compared with Vicki's father!'

Guy managed to smile and even as he did so, the sudden thin notes of a child's cry fell upon the tense silence.

Guy rushed to the door.

'You won't,' said Nadia, 'be allowed up there yet!'

He listened in the hall, returned and ran his fingers through his hair as though the inactivity would send him insane.

'No more after this,' he said hoarsely.

Nadia's heart was hanging on a thread; she felt physically ill almost as though she were sharing Vicki's experience, but she teased:

'Every man in love with his wife says that!'

'I know,' he agreed. 'I'm behaving true to type ... never again will I ridicule the old music hall jokes! Here's someone – ah–'

Doctor Weldon, friend of Guy's, a brilliant gynaecologist, came forward and his beaming smile told its own story.

'Congratulations, Guy! A son! And Vicki's fine. Seven and a half pound monster.' He looked across at Nadia. 'I suppose you've been giving moral support to this wilting specimen,' he added jocularly.

'She has.' Guy seemed to stretch to his full height again; the strain vanished miraculously from his face. He breathed heavily and sat down, rather like a sack of flour, in the nearest chair. 'It seemed like a century.'

Doctor Weldon glanced at the clock.

'Only just after midnight. Most respectable time.' He nodded. 'You can go up now.'

Guy grinned boyishly and ran up the stairs two at a time.

A second later he stood hesitantly on the threshold, then encouraged by the nurse who left the room, moved forward to Vicki's side.

'Darling – oh *darling!*'

Her eyes, starry even in their tiredness, met his adoringly. Then together they studied the morsel of humanity that lay in the crook of her arm.

'Our *son*,' she breathed.

Guy's heart swelled with a sudden, stabbing pride. It had always been so easy to dismiss the vapourings of proud fathers and smile a little indulgently, but now, the experience shared, he felt a surging of emotion, new, humbling.

'Thank God, it's all over,' he whispered. 'Oh, my sweet, these hours have been … are you all right?' He added softly: 'I'm not making much sense – am I?'

'I don't want you to.'

He bent and kissed her.

'I'm so – *happy*,' she whispered. 'So *happy*.'

Their eyes met suddenly in understanding. A memory stirred to which silent homage was paid; a name echoed softly between them.

Then:

'We're – *parents,*' Vicki exclaimed, jubilantly. 'I feel most terribly *important.*' A little laugh. 'Do you?'

'Important, light-headed and so thankful–' He held her hand against his cheek. 'And he'll grow up here, my darling...'

She sighed almost in reverence.

'The first of our *family.*'

Guy groaned.

They smiled together.

'A woman always has her way,' she added just before the nurse came in to whisk off the child and send Guy meekly downstairs.

Vicki lay there, at peace. This was living ... this rich fulfilment, this heritage of love and faith. Her son and Guy's ... a part of them to perpetuate their happiness.

And Old Meadows impregnable, secure, lay bathed in moonlight. Outside in the crisp night air, Guy looked up at the dimly lighted window... Here, he thought, with a sense of humble thankfulness, was his world, his kingdom.

The publishers hope that this book has given you enjoyable reading. Large Print Books are especially designed to be as easy to see and hold as possible. If you wish a complete list of our books please ask at your local library or write directly to:

Dales Large Print Books
Magna House, Long Preston,
Skipton, North Yorkshire.
BD23 4ND

This Large Print Book, for people
who cannot read normal print,
is published under the auspices of

THE ULVERSCROFT FOUNDATION

... we hope you have enjoyed this book.
Please think for a moment about those
who have worse eyesight than you ...
and are unable to even read or enjoy
Large Print without great difficulty.

You can help them by sending a
donation, large or small, to:

**The Ulverscroft Foundation,
1, The Green, Bradgate Road,
Anstey, Leicestershire, LE7 7FU,
England.**
or request a copy of our brochure for
more details.

The Foundation will use all donations
to assist those people who are visually
impaired and need special attention
with medical research, diagnosis
and treatment.

Thank you very much for your help.